The Canal Whisperer

Stefaan Declerck

Copyright © 2024 by Stefaan Declerck

This is a work of fiction. The characters, events, and places described herein are purely imaginary and are not intended to refer to specific places, or to specific persons alive or dead. All rights reserved. No part of this publication may be reproduced, distributed or transmitted in any form or by any means, including photocopying, recording, or electronic or mechanical methods without prior written permission of the publisher except for brief quotations embodied in critical reviews.

Contents

1. A Darkened Past — 1
2. A Mysterious Drowning — 17
3. Rumors and Whispers — 31
4. The Inspector's Doubts — 49
5. A Reluctant Ally — 63
6. A Confrontation — 83
7. Unlikely Companions — 97
8. The Guild's Secrets — 113
9. A Glimmer of Truth — 127
10. The Artist's Plight — 143
11. Eva's Discovery — 153
12. The Locket — 169
13. Shadows of the Past — 183
14. The Guild's Vendetta — 199
15. A Desperate Search — 215

16. A Tangled Web	229
17. A Crushing Setback	245
18. Helena's Resolve	257
19. A Dark Revelation	265
20. Willem's Despair	279
21. The Final Confrontation	291
22. The Truth Unveiled	305
23. A new Dawn for Brugge	315
24. Rebirth	333
Also By	337
About the Author	339

A Darkened Past

Before dawn breaks, I find myself waking up, not because of an alarm, but due to the natural rhythm to which my life has been synchronized after years of living closely with nature. The quietness of my simple home is occasionally disturbed by the creaking sounds of its old wooden structure, sounds that I find reassuring as they remind me of the cottage's long-standing history. From outside, the soft sounds of the canals at a distance reach me, a gentle and constant background noise that feels like a lullaby.

A sliver of pale light sneaks through the shuttered windows, painting elongated shadows across the room's sparse furnishings. Rising from my bed, my body protests with aches from the previous day's toils, and I shiver as the early morning cold seeps into my bones like an uninvited ghost.

In the stillness, I dress quietly, pulling on well-worn garments that have molded to the contours of my labor-hardened frame. My hands, marked by years of net casting and line hauling, fumble with the familiar buttons, the hard skin a testament to a life spent at sea.

In the kitchen, a small pot sits atop an unlit stove. Striking a match, I watch with quiet satisfaction as the flame catches the kindling. The growing fire begins to challenge the room's chill. I set the water to boil, the soon-to-emerge aroma of coffee infusing the air with comfort that feels like an old friend.

The wooden floor creaks underfoot as I gather my fishing gear: nets neatly coiled, hooks glinting in the dim light, and a fishing rod that has been my steadfast companion through countless dawns. Each piece is stowed with care in my weathered satchel, a ritual of preparation for the day's labor.

Clasping a steaming mug of coffee, its warmth seeps into my hands, each sip sharpening my senses and sweeping away the remnants of sleep. Memories drift in, witnesses of a time when this cottage echoed with more voices than just my own. But such thoughts are fleeting, slipping away like elusive fish in the deep.

Stepping outside, the brisk morning air greets me, a swift reminder of life's persistent flow. The horizon is now tinged with the first light of dawn, a slow but inevitable herald of the day ahead.

I make my way to the canal where my boat, De Zilverreiger, waits patiently. She's a vessel bearing the scars and stories of many years, much like myself. Once respected, her name is now whispered with a mix of reverence and superstition.

Caressing her timeworn sides, I board and push off from the bank, gliding into the canal's embrace. The water is a mirror this morning, reflecting the awakening sky's blush of pinks and oranges. Each stroke of my oars is a meditation, distancing me from the murmurs of witch hunts and unjust accusations that haunt my shores.

As Brugge stirs to life, its historic beauty emerges from the night's shadows. I am a part of this city, yet apart from it, acutely aware of its allure and its darker undercurrents.

Reaching my favorite spot, a secluded nook where willows weep into the still waters, I begin my day's work. Each action is methodical, honed by years of practice: casting nets, inspecting lines, baiting hooks. Here, on the water, I shed the weight of my tarnished family name, finding solace in the simple identity of a fisherman.

The nets, submerged and still, hold the morning's humble bounty. With the ease of long practice, I tie De Zilverreiger to the jetty, securing her with a knot that has held through countless tides. Slinging my satchel over my shoulder, I feel the weight of the day's work seep into my bones. The fish inside are more than a meal; they are the coins of my trade, a way to carve out a living on the margins of a society that looks askance at my lineage.

I tread the path to the old town square, where the streets are waking to a new day. Shopkeepers are slowly opening their stores, awnings unfurling gracefully. Morning greetings are exchanged by early risers, their words floating through the air like seeds on a breeze. The scents of fresh bread from the bakeries and the salty smell of fish in my sack weave together, illustrating the enduring patterns of daily life.

I walk with a purposeful stride, my gaze not lingering on faces or storefronts. Yet I remain acutely aware of the subtle dynamics around me. Children dash by, their laughter a vivid splash of innocence in the morning's tapestry. Their unburdened spirits, untouched by the shadows that haunt my family's name, spark fleeting envy in my heart.

Soon, the familiar outline of the Simon Steven square unfolds before me, its historic houses standing sentinel around its edges. Dominating the square is a monument, a spire of stone that seems to accuse the heavens. It is a relic from a time when justice was contorted into a public spectacle when fear was stoked like the flames that once consumed lives here.

Despite myself, I pause. My eyes trace the monument's stark lines, rising to where names are etched into its unforgiving surface—names that share my blood. It's then that the whispers start, curling through the air like morning mist.

"Van Aarden," they murmur, a name once spoken with respect, now tinged with the chill of suspicion.

The stares of the townsfolk follow me, heavy with unspoken questions and age-old fears. I stand in the shadow of history, marked by a past that clings to me like a spectral shroud. I don't need to turn to feel their cautious retreat, their silent prayers warding off a darkness long past but never forgotten.

I elbow my way through the bustling crowd, heading towards Brugge's vibrant fish market, where the air is tinged with the salty embrace of the sea. All around me, the market is alive with a symphony of sights and sounds. Fishermen, their voices robust and full of life, compete to sell their catches, their shouts intertwining with the raucous cawing of gulls circling overhead. Shoppers, seasoned in the art of negotiation, engage in a lively exchange of words, each trying to strike the best deal.

In this boisterous chorus, my voice barely registers a quiet note amidst the din. I arrange my day's catch on my familiar, worn stone stall – a modest display of fish that gleam under the morning's soft light, their scales reflecting my dedication and silently challenging the whispers and wary glances thrown my way.

"Fresh haddock," I call out half-heartedly, feeling like I'm casting nets into barren waters, skeptical of attracting much interest.

A woman approaches, her eyes scanning my fish before cautiously meeting mine. There's a flicker of recognition, quickly masked by a polite, yet distant smile.

"How much for the mackerel?" she inquires, her voice betraying none of her inner turmoil, though her hands, trembling slightly as she points to the fish, tell a different story.

"Two stuivers each," I respond evenly, carefully wrapping the chosen mackerel in a paper, its cool, slick skin a familiar sensation.

She places the coins on the stall with deliberate precision, avoiding any direct contact. "Thank you," she says softly, quickly retreating into the crowd, her relief at leaving my presence almost tangible.

As she disappears, I'm struck by the deep divide between us, a chasm wider than the canals of Brugge. My name lingers in the air, a ghostly presence that refuses to fade.

"Willem Van Aarden." The whisper comes, a chilling breeze in the warmth of the bustling market.

I tense but remain facing forward, knowing too well the mix of curiosity and fear that likely colors the faces of those around me. My family's story is one of whispered legend, a dark fable told in hushed tones.

A man approaches next, his presence marked by an exaggerated casualness. "Eels today?" he inquires, his gaze scrutinizing my catch.

I nod towards a bucket of writhing eels. "Caught fresh this morning."

He selects a few and then remarks, his voice low but sharp, "The Van Aarden name used to mean something different here."

Our eyes meet, two souls navigating an unspoken sea. "It still does," I reply, my voice a quiet assertion of my identity.

He pays and disappears into the crowd, leaving me to face a morning punctuated by brief exchanges and longer spells of solitude, as others steer clear of my stall, guided by old fears and deep-seated prejudices.

In these moments of quiet, I retreat into memories of better times – my father's laughter echoing through the market, my mother haggling over spices, my sister's joy at treats bought with hard-earned coins – all from a time before fear eclipsed love.

A young boy, unburdened by the town's history, approaches. "Are you really a witch?" he asks with childlike frankness.

The market holds its breath around us, waiting for my answer.

I lower myself to his level, meeting his gaze. "No more than you are," I say gently, acknowledging our shared humanity.

He seems to ponder this, then nods, accepting the answer. As he turns to leave, he looks back. "I like your fish," he says, his words cutting through the years of suspicion and fear.

His departure leaves a trace of laughter in the air, a fleeting warmth that for a moment lightens the weight of history and judgment.

As the day moves towards midday, the activity in the market starts to slow down. At my stall, there are only a few mackerel and trout left, lying on a bed of crushed ice, but there are no customers in sight. Trying to sell the remaining fish is becoming more difficult; the reputation of my family name, Van Aarden, seems to cast a shadow over my efforts, making my pitches to potential buyers seem strained and ineffectual.

I'm about to close up for the day when a figure casts a shadow over my stall. I tense up instinctively, then look up to see Father Emile, his gentle face framed by a smile that doesn't quite mask the underlying sorrow in his eyes.

"Good day, Willem. Fine-looking fish you have there," he says softly.

"Father Emile." I acknowledge him, a hint of wariness in my voice. Our pasts are intertwined, his role as a spiritual guide contrasting starkly with my family's tainted history.

He looks over the fish, nodding with genuine admiration. "No one knows these waters like you. I've always said you have a gift."

The word 'gift' irks me, suggesting my skill is something mystical rather than earned through experience. I bite back a sharper reply, opting instead for neutrality. "The fish run well this time of year."

An uncomfortable silence falls between us, heavy with unspoken words. Father Emile finally breaks it. "Well, I shouldn't keep you. Just wanted to see how you were."

I nod, my body already half-turned from him. "As well as can be expected."

"Good, good," he says, but he lingers, clearly wrestling with something more he wants to say. My patience wears thin.

"Willem..." he starts hesitantly, "Dark days may come again, but the Lord's light still shines if you let it."

I stiffen, a rush of old anger surging up. The well-intentioned words feel like a hollow attempt to mend deep, old wounds. But I keep my composure, my response cold yet polite. "We all walk in shadow and light, Father. I prefer to rely on my own feet to find my path."

Father Emile recoils slightly but regains his composure. "Of course, of course. I meant no offense." He sighs, the weight of sadness in his eyes deepening. "I know you bear heavy burdens from the past. As do I."

This shared acknowledgment of pain momentarily bridges the gap between us. I relent slightly. "The past is done. All we can do is carry on as best we can."

"Well said," he agrees, patting my shoulder briefly before retracting his hand. "You know you can always seek refuge within the church's walls should you need it."

I nod, my response tight-lipped, grateful but not willing to accept his offer. He seems to understand.

"Go well, my son." He offers a final, faint smile before blending back into the thinning crowd.

I exhale slowly, feeling both drained and strangely comforted by our exchange. The priest's genuine concern offers a small solace, yet it reopens wounds I struggle to keep closed.

Packing up my stall, thoughts swirl in my head, a mix of "Van Aarden," "witch," and "devilry" - a toxic brew I can't seem to dilute.

I shoulder my satchel and head towards the canal, seeking the solitude it offers. Father Emile's parting words echo in my mind, a bitter reminder of the church's role in my family's tragic past.

No, I decide, I will face what comes on my terms. The canals, with their quiet understanding, are more comforting than the church's hallowed halls.

I'll keep to my secrets, just as the church clings to theirs. In the quiet flow of the water, I find a peace that eludes me in the shadow of the steeple.

***

The afternoon sun casts a golden sheen over the still waters of the canal, where I find my familiar haven - a secluded bank, shrouded by willow branches that offer a comforting blend of shade and solitude. Settling down, I rest against a tree whose roots cling to the earth like ancient, gnarled fingers.

In this quiet spot, the persistent murmurs that follow me through Brugge's streets seem to fade. The gentle lap of water against the bank and the soft rustle of leaves combine into a tranquil whisper, offering a temporary respite from the turmoil in my mind.

I unpack my modest lunch - bread, cheese, and smoked herring. The simplicity of the meal is grounding, and I savor each bite, my gaze drifting over the calm expanse of the canal.

Memories of a distant childhood surface, times when my father and I would sit here, sharing meals in companionable silence. I recall how he would point out the fish leaping from the water, eager to share his knowledge with his attentive son.

His large, calloused hands would animate his stories, detailing the depths of the canal, and the ebb and flow of its currents. His voice, deep and warm, still echoes in my mind, filled with the wisdom of a life lived in harmony with these waters.

My mother's gentle admonitions about neglecting Bible lessons for "silly fish tales" often rang in the background. Yet, her tone betrayed her delight at the bond between father and son, united by a mutual love for the water.

Even my sister Anna would join us at times. Her protests against such 'unladylike' pursuits were always met with playful threats from our father to toss her into the water, her shrieks of mock outrage echoing across the canal and sending birds into flight.

A lump forms in my throat, the echo of laughter long silenced, a family torn apart by fear and superstition. This once joyful place now holds only ghosts - memories of a lost family, a stolen innocence.

Closing my eyes, I bask in the dappled sunlight, attempting to conjure the sound of Anna's laughter. But it fades too quickly, like a dream at dawn.

Sometimes, solitude is a healing balm; other times, it cuts deeper with each year that passes.

My reverie is shattered by the crunch of footsteps. Opening my eyes, I see a group of local boys approaching, their youthful bravado evident in their posture. The leader, a tall boy with unruly blond hair, exudes malice.

"Well, if it isn't the witch boy," he taunts, his voice drawing laughter from his companions.

I tense, my hand gripping the remains of my lunch. Their taunts are not new; I've borne their cruelty before. Most in Brugge whisper behind backs; these boys, fueled by youthful ignorance, confront openly.

"That's him alright," another chimes in, "devil worshippers, all of them."

I remain silent, my gaze fixed on the tranquil canal, a stark contrast to the rising anger within. Years of enduring such torment have taught me that retaliation only breeds more hostility.

The leader steps closer, now looming over me. "Is it true? Can you hex people?" He's mocking, yet a flicker of doubt underlies his bravado.

I look up, meeting his gaze calmly. "People say many foolish things in fear." My voice is even, a product of years of holding back anger.

The boy hesitates, taken aback by my response, but quickly masks it with a scowl. "We're not afraid of you, witch boy. Prove it, curse me!"

Their jeers grow louder. I stay seated, outwardly calm but inwardly seething, wanting to defend my family's honor.

But I know better. Speaking softly, I urge them to leave me be, packing up my things.

"There's no truth in those tales," I say as I stand, slinging my satchel over my shoulder. I walk away without looking back, their laughter and insults fading with each step.

My shoulders stay tensed, braced for a blow that never comes. It's a familiar cycle - accusations, internal rage, the helplessness of being misunderstood. When will the shadow of the past lift?

I head towards my boat, seeking the solitude of the waterways. But even here, in the beauty of Brugge, the whispers of hatred linger, tainting even my most cherished memories.

True solace seems ever out of reach, as the city's canals echo with stories of a past that refuses to stay buried.

***

As I step aboard my trusty boat, the familiar creak of its timeworn planks greets me like an old friend's complaint. I untie the mooring rope with well-practiced hands and gently push off from the bank, feeling the boat yield to the canal's tender embrace. The oars feel right in my calloused hands, as natural as an extension of my limbs, guiding me along the serene waterway.

The sun has just dipped below the horizon, leaving the sky in that serene state of twilight where the day's noise surrenders to the evening's calm. The water's surface glows with the last embers of daylight, ripples of gold and crimson dancing under a deepening purple sky. Stars begin to dot the heavens, twinkling faintly like distant guardians guiding sailors home.

Solitude envelops me, a welcome relief from the day's weight. Here on the water, I'm no different from any other soul-seeking passage; there are no judgmental stares or whispered curses, just the soothing sound of water caressing the hull and the distant calls of marsh birds.

Gliding past clusters of bulrushes, their feathery tops nodding in the gentle breeze, I witness the sudden grace of a heron taking flight. Its majestic wings stir the water, leaving ripples in its wake, and I watch, envious of its effortless freedom.

The familiar outlines of Brugge's spires recede into shadowy silhouettes, their importance and the city's troubles seeming insignificant from this distance. Here, the canal and I are in harmony, old friends sharing unspoken stories.

As I rest the oars inside the boat, my fingers trace the scars and stories etched into its wooden frame. Each mark is a memory: the first time my father entrusted me with the oars, the storms we've braved together. These recollections are as vivid as if they happened yesterday.

The past comes alive in the twilight; my mother's smiling face on the shore, her dress billowing in the wind, my sister's excited squeals as she spots fish below, and my father's proud, bearded face as he guides my hands on the oars. "She's yours now, son," his voice seems to resonate across the years. "Treat her well and she'll always see you home."

I stroke the gunwale, a silent promise to both the boat and my father's memory. Here, away from the whispers and stigma, I am still Willem Van Aarden, my father's son, a man of the water.

The stars above, bright and unwavering, anchor me in the vastness of the night. Orion's belt, Polaris - these celestial guides have steered me through many a night when the land and its troubles felt worlds away.

A shiver runs through me as a breeze picks up. I pull my jacket closer, lost in thought. What will I return to on land? More distrust and whispered accusations? Out here, at least, such judgments hold no sway.

Reaching for the oars, my hand brushes against something unexpected - a deliberate carving in the wood. A chill runs down my spine as I recognize the symbol: a pentagram, a witch's mark, crudely etched into my sanctuary. Anger and disbelief surge within me. Who would dare violate my boat, my refuge, with such a hateful sign?

I look towards the shore, half expecting to see a figure lurking in the fading light, but the canal is quiet, indifferent to my turmoil. I touch the symbol, feeling the anger boil inside me. This deliberate act of malice has seeped into my haven, marking it just as the whispers have marked me.

But I force myself to calm down, refusing to give the perpetrator the satisfaction of seeing me rattled. This scar on my boat, like the whispers, is now part of my narrative, a symbol of the ignorance and fear I face.

For now, the witch's mark will stay, a blemish on the boat's weathered skin. Yet I refuse to let it drive me from my place of peace. These waters, with their quiet understanding, remain my true sanctuary, impervious to the world's misconceptions and fears.

The canal moves through Brugge smoothly, resembling a peaceful thread of silk, leading me toward my home as daylight begins to fade. My boat moves easily over the still water, with the oars cutting through methodically, their movement creating a steady beat that resonates in the dimming evening light. In the distance, my simple cottage becomes visible, its lantern casting a welcoming glow into the dusk, standing out as a lone light amid the encroaching darkness.

I bring the boat to rest at the dock with a final, firm stroke of the oars. The ropes groan softly as they strain against the wooden posts, a gentle disturbance in the evening's stillness. Shouldering my satchel, I step onto the bank, the well-worn planks familiar beneath my feet.

The cottage door opens with a soft creak of rusty hinges, revealing a dimly lit interior filled with the musty scent of mold and the stagnant air of disuse. This place, once full of life and laughter, now holds only the faded echoes of its former glory, worn down by years of neglect and sorrow.

Inside, the remnants of my family's past clutter every surface. Stern-faced ancestors stare down from dusty frames, their judging eyes following me as I move through the room. An old spyglass, its brass dulled by time and salt, rests forgotten on the mantle. Cobwebs veil the delicate china, once a proud heirloom of the women in my family.

Each object whispers tales of a proud heritage, of a lineage that once stood for something more than whispered rumors and sideways glances. Here, away from the freedom of the canal, the ghosts of my past press uncomfortably close.

Approaching the cold hearth, I pause before a portrait that captures my family in happier times. My father's kind yet stern face, my mother's gentle smile, my sister Anna's youthful inquisitiveness, and there I am, a solemn, young version of myself. The painting, stained with mildew and cracked with age, is a bittersweet reminder of what once was.

I run my fingers over their painted faces, tracing the contours as if to keep their memory alive through touch. These portraits are not just images; they are the last vestiges of a family torn apart by fear and hatred.

"Sorry," I whisper to them, a lone apology for all that was lost – our standing, our legacy, and most of all, their lives. In this cottage, only echoes remain, tended by the sole survivor of our line.

Turning away, I make my way to the kitchen to prepare a simple meal. The routine tasks bring a semblance of normalcy, a brief respite from the memories that haunt these walls.

As I eat alone by the fire, the shadows of the past loom close. The fire's flickering light is a stark reminder of the flames that consumed my family, yet it also offers a small comfort against the night's chill.

The day's events replay in my mind – the veiled hostility at the market, the priest's well-meaning but unwelcome words, the thoughtless cruelty of children. In Brugge, suspicion runs deep, a legacy of fear that clings to my name.

I ponder the irony of the fire, both a symbol of my family's destruction and my sole companion in solitude. I am a living contradiction – an outcast yet a survivor, bearing a name that evokes both fear and pity.

Outside, the night deepens, and I sit, lost in thought. The idea of a different future, free from the burden of my family's past, flickers at the edge of my consciousness. It's a fragile hope, but it's mine to hold onto in the darkness.

For now, I endure. I tend the flames, honor the memories, and navigate the waters of my existence. They could not extinguish my spirit entirely. As long as I live, the name Van Aarden remains, a defiant testament to survival.

A Mysterious Drowning

The stillness of the early morning was abruptly broken by a scream of terror that cut through the peaceful atmosphere of Brugge, disrupting the tranquility of the city. Martijn Janssen stumbled back in shock, nearly dropping the heavy ring of keys in his hand. His usual morning routine of unlocking the bakery and preparing the ovens for the day's work had been violently disrupted by the ghastly sight before him.

A body floated face down in the canal, bobbing gently in the cool waters. Martijn stared in disbelief, his eyes unable to break away from the swollen, discolored flesh and the dark coat that billowed around the lifeless form. How was this possible? The canal was usually so serene this time of morning, with only the occasional ripple marring the glassy surface.

Martijn's mind reeled, unable to comprehend the horror of the situation. He had to alert someone, had to get help. The authorities needed to be informed. Heart pounding, Martijn turned and ran towards the constabulary's office nearby.

Constable Hendrik De Jong was just settling down at his desk with a cup of coffee when the bakery's door burst open violently. He was on his feet in an instant, startled by the sudden intrusion. Martijn stood in the doorway, chest heaving, face pale, and eyes wide with panic.

"There's...a body...in the canal..." Martijn gasped out between gulps of air.

Hendrik set his jaw, immediately grasping the severity of the situation. Setting his coffee down, he strode towards Martijn with urgency. "Show me where."

The two men hurried to the grim scene by the canal's edge. Hendrik's sharp eyes quickly scanned the surrounding area before focusing on the floating corpse. His experienced gaze took in every detail - the expensive coat, the leather boots, the pale skin, and the grotesquely bloated flesh.

Hendrik placed a steadying hand on Martijn's shoulder. "Go and fetch Doctor Van Houten, quickly now. I'll secure the scene." Martijn nodded mutely, still shaken, and rushed off.

With practiced swiftness, Hendrik barricaded off the area, knowing the curiosity of townsfolk would soon draw a crowd. He kept his movements brisk and efficient as he took notes, documenting the scene while taking care to preserve any potential evidence. In the distance, the clatter of approaching hooves marked the arrival of more constables.

Hendrik briefed them rapidly and assigned tasks. "Karel and Lukas, interview the witness and look for anyone who may have seen something. Pieter, examine the body more closely but don't move anything yet. We'll wait for the doctor."

The men dispersed, the quiet morning now a hive of activity. Hendrik stood watchfully as the doctor arrived, trailed by a visibly unsettled Martijn.

Doctor Van Houten's examination was thorough but brief, his experienced eyes taking in the pertinent details. He estimated the time of death to be approximately eight to ten hours prior. There were no immediate signs of violence that he could detect externally, but he would need to conduct a full examination back at his surgery.

Hendrik nodded, mentally filing away the doctor's initial assessment. His gaze swept over the canal again, questions swirling in his mind. Who was this man? How did he end up here? Was this an accident, suicide, or something more sinister?

Doctor Van Houten departed to conduct the autopsy as the punt disappeared down the canal. Hendrik posted guards to keep the scene secure as he headed to the constabulary to begin piecing together this puzzle.

The day passed swiftly in a flurry of activity. Witness statements were taken, missing person reports perused, and leads followed to no avail. The victim's soggy belongings were inventoried, offering a few clues aside from a silver pocket watch and a few coins.

It was evening when Doctor Van Houten arrived with his preliminary results. The inside of the man's lips showed indications of poison, but no external injuries were found. "I'll need to conduct more tests to pin down the exact substance," he informed Hendrik. "But I suspect poison is likely the cause of death."

Hendrik's jaw tightened. This was no accident - it was murder. He redoubled his efforts, working long into the night to uncover any information he could. But as dawn's light peeked over the gabled rooftops, the mystery remained whole.

***

News of the grisly discovery spread through Bruges like wildfire, carried on hushed whispers and gossiping tongues. By mid-morning, a sizable crowd had gathered along the edge of the canal where the drowned man's body still lay, submerged just below the surface.

Murmurs rippled through the crowd as people craned their necks to catch a glimpse of the pale, bloated form drifting lifelessly in the murky water. Some made signs of the cross, others shook their heads and clicked their tongues in disapproval. The animation of the crowd contrasted starkly with the terrible stillness of the dead woman, her open eyes staring vacantly skyward.

"Another one taken by the canals..." said Johan, a fishmonger's son, to no one in particular.

"This makes three in as many weeks," replied a butcher named Frans grimly.

The mood was uneasy, tensions simmering just below the surface. In the shadows of alleyways and arched doorways, suspicious glances were exchanged and accusations whispered. Fear and superstition clung to the crowd like morning mist.

In the distance, past the tightly packed guild houses along the canal, Willem Van Aarden's cottage was just visible - a ramshackle, solitary structure on the outskirts of town. More than a few wary gazes settled on it. Willem's family history made him an easy target for the frightened townspeople's suspicions.

"Old Van Aarden has always been a strange one, keeping to himself like he does," muttered a fishwife to her companion.

"Shame what happened to his family all those years ago, but it left a mark on the poor lad, that much is clear," her friend replied, shaking her head.

"Still, strange goings-on around that cottage of his. My cousin's wife swears she saw ghastly lights moving about his property late one night. Unnatural, she said."

Their voices dropped to barely audible whispers. "You don't think he could be involved in these dreadful drownings, do you?"

***

Eva Van der Meer, a mid-20-year-old seamstress from a modest family in Brugge, climbed the creaky attic stairs, lantern in hand, taking care not to stir up too much dust. She paused on the landing, surveying the jumbled assortment of trunks, furniture, and other relics that crowded the space. Somewhere in this attic, she was certain she could find clues about her grandmother's past.

She began her search, lifting the lids of old steamer trunks and rifling through their contents. In one trunk she found musty gowns and ladies' hats from decades past. Another contained a collection of dusty books and faded sheet music. She examined each item, hoping for some revelation, but found nothing of note.

As she moved deeper into the attic, she spied a small wooden box peeking out from under a moth-eaten blanket. Kneeling down, she pulled it out and carefully opened the lid. Inside lay an assortment of trinkets - coins, buttons, dried flowers - along with a bundle of letters tied with a faded pink ribbon. She untied the letters and fanned through them. The elegant script and dated contents affirmed they were her grandmother's correspondence from her youth.

Beneath the letters, something heavy slid to the bottom of the box. Eva retrieved it - an antique locket on a delicate golden chain. Intricate engraving adorned the oval face of the locket. She ran her fingers over the engraving, mesmerized by the swirling design. With trembling fingers, she pried open the locket. Inside was a portrait of a serious young woman with eyes that bore a striking resemblance to her own.

"It's her, it must be," Eva whispered. This was the first image she had seen of her grandmother as a young woman. She studied the portrait, enthralled by the connection she felt across generations. What had her grandmother been like then? What secrets did she hold? Eva's mind swirled with questions.

She turned her attention back to the letters, skimming their contents for any mention of the locket. The first several yielded no clues, dominated by talk of suitors, social affairs, and family happenings. But tucked halfway through the stack, she discovered what she had been searching for. It was a letter addressed to her grandmother from someone named Isaac, thanking her effusively for sending the locket and emphasizing how much it would mean to have a token of her affection so close to his heart.

Eva's pulse quickened. This was it - evidence of a suitor from her grandmother's past, someone who had clearly adored her enough for her to gift him such an intimate item. She read on, hungry to learn more about this Isaac and the role he played in her grandmother's life. But annoyingly, his identity remained a mystery, referenced only briefly and in passing, as if her grandmother had known him so well his full name was unnecessary.

Eva quickly searched through the remaining letters, hoping for more clues, but found nothing further. She sat back on her heels, frustrated and intrigued. Who was this Isaac? What had become of him and the love implied in his lyrical letter?

Determination welled up within her. The locket and these letters were clues, and she resolved to get to the bottom of the mystery they presented. There must be more to the story, and she would uncover it. She clasped the locket securely in her hand, feeling somehow closer to her grandmother through this unique object she had held so dear.

Eva gathered up the letters and carefully placed them back in the wooden box. As she did, she noticed some initials etched inside the lid: E.V.D.M. - her grandmother's initials. This box truly was filled with her most treasured personal effects. Holding the lantern aloft, Eva cast her gaze around the shadowy attic, wondering what other secrets might be hidden up here, waiting to be found. She would have to explore further, peel back each layer in this space that time had preserved.

For now, her most valuable discovery was nestled securely in her pocket, the metal still warm from her touch. She had found the first clue, and with it, a connection that made her feel closer than ever to the grandmother she realized she hardly knew. Descending from the attic, Eva's mind swirled with newfound curiosity about the woman who had once occupied her world so completely, and the untold stories that the locket signified, waiting to be unlocked.

***

Back at the canal, Constable Hendrik De Jong began his preliminary investigation. The victim's name has been identified as Pieter De Smet. He examined the body, noting certain peculiarities that suggested this wasn't a simple case of accidental drowning. The victim's clothes were immaculate, suggesting he had been well-dressed before entering the water. His hands were clenched tightly into fists, and there were bruises on his wrists and ankles from struggling against something unseen.

Hendrik's mind raced as he considered these details. He knew that drowning victims typically didn't fight back; they succumbed to the water due to lack of air or exhaustion. But these bruises... they suggested a struggle, a fight for survival. And what about the immaculate clothing? It was unusual for someone to drown in their finest attire.

As he continued his examination, Hendrik noticed something suspicious about the water itself. There were small, dark particles suspended within it, almost like grains of sand. He collected a sample and sent it off to the lab for further analysis.

Meanwhile, word of the drowning spread throughout Brugge like wildfire. People gathered at the scene, their faces etched with concern and fear. Among them were Pieter De Smet's family and friends - his wife, Maria; their two children; and several close friends from the local artisan community where Pieter had made his name as a master blacksmith.

Maria clung tightly to her husband's eldest son, her eyes red-rimmed with tears as she whispered prayers for her husband's soul. The children looked lost and bewildered, struggling to comprehend the sudden absence of their father. Friends from the artisan community exchanged worried glances, their livelihoods intertwined with Pieter's success.

Hendrik felt a pang of sympathy for them but knew he had a job to do. He approached Maria cautiously, offering condolences and assuring her that everything possible would be done to find out what happened to her husband. She nodded numbly, barely registering his words as she continued to cling to her son.

As he turned his attention back towards the investigation, Hendrik received a call from Inspector Gerard De Vries requesting his immediate presence at police headquarters for a briefing on the case details and updates on ongoing investigations into other murders in town. Reluctantly leaving the scene behind him, Hendrik made his way through Brugge's cobblestone streets towards De Vries's office in City Hall.

***

Eva clutched the antique locket in her palm as she hurried along the cobblestone streets towards the Brugge Central Library. Though she had lived in the city her whole life, the building's neo-Gothic facade never failed to impress her with its arched windows and intricately carved stonework. She hoped the vast collection of books and documents within its walls might shed some light on the mysteries of her newfound treasure.

The librarian, an older gentleman named Monsieur Dubois, peered at Eva over his spectacles as she breathlessly explained her request.

"Let me take a look at this locket of yours," he said, extending a gloved hand.

Eva placed the oval-shaped locket in his palm. He examined it under a magnifying glass, taking note of the tarnished silver exterior and the strange inscription etched along the edge that Eva had puzzled over.

"Very interesting. This appears to be quite old, likely dating back to the late 18th century if I had to wager a guess. And these markings..." He furrowed his brow. "They look to be some kind of cipher or code."

"Can you make out what it says?" Eva asked eagerly.

Monsieur Dubois shook his head apologetically. "I'm afraid cryptanalysis is not my area of expertise. But let me consult our resources, and I may be able to point you in the right direction."

Eva followed the librarian through the grand, high-ceilinged rooms as he searched the catalogs and made notes, periodically adjusting his spectacles. After some time, he presented her with a stack of heavy, leather-bound volumes.

"These texts on local history, symbols, ciphers, and jewelry crafting techniques of the era may help shed some light on your locket's origins and meaning," he explained.

Eva's eyes lit up. "This is wonderful, thank you!" She found an oak table near a window overlooking one of Brugge's many picturesque canals and got to work.

The hours slipped by as she pored over page after page, taking meticulous notes in her journal. A picture slowly began to emerge of secret societies and encrypted messages popular among the aristocracy in 18th-century Belgium. She found several books analyzing symbols common in lockets of the period - flowers for love, birds for freedom, and stars for guidance.

When the light outside began to fade, Eva reluctantly packed up her notes. Though she was bursting with new insights, the locket's full meaning still eluded her. As she bid Monsieur Dubois goodnight, he gave her an encouraging smile.

"Come back anytime, my dear. I do love a good mystery, and I have a feeling you're on the cusp of a breakthrough."

Eva clutched the books to her chest, smiling. The librarian was right - she could sense the answers were close. She just needed to dig a little deeper. As she stepped outside, a light rain began to fall, misting the cobblestones. Somewhere in the distance, a clock tower chimed, signaling the night's descent on the somber beauty of Brugge.

Eva made her way down the winding cobblestone streets, still lost in thought about the clues she had uncovered at the library. The cool night air helped clear her mind after hours of intense research. As she passed by the town square, she noticed a small crowd gathered near the central fountain. Their voices echoed solemnly under the vaulted archways.

"Such a tragedy, and so unexpected," Martijn Janssen, the owner of the local bakery, was saying to the butcher, Monsieur Dumont. "Pieter was so young and full of life."

Monsieur Dumont shook his head gravely. "No one deserves an end like that, especially not drowned in these waters we've known all our lives."

Eva slowed her pace to listen. So the rumors were true - Pieter De Smet's body had been found in the canals just this morning. She shivered, despite her woolen shawl.

"Mark my words, there's something sinister behind this," came the raspy voice of Old Jacques, the lamplighter. "Healthy young men don't just drown on a clear summer night."

Other hushed voices echoed this sentiment. Though the details were scarce, everyone seemed to agree on one thing: Pieter's death was no ordinary accident.

As Eva continued, she overheard the same ominous theories swirling through the streets - a vengeful spirit was taking men into the waters; someone was exacting revenge for an old family feud; a demonic ritual was behind it. Though she knew most were born of superstition, she couldn't deny the unease creeping through the town.

Nearing her family's modest row house, Eva's thoughts returned to her grandmother's locket tucked safely in her pocket. She quickened her pace, eager to add this new piece to the puzzle. Passing beneath the stone archway, she entered the small courtyard dotted with her mother's herbs and flowers. The scent of rosemary hung in the air.

Inside, she found her parents speaking in hushed voices in the kitchen. They broke off when Eva entered, their faces etched with worry.

"You've heard about Pieter, I take it," said her father. Eva nodded.

"First Diederik, now Pieter," her mother sighed. "If only we knew what evil has come to Brugge."

Eva excused herself and hurried to her room before they could ask any questions. She didn't have time to get drawn into ominous speculations. Spreading her notes and books across the bed, she lit a candle and continued her work into the night. If her instincts were right, her grandmother's locket might hold a vital clue, not just to the family's hidden past, but to the darkness now gripping the town...

Eva rubbed her eyes wearily as the church bells chimed two in the morning. She had filled several pages with details on 18th-century symbolism, but the locket's meaning continued to elude her. As her eyelids grew heavy, the dancing candle flame seemed to hypnotize her. She thought she saw a shape flicker across the wall - a hooded figure gliding silently down stone steps into shadowy water. But when she blinked, it vanished.

Must be dreaming, she thought vaguely as she drifted off to sleep surrounded by leather-bound books and the glow of the dying candle. She dreamed of a gloved hand holding an ornate locket, then dropping it into murky depths. Just before it was swallowed by darkness, it opened to reveal a secret hidden within…

Rumors and Whispers

The damp chill of the morning air cuts through my worn fisherman's coat as I make my way down the cobblestone streets. I keep my eyes low, avoiding the scrutinizing glares that seem to follow my every step. The fog drifting over the canal blankets the city in an eerie haze, one that seems to magnify the hostility brewing beneath the surface.

As I pass the bakery, the murmurs begin. Voices drop to hushed whispers, only to rise again as I move farther down the road. I don't need to hear the words to know what they say. The Van Aarden name carries a bitter stigma in this city, one that lingers no matter how many years go by.

I quicken my pace, eager to escape the oppressive weight of their judgment. The lonely tap of my boots echoes off the buildings lining the narrow alley. This was the same route my father walked every morning before...before the accusations came. I can almost see his silhouette ahead of me - tall, broad-shouldered, with a warm smile few were privileged to see.

The further I get from the town center, the more the vise grip on my chest loosens. I breathe deeply, letting the damp air fill my lungs. The canal comes into view, its gentle current breaking the stillness of the morning. My worn fishing boat bobs softly in the water, awaiting its captain.

As I begin prepping the boat for the day's catch, I catch a flash of movement down the canal. A curtain in the window of a brick townhouse draws shut. I wonder if it was Madame Dutoit, the widow of the magistrate who condemned my family. Does she still peek through her lace curtains, watching for any misstep? For any hint of guilt?

I cast off, letting the momentum carry me into the open waters. The rhythmic slosh of the oars soothes my unease. Out here, judgment gives way to solitude. There are no prying eyes or hushed condemnations, only the company of the wind and the steel-gray sky reflected on the surface.

The canal bends, the town disappearing from view. I breathe easier now. The Van Aarden name means nothing out here. I am just another fisherman, destined to harvest from the brackish waters until my final days. My father taught me the contours of this canal, every eddy and secret depth. We spent countless dawns together, silently casting our nets as the rest of Brugge slept.

I wonder if he ever felt the eyes on him, heard the whispers. If he did, you'd never know. He had a quiet strength, an ability to let judgment roll off of him like raindrops. I envy that resilience now. The stares, the unspoken accusations - they burrow under my skin, an itch I cannot scratch.

My father's old pipe, kept carefully wrapped in oilskin, sits unused at the bow. I bring it to my lips and breathe deeply, hoping to conjure him, if only for a moment. The faint scent of tobacco lingers in the creases. What would he make of the unease gripping Brugge? Is the suspicion once again creeping through its veins?

A splash in the distance pulls me back. A pair of swans glide by, oblivious to the turmoil of man. I tug my woolen cap lower and grip the oars once again. There are fish to catch and mouths to feed. No use dwelling on what cannot be changed. I've spent too many years looking back. Somehow I must find a way to move forward.

The rhythmic cast and pull of the nets offer escape, if only temporarily. The sun breaks through the clouds overhead, glittering on the ripples below. I lose myself in the work, muscles straining against the pull of the current.

A gnarled hand on my shoulder startles me from my reverie. I turn to see old Claude, his weathered face crinkled into a smile. "Quite the haul today," he remarks in his gravelly voice. I nod, unsure how to respond. Claude is the only fisherman to share these waters with me. A widower with no family left, he keeps to himself, seemingly indifferent to town gossip.

"Best be getting back," Claude notes, nodding toward the lightening sky. I gut the fish in silence, their silver scales glinting in the dawn light. We work side by side, a quiet camaraderie passing between us. Claude's is the only company I welcome out here.

The sun rises higher as we make the return journey, its rays glittering on the ripples. The fog has retreated for now, the buildings of Brugge coming into sharper relief. The church spires loom high above the terracotta rooftops, shadowy sentinels over the waking city. I feel the familiar tension creeping back in.

Claude gives a parting nod before mooring his boat. "Chin up, boy," he remarks with a squeeze of my shoulder. Before I can respond, he disappears down the canal bank. I wish I could borrow some of his stoicism, his way of letting the current take him where it may.

With a deep breath, I turn my boat toward the market docks. The day's catch will fetch a decent price, but more importantly, it's a sign of normalcy. I cannot control what others think or say, only how I respond. One foot in front of the other, I remind myself. Keep moving forward.

As I make my way among the crowded stalls, the murmurs begin anew. I keep my eyes trained straight ahead. My name may carry a stigma, but I cannot allow it to define me. I am more than the tragedy that befell my family. Their legacy will not be my destiny.

***

Inspector Gerard De Vries stepped off the train onto the platform of Brugge's bustling station. He paused for a moment, taking in his surroundings. Despite the crowds of travelers hurrying to and fro, there was an unmistakable stillness in the air, as if the city were holding its breath.

De Vries hoisted his leather satchel higher on his shoulder and made his way through the station. He had an appointment with one of his constabulary about a series of troubling deaths - drownings in the city's famed canals that, according to the briefing he'd received, had the townspeople stirred up and on edge.

As he exited the station, the cobblestone streets and ornate gabled buildings of Brugge unfolded before him. De Vries couldn't help but admire the city's aged beauty, like a meticulously preserved relic from centuries past. Yet there was something somber in the medieval alleys and waterways that didn't sit quite right with the detective. An unease seemed to lurk beneath the picturesque facade.

When De Vries arrived at the police station, Constable Hendrik De Jong was already waiting for him. De Jong greeted him with a firm handshake and wasted no time delving into the details of the case.

"Three canal drownings in as many weeks," De Jong explained, leading De Vries to a desk where a folder of notes lay. "All young men, all after dark. No signs of a struggle, no wounds. It's the damnedest thing."

De Vries flipped through the case notes, his eyes scanning over the details. "No indications of suicide?" he asked.

De Jong shook his head. "None whatsoever. All signs point to foul play, but we can't figure out how someone is getting to these men without a fight."

The detective's eyes narrowed in thought. "No witnesses? In a city like this?"

"Most folks are home by dusk these days," De Jong said. "Afraid they might be next if they linger by the canals at night."

De Vries considered this information. If fear was already seizing the locals, solving this case quickly would be crucial before panic spread further.

"What about suspects?" he inquired, eager to start eliminating possibilities.

De Jong hesitated before responding. "Well, there's been some murmurings about Willem Van Aarden."

The name meant nothing to De Vries, but the constable's tone indicated local significance. "Go on," he prompted.

"The Van Aardens have a bad reputation in Brugge, on account of the witch trials some centuries back," De Jong explained. "Whole family was executed, accused of dark magic. Willem is one of the last of the bloodlines. Keeps to himself mostly, and works as a fisherman. But folks have been wary of him since the drownings started."

De Vries absorbed this carefully, unwilling to prematurely pass judgment. "Is there evidence directly linking him to the murders?"

De Jong shook his head. "None yet. But he's been seen near the crime scenes, being a fisherman and all. And people figure it's no coincidence, him being a Van Aarden descended from witches and these drownings happening."

The detective considered pressing for more information but decided to reserve judgment for now. He'd need to speak to Willem himself before determining if he was a true suspect or simply a convenient scapegoat for the town's fear.

For now, his priority was examining the sites where the bodies had been found. De Jong led him to a map marking each location, spaced out along the snaking waterways that crisscrossed Brugge. De Vries traced them with a finger, searching for any hidden pattern or meaning.

"I'll need to visit each site myself," he declared. "See if there are any details your men may have overlooked."

De Jong nodded. "Of course. My men can take you there straight away."

Within the hour, De Vries found himself being rowed along the very canals where the mysterious drownings had occurred, their waters now placid and innocuous beneath the afternoon sun. He studied the ancient buildings lining the canal banks, imagining what secrets their aged facades concealed.

At the first crime scene, De Vries disembarked and scrutinized every inch along the narrow quay. Other than a few lingering candle tributes left by grieving locals, there was little evidence remaining from the drowning weeks earlier.

De Jong watched De Vries work with reserved curiosity. "We searched thoroughly but found nothing of note," he commented. "Just like the others."

De Vries remained silent, intent on his examination. He crouched low near the water's edge, peering into the depths below. The canal's surface was an opaque green, revealing none of its secrets.

"The canals appear shallow along the edges," mused De Vries. "Yet the reports state all the victims were found fully submerged."

De Jong nodded grimly. "They must have been dragged out farther, into the deeper middle channel. But we found no marks to suggest such a struggle."

The lack of physical evidence was troubling, but De Vries pushed aside his frustration. He would need to approach this investigation with logic and patience. There was something here not yet discovered, some unseen thread connecting these deaths; he need only find the loose end and begin to unravel it.

For now, he could only continue his examination of the remaining crime scenes, searching for patterns and anomalies. De Vries finished his inspection of the first site, and then turned to De Jong. "Take me to the next one."

The constable dipped his head and led the detective back to the waiting boat, the old floorboards creaking under their footsteps...

***

The clamor of the fish market surrounded me as I arranged my catch on the ice. Silverfish tails flipped lazily despite the ruckus. My rough hands worked quickly, nestling each fish into the icy bed. I had hauled in a fine catch today - mackerel, sea bass, mullet. My small wooden boat had lurched under their weight when I pulled the nets.

I kept my head low, focused on my task, though I could feel the eyes on me. The bustling crowd gave me a wide berth, unconsciously forming a bubble around my stall. I was used to the pitied looks and hushed whispers by now. "The Canal Whisperer," they called me. An omen of death.

A chill morning mist still clung to the canal, dampening the cobblestones. Despite the thick woolen sweater chafing my neck, I shivered. Ominous fog always reminded me of that night, when they came for us. I shook off the dark memories, rubbing my hands together for warmth.

The market's familiar sounds washed over me - vendors singing their wares, customers haggling for the best price. But around my stall, there was only silence. Wary eyes followed my every move. Passersby crossed the street to avoid me. I kept my gaze down. Their fear and distrust was an open wound that never fully healed.

I busied myself arranging the fish, focusing on each task. Gutting knives flashed as I sliced open bellies with practiced ease. The scent of fish guts mingled with the smell of the sea. My hands were soon slick, scales sticking to my skin.

Despite my hunched posture, I was acutely aware of two women nearby gossiping in hushed tones. "That's him, isn't it? The canal murderer?" one asked. I gritted my teeth, my jaw tightening as I forced myself to keep working. Their whispers were like papercuts, small but unrelenting.

A man in a bowler hat approached my stall but stopped short, eyeing the fish warily as if they too were cursed. He turned abruptly and hurried away. My shoulders slumped. Another sale was lost.

Out of the corner of my eye, I saw a mother pull her child closer as they scuttled past. The boy gawked at me, eyes wide. "Don't look at him," the mother scolded, yanking the boy's hand. My hand unconsciously went to the brand on my chest, forever marking me as the last descendent of a witch.

I let out a slow breath, watching it fog before me. I could not blame them for their judgment and fear. Not when I had known the depths of darkness fear can lead to. The early loss of my parents and sister had ignited a wildfire of anger within me, burning for far too long. It was only recently that I had found a kind of peace, a stillness within. But their whispered accusations about witchcraft threatened to reignite the flames.

A commotion at the end of the market caught my attention. I looked up to see Inspector De Vries's hulking form pushing through the crowd, his black coat flapping. Our eyes met for a moment before I dropped my gaze once more. The Inspector's arrival in Brugge signaled a reckoning was coming, for me and this town. Justice cast a long shadow, and I had dwelt in the darkness for too long.

With a sigh, I laid down my gutting knife, wiping my hands on my trousers. The fish were arranged on the ice, their dead vacant eyes staring at nothing. Despite the fine catch, my stall remained empty of customers save for a mangy grey cat nibbling at entrails cast aside.

"Well Soot, at least you're not afraid of me," I murmured, scratching the cat behind her ear. She purred, arching her back. I packed away my tools, getting ready to close shop for the day. My catch would feed only me and Soot tonight.

***

Inspector Gerard De Vries stood at the edge of the bustling market square, his keen eyes taking in every detail. The town was a picturesque blend of history and modernity, with cobblestone streets lined with ancient buildings and vibrant shops. But there was an undercurrent of unease that ran through the place, like a dark current beneath the surface of the tranquil canals.

His gaze lingered on Willem Van Aarden, who stood nearby, selling fish from a small wooden stand. De Vries couldn't shake off the feeling that something about Willem seemed off. He had heard whispers about the man's ancestors being accused of witchcraft and executed, and now, with the mysterious canal murders happening in town, Willem found himself at the center of suspicion.

As De Vries continued to observe Willem, he noticed how people moved away from him, casting sidelong glances filled with fear and mistrust. It was clear that Willem family's past weighed heavily on him and on those around him.

De Vries jotted down his initial observations in his notepad. He knew he had to approach this situation with an open mind and a non-judgmental attitude. He had come to Brugge to solve a crime, not to make assumptions or jump to conclusions based on hearsay or prejudice.

He turned his attention to the market stalls around him, taking note of the various vendors selling their wares. The scent of fresh bread and brewing coffee filled the air, mingling with the sounds of laughter and chatter from patrons enjoying their morning shopping routine. Despite the apparent normalcy of it all, De Vries couldn't shake off a sense of disquiet that lingered at the edges of his consciousness.

As he continued to walk through the market square, De Vries took note of other townsfolk going about their daily routines. He saw children playing near a fountain, couples strolling hand-in-hand along the canalside pathways, and elderly women chatting animatedly outside a bakery. Yet beneath this veneer of normalcy lay a simmering tension that seemed to permeate every aspect of life in Brugge.

He approached a group of locals gathered around a newsstand, listening intently as a man read aloud from a newspaper article about the latest developments in the canal murders case. As De Vries drew closer, he could hear snippets of conversation that hinted at fear and suspicion towards Willem Van Aarden - accusations that seemed unfounded yet impossible to ignore given his family history and proximity to the crime scenes.

Despite these troubling signs, De Vries resolved to maintain an objective perspective on Willem's involvement in the murders case. He knew better than to jump to conclusions based on circumstantial evidence or unfounded rumors - especially when dealing with such sensitive matters as witchcraft accusations and capital punishment cases from centuries past. His mission was clear: solve these murders without letting personal biases cloud his judgment or compromise his duty as an investigator dedicated to upholding justice for all citizens of Brugge.

***

Elsje, with her years etched deeply into her face and hands, moved towards me with a careful step. Her fingers, twisted from time and toil, hinted at a life filled with hard work and perhaps, untold stories. Despite her age, there was a keen sharpness to her gaze and a wit in her words that belied the fragility her appearance might suggest. She approached, not with the hesitance of the elderly, but with a deliberate, measured caution that spoke of wisdom and a deep understanding of the world around her. Her eyes twinkled with malicious glee as she leaned in close, her breath hot against my ear.

"Willem Van Aarden," she hissed, her voice barely above a whisper. "I've been keeping an eye on you."

I stiffened, my heart pounding in my chest. I knew what was coming. Elsje was notorious for her cruelty and her penchant for spreading rumors.

"What do you want?" I demanded, trying to keep my voice steady.

Elsje cackled maniacally, her laughter echoing through the quiet cobblestone streets of Brugge. "Oh, Willem," she purred. "You're just the man I wanted to see."

Her words sent a shiver down my spine. I had heard whispers about Elsje's involvement in the recent tragedies that had befallen our beloved city. The drownings in the canals had cast a pall over Brugge, and now it seemed that my own family's dark past was being dragged into the light.

"What do you want from me?" I repeated, my voice growing more urgent as the tension mounted.

Elsje leaned in even closer, her breath hot against my cheek. "I want to know everything about your family," she whispered menacingly. "Especially your grandmother."

My heart leaped into my throat at the mention of my grandmother. She had been a mysterious figure in our family's history, shrouded in secrecy and whispered about in hushed tones. But now it seemed that Elsje was determined to uncover the truth about her past, no matter the cost.

"You leave my family out of this," I warned, my voice rising with anger and indignation. "I won't stand for you spreading lies about them."

Elsje sneered at me, her eyes glinting with malice. "Oh, Willem," she hissed again. "You're just the man I wanted to see." She wagged a gnarled finger at me before turning away, leaving me standing alone on the cobblestone street with a sinking feeling in the pit of my stomach.

***

Inspector Gerard De Vries stood in the grand office of Brugge's mayor Elisabeth De Groote. The room felt like a warm embrace, its walls telling stories through the intricate tapestries that hung with grace, each thread woven with tales of the city's grand past. The wooden furniture, ornate and lovingly crafted, spoke of skilled hands and timeless artistry, bearing witness to the richness of the city's heritage. Every piece seemed to hold a memory, inviting you to sit and listen to the whispered legacies of times gone by. This was not just a room; it was a sanctuary where history breathed and danced in the light, inviting all who entered to become part of its enduring story.

"Good morning, Mayor," De Vries began, his voice firm yet respectful. "I trust you're well?"

The mayor nodded, a hint of concern in her eyes. "Indeed, Inspector. But I must admit, these recent events have taken their toll on our beloved town."

De Vries nodded solemnly. "I understand your sentiments, sir. The murders in the canals have cast a pall over Brugge, and I am here to discuss how we might bring some measure of closure to the victims and their families."

The mayor leaned forward in her chair. "Tell me more about your investigation so far."

De Vries paused for a moment to gather his thoughts before continuing. "Well, we've interviewed countless individuals within the community.

We've also examined the crime scenes meticulously, searching for any clues that might lead us to the perpetrator."

"And what have you discovered?" the mayor asked anxiously.

"Unfortunately, not much," De Vries admitted. "But I believe there is more to this case than meets the eye. I suspect that the Van Aarden family's dark past may be connected to these murders in some way."

The mayor's expression darkened at the mention of the Van Aardens. "That family has always been shrouded in mystery and suspicion," she said grimly. "Their tragic history with witchcraft has cast a long shadow over Brugge."

De Vries nodded gravely. "Indeed, it seems that their misfortunes have not been limited to mere superstition and gossip. The recent drownings have only served to exacerbate the fear and mistrust that already exists within the community."

The mayor sighed heavily. "It seems as though we are fighting an uphill battle against an invisible enemy."

De Vries nodded sympathetically. "I understand your frustration, madam. But rest assured that I will leave no stone unturned in my pursuit of justice for these victims and their families."

As they continued their discussion, De Vries couldn't help but feel a sense of unease growing within him. There was something about Brugge that felt off-kilter as if it was hiding something beneath its picturesque facade. He knew he would need all his skills as an investigator to uncover the truth behind these mysterious murders and bring peace to this troubled town once and for all.

***

The cobblestone under my heavy boots resonates with memories. Those memories echo a time when my family's name held respect, not whispers of witchcraft. I walk the familiar path towards the canal, the same waterways where my ancestors fished, and where recent horrors unfolded.

In my satchel, a humble lunch awaits - a thick slice of coarse bread, a wedge of sharp cheese, and a flask of ale. My fingers trace the initials carved into the wooden bench by the canal. They're old, weather-worn like me. 'V.A.', they read. Van Aarden.

I settle down on the bench, facing the placid water that hides such terrible secrets. I break off a piece of bread, its rustic crust surrendering to my calloused grip. The cheese offers a sharp contrast to the bread's stolidity, its tang an echo of Brugge's character - quaint charm on the surface with a sharp undercurrent.

I take a swig from my flask, feeling the ale's warmth seep into me. My gaze settles on the rippling canal. This is where they found them - innocent souls claimed by this silent killer.

Brugge's canals are my sanctuary and my prison, their waters reflecting at me the scornful glances of the townsfolk. They whisper behind their hands as I pass by. I'm the outsider in my town; an outcast bearing an ancestral sin.

A gaggle of children pass by, their laughter echoing through the narrow alleyways. They pause to stare at me - their innocent eyes wide with curiosity and fear - then scamper away when I meet their gaze.

I let out a soft sigh that fogs up in the cold air. The chill doesn't bother me; it's another feeling entirely that sends shivers down my spine - loneliness.

My mind drifts back to those horrific days when the world I knew crumbled. My parents couldn't stand the never ending accusations and suspicious of the city anymore. Taking my sister with her, they jumped into the sea and drowned themselfs.

The weight of their loss bears down on me, a constant reminder of the injustice that took them from me. But within me, a fire smolders. A fire-forged from pain, hardened by years of isolation, and kept alive by the desire for justice.

I take another swig of ale, letting it wash down the bitter taste of past injustices. But there's no ale strong enough to wash away the scars etched deep within my soul.

I stare at my reflection in the canal's mirror-like surface, seeing beyond the rugged exterior to the resilient spirit beneath. I am Willem Van Aarden, I remind myself. The last of my line, carrying a name stained with suspicion and a heart filled with resolve.

In this town that's turned its back on me, among these waters that whisper tales of dread, I stand alone. Yet, I'm not defeated.

My lunch is over; only crumbs remain on the parchment paper. I stand up, brushing off invisible dust from my worn trousers. The afternoon sun casts long shadows on Brugge's cobblestones as I leave my solitary spot by the canal.

***

Inspector Gerard De Vries stood at the edge of the canal, his eyes scanning the murky waters. The site of the drownings was eerily quiet, with only the distant sound of a boat passing by breaking the silence. He had been tasked with solving this baffling case, and he was determined to leave no stone unturned in his search for answers.

He ordered a thorough re-examination of the area, looking for any overlooked clues or evidence that could shed light on the mysterious deaths. His team carefully combed through the murky waters, searching for anything that might have been missed during the initial investigation.

As they worked, whispers of fear and suspicion filled the air. The townsfolk were terrified, and their anxiety was palpable even from a distance. Patrons at a local café huddled together, their voices low as they discussed the latest drowning and their fears of a murderer in their midst. Their conversation was a mix of fear, superstition, and suspicion, reflecting the growing anxiety that gripped Brugge.

De Vries was deep in thought as he reviewed the evidence gathered so far. He knew that this case would be complex, but he was determined to uncover the truth behind these gruesome deaths. As he pondered his approach to the investigation, he couldn't shake off a nagging feeling that there was more to this story than met the eye.

The day wore on, and De Vries found himself immersed in his work. He interviewed witnesses and suspects alike, searching for any clue that could lead him closer to solving this enigma. As he delved deeper into the case, he began to realize that Willem's family history was intertwined with Brugge's dark past - a past marked by witchcraft accusations and executions. This realization sent chills down his spine as he considered its implications for Willem's current predicament.

The Inspector's Doubts

Before the first light of dawn has a chance to peek through the windows, Inspector Gerard De Vries finds solace at his desk within the quiet walls of the Brugge police station. Illuminated by a lone lamp, its warm light bathes the desk in a cozy glow, bringing a touch of comfort to the otherwise cold room. Around him, case files lay scattered, each a silent testament to stories of sorrow plucked from the city's canals. The station enveloped in an almost reverent hush, is disturbed only by the occasional groan of the aging wood underfoot and the gentle, rhythmic scratching of his pen as he diligently records the night's solemn tales. In this moment, Gerard is more than an inspector; he's a keeper of stories, each mark of his pen a homage to the lives entwined with the city's watery veins.

De Vries turns a page, his eyes scanning the meticulous notes he's taken during the investigation. The statements from townsfolk about Willem Van Aarden's movements on the nights of the drownings form a puzzle that refuses to fit neatly together. Some claim to have seen Willem's silhouette against the moonlit water, while others are certain the fisherman was nursing a drink in solitude at The Gilded Carp.

The inspector leans back in his chair, fingers steepled against his lips. A discrepancy glares at him from the parchment; it is as though Willem has been in two places at once. De Vries understands all too well the elusive nature of memory, shaped and reshaped by the whispers and wary looks that thread through the fabric of human interaction. He's learned, through years of sifting through stories and testimonies, that what we remember isn't always the pure truth but rather a mosaic, colored by emotion and perception. To him, memory is like water, slipping through fingers, taking on the hues of the containers it fills. This awareness guides him as he navigates the complex waters of his investigations, always mindful of the subtle ways in which the truth can be shaded and altered by the very nature of recollection. He pulls out another statement, this one from an old woman who insists she saw Willem walking towards his boat, a shadow among shadows, on a night one of the bodies was found. But there is something about her words, a hesitance that didn't sit right with him during her interview.

Another witness, a young boy who helps at the market, speaks of seeing Willem miles away from the scene, caught in an animated discussion with an unknown traveler. This boy has no reason to lie; his innocence shines through his statement like sunlight through stained glass.

Inspector De Vries makes notes in the margin, underlining and circling key phrases. He draws connections with lines that crisscross like the canals themselves. A pattern begins to emerge – one that suggests Willem's presence near the waterways might be more than mere coincidence.

Yet doubt lingers like morning mist. The inspector retrieves his pocket watch from its resting place on the desk and flips it open; its ticks are steady and reassuring against the murmur of suspicion that fills his mind. He reminds himself not to be swayed by conjecture or superstition; facts are his steadfast companions in this dance with uncertainty.

The early morning fog clings to the fields like a shroud as Inspector Gerard De Vries navigates the narrow dirt road leading to Willem Van Aarden's cottage. His carriage rattles over uneven ground, the sound muffled by the dense air. He reins in his horse as the cottage comes into view, a solitary silhouette against the waking sky.

De Vries steps out, noting the stark simplicity of the dwelling. The thatched roof sags slightly, weighed down by time and weather. A small garden, more practical than ornamental, bears a testament to Willem's self-reliance. The inspector's breath forms a cloud in the chill as he approaches, his boots leaving crisp impressions on the frost-covered ground.

He knocks on the weathered door. Moments pass before it creaks open, revealing Willem standing on the threshold. The fisherman's eyes are guarded yet curious, his posture as sturdy as the doorframe he fills.

"Mr. Van Aarden," De Vries begins, tipping his hat respectfully. "May I have a moment of your time?"

Willem's nod grants entry into his world—a world that seems at odds with the rumors swirling around Brugge like autumn leaves in the wind.

The interior of the cottage is as unassuming as its owner. A fire crackles in a stone hearth, warding off the morning's bite. The furnishings are sparse: a wooden table worn smooth by use, chairs that favor function over form, and shelves lined with various tools of a fisherman's trade.

De Vries takes a seat at Willem's invitation, observing how the man moves with an ease that belies his rugged exterior. There is care in how he places two cups on the table and pours steaming tea from a kettle into each one.

The inspector warms his hands against his cup, savoring the heat that seeps into his skin. He watches Willem sit across from him with an air of resignation—as if this interview is yet another tide he must endure.

"I'll come straight to it," De Vries says after a sip of tea that tastes of herbs and honesty. "The town is uneasy with these drownings, and your name has surfaced more than once."

Willem meets De Vries's gaze squarely. "I understand why they suspect me," he replies, his voice steady like the earth beneath him. "But I had no part in those deaths."

De Vries nods, noting not just what Willem says but how he says it—without haste or heat, like a man who has weathered many storms and has learned when to sail and when to anchor.

"And where were you on those nights?" De Vries asks.

"I was out on my boat most times," Willem answers without flinching from the inspector's scrutiny. "The water... it brings me peace."

"A solitary pursuit," De Vries muses aloud.

Willem's lips curve into something that might be considered a smile in another life—one less marked by loss and suspicion. "It's been my way for years."

The inspector leans back in his chair, considering this man who seems more at home with tides than tales spun by fearful townsfolk. There is an aura of solitude about Willem that speaks not of guilt but of someone accustomed to being apart from others.

"You understand I must ask these questions," De Vries continues. "Your family history with... witchcraft accusations—it casts a long shadow."

Willem's face tightens imperceptibly at this reminder of past wounds but his voice remains even when he speaks. "I live with my ancestors' shadows every day; they darken my door no matter what I do."

De Vries nods slowly; there is weight in Willem's words that goes beyond resentment or anger—a resignation forged through years of being marked by history's cruel pen.

"Have you seen anything unusual? Anyone near the canals at night?" De Vries probes gently.

"I keep to myself," Willem states simply. "But Brugge has many secrets; some walk in daylight while others prefer shadows."

There is truth there—De Vries feels it keenly. The canals do whisper secrets meant for those willing to listen.

The inspector finishes his tea and stands, placing his hat back atop his head. "Thank you for your time and candor, Mr. Van Aarden."

Willem rises too, showing De Vries to the door with quiet dignity.

As De Vries steps back into his carriage and guides it away from Willem's humble abode, he carries with him more questions than answers—a common currency in his line of work but one that feels particularly burdensome today.

And so Inspector Gerard De Vries leaves behind Willem's cottage.

***

The carriage trundles away from Willem's solitary dwelling, the morning mist parting reluctantly before the steadfast horse. Inspector Gerard De Vries sits with a pensive air, the warmth from the fisherman's tea lingering in his core. His thoughts weave through the facts and rumors.

He spots a group of local fishermen by the canal, their nets casting wide over the still water, and instructs his driver to halt. Stepping down onto the dew-kissed grass, De Vries approaches them, his presence commanding yet unobtrusive.

"Morning," he greets, tipping his hat to acknowledge their labor.

The fishermen turn, their expressions a mix of curiosity and caution. One by one, they nod in response, their hands never ceasing their rhythmic toil.

"I'm Inspector De Vries," he introduces himself formally. "I'd like a word about Willem Van Aarden if you have a moment."

The name hangs in the air, a baited hook waiting for a catch. The fishermen exchange glances; one spit into the canal, another shrugs as if to shake off an unwelcome chill.

"He's an odd one," mutters the eldest among them, his face weathered like the hull of an old ship. "Keeps to himself."

"But he knows these waters better than anyone," chimes in a younger fisherman with bright eyes and hands calloused by nets and ropes.

"Has he ever seemed... out of sorts to you? Or been seen with strangers?" De Vries inquires, watching their faces closely for any flicker of insight.

"Nah," another replies after a moment's hesitation. "Willem's as steady as they come. Doesn't mix much with others."

The inspector notes the undercurrent of respect in their voices despite their wary demeanor. It is clear they hold no particular fondness for Willem but neither do they condemn him outright.

"Ever known him to act violently?" De Vries probes further.

Laughter breaks from one fisherman's lips before he can stifle it. "Willem? He'd sooner fight a fish than a man."

De Vries's eyes narrow slightly—not in suspicion but contemplation. These men, sculpted by countless days beneath the open sky and against the backdrop of ceaseless waters, stand as embodiments of honesty. Their experiences have forged them into unwavering pillars of candor, their every word resonating with the depth and gravity of the life they've led. Though they may not fully grasp the impact of their voices, the authenticity and earnestness that lace their speech imbue their words with a significance that is felt, if not always acknowledged. In their presence, one can't help but sense the profound truth of their lived experience, a testament to the unvarnished reality of life at sea.

"Thank you," De Vries says after a few more questions yield nothing substantial. "Your cooperation is appreciated."

He tips his hat once more and returns to his carriage. As it rolls away, De Vries feels the tendrils of skepticism tightening around his thoughts regarding Willem's guilt.

A familiar unease settles over him as he recalls another case from years past—a case that had gnawed at his conscience with sharp teeth until justice had been served correctly. He was younger then, more prone to be swayed by public outcry and less tempered by experience.

It had been in another town much like Brugge where whispers turned into shouts that condemned an innocent man. The suspect was much like Willem—aloof and enigmatic, easy fodder for suspicion in times of fear.

De Vries remembers walking through streets thick with accusation, each gaze upon him demanding swift resolution. The suspect's eyes had been much like Willem's when they first met: resigned yet holding a flicker of hope that someone would listen—listen—to what wasn't being said.

The inspector had delved deep into that case, picking apart alibis and testimonies with meticulous care. It was only when he uncovered an overlooked piece of evidence that the true culprit was revealed—a person above reproach in the eyes of the public but rotten beneath their respectable veneer.

That case taught De Vries more about justice than any textbook or lecture; it showed him how easily the truth can be shrouded by fear and how vital it is to question every assumption, especially when lives hang in balance.

Now here he is in Brugge, facing echoes of that long-ago challenge. The whispers around Willem are too reminiscent of those previous cries for vengeance against an easy target.

De Vries leans back against the leather seat, closing his eyes as if to sharpen his mind's focus. He will not allow past mistakes or town gossip to cloud his judgment—not while there is still work to be done and truth to be unearthed.

***

Back at the police station, the atmosphere is rich with the familiar, comforting scents of ink and aged wood. These smells mingle and permeate the space, creating a tangible sense of history and diligent work that has unfolded within these walls. The air, thick with these aromas, seems to carry the weight of countless stories, whispered secrets, and the silent presence of those who have passed through, leaving behind traces of their endeavors. It's a space where the past and present meet, enveloped in the essence of tradition and the persistent pursuit of truth. Inspector Gerard De Vries strides into the dimly lit office, his mind churning with the morning's revelations. Constable Hendrik De Jong looks up from a stack of papers, his face etched with concern.

"Any luck, Inspector?" Hendrik asks, setting aside the paperwork.

De Vries removes his hat, placing it on the desk with a thoughtful tap. "Luck is not what we need, Hendrik. We need clarity—and we're sorely lacking in that department."

Hendrik leans back in his chair, nodding slowly. "The town's whispers are growing louder by the day."

De Vries takes a seat across from him, folding his hands on the desk. "We cannot allow rumors to dictate our investigation," he asserts firmly. "What we require is evidence, hard and incontrovertible."

Hendrik meets De Vries' gaze, the unspoken understanding between them clear. They have been down this road before—different case, same cloud of suspicion.

"The townsfolk are convinced Willem's involved," Hendrik says with a sigh. "But I've known him for years; he's not capable of such violence."

De Vries nods in agreement. "I've spoken with him and others who know him. His demeanor does not strike me as that of a guilty man. And the fishermen by the canal—none could recount a single instance where Willem acted with aggression."

Hendrik rubs his chin thoughtfully. "Still, we can't dismiss him outright without evidence to clear his name."

"Which brings us to our next course of action," De Vries replies as he stands up. "The autopsy reports—have they been finalized?"

"Yes, they're on your desk," Hendrik answers, pointing to a folder bound in red string.

De Vries moves to his desk and sits down, unraveling the string with deliberate care. He spreads out the documents, each page a silent testament to a life cut short.

Hendrik stands behind De Vries, peering over his shoulder as they pore over the medical examiner's findings. The inspector's finger traces down the lines of text, pausing at each victim's time of death.

A frown creases De Vries's brow as he leans closer to the parchment. "This doesn't align," he murmurs more to himself than to Hendrik.

"What doesn't?" Hendrik inquires, leaning in further.

"The estimated times of death—they vary widely." De Vries taps the paper for emphasis. "And not one coincides with when Willem was seen near the canals."

Hendrik squints at the scrawled handwriting that details each victim's final moments. "Are you saying these drownings didn't happen at night?"

"It appears so," De Vries replies, sitting back in his chair with a heavy sigh. "Which means our killer might have struck at different times, perhaps even during daylight hours."

Hendrik's expression turns grim. "That would make finding witnesses all the more difficult."

De Vries nods slowly. "Indeed." He scans through more pages before halting once again.

"And there's something else," he says quietly. "Look here—signs of struggle are absent on most victims but present on others." He points out bruising on one victim's arms and scratches on another's face.

Hendrik leans closer, his eyes narrowing as he takes in the details. "So some fought back while others didn't—or couldn't."

"That inconsistency troubles me," De Vries admits as he continues reviewing each page meticulously.

"Could it be that some were taken by surprise?" Hendrik suggests.

"Possibly," De Vries concedes. "Or it could indicate that we're looking for more than one assailant."

In the room, a hush settles, broken only by the soft noise of shifting papers, as they both pause to contemplate this newfound perspective. It's a moment of reflection, where the air itself seems to hold its breath, charged with the realization of a complexity that deepens the enigma they're entangled in. This silence is more than an absence of noise; it's a shared space of understanding between them, a mutual recognition of the intricate puzzle that lies ahead. As they sit in quietude, the rustle of the documents serves as a reminder of the ever-evolving mystery that binds them, weaving a thread of anticipation through the stillness.

After several long moments spent dissecting every line and note within the autopsy reports, De Vries leans back in his chair and exhales slowly.

"We must re-examine every piece of evidence we have thus far," he declares resolutely. "And we must do so without prejudice or preconceived notions."

***

Inspector Gerard De Vries stands at the edge of the canal. His sharp eyes are scanning the water's surface as it laps gently against the moss-covered stone. The early afternoon sun casts a deceptive serenity over the scene, but De Vries is not swayed by the peaceful facade. This very canal has cradled the lifeless bodies of victims, secrets submerged in its murky depths.

He kneels, peering into the water where shadows dance with the ebb and flow. De Vries has been here before, but something nags at him—a whisper of something missed, a detail overlooked. His gaze is methodical, moving from the water to the bank and then to the cobblestone path that runs alongside it.

De Vries spots a small alcove obscured by reeds, barely noticeable to an untrained eye. He moves closer, pushing aside the verdant curtain to reveal a narrow recess in the canal wall. A flicker of intuition tells him this is a place someone might hide or be hidden.

He crouches down, examining the space more closely. The mud inside the alcove is undisturbed, save for the delicate trails left by snails and insects. But there—just at the edge where shadow meets sunlight—is an indentation that seems out of place. It's subtle, yet to De Vries' keen observation, it stands out as a silent scream in a quiet room.

He reaches out, fingers brushing over the irregularity. It's a footprint—partially and eroded by water but unmistakably human. The size suggests someone small or perhaps a child; certainly not a man of Willem's sturdy build.

De Vries senses a thread unraveling in the web of suspicion surrounding Willem Van Aarden.

His attention shifts as voices drift toward him from further along the canal—a group of townsfolk gathered in a heated discussion. Their words are carried by the breeze, laced with fear and accusation.

"He's got that look about him," one woman says sharply. "The same look his witch ancestors must have had."

De Vries rises to his full height and makes his way toward them, his presence commanding even before he speaks.

"Good day," he interjects as he approaches, his tone courteous yet firm enough to cut through their gossip.

The townsfolk fall silent, their eyes wide as they recognize him.

"Inspector De Vries," one man nods, an attempt at casual respect that doesn't quite mask his discomfort.

"I couldn't help but overhear your conversation," De Vries says evenly. "It seems you have strong opinions about these tragedies."

The woman who spoke earlier steps forward defiantly. "We know what we see," she asserts. "Willem's family cursed this town long ago—it's no surprise he's following in their footsteps."

De Vries meets her gaze squarely. "And what exactly do you see? Because thus far, all I have encountered are whispers without substance."

She opens her mouth to retort but falters under his scrutinizing stare.

"Suspicion is not evidence," De Vries continues in a tone that brooks no argument. "And fear can often mislead good judgment."

The group exchanges uneasy glances as they grapple with his words.

"I urge you all to consider facts over folklore," De Vries adds before nodding curtly and leaving them to their reflections.

***

As evening descends upon Brugge, Inspector Gerard De Vries finds himself seated at a corner table in The Gilded Carp tavern. The low hum of conversation mingles with the clink of glasses and occasional laughter—a symphony of life carrying on despite darkness lurking beneath its streets.

He sips from a glass of local ale, its bitter tang grounding him in thought. Today has yielded more questions than answers; however, each question slowly chips away at false certainties and carves space for truth.

De Vries opens his notebook—the leather cover worn from years of service—and begins to write. His penmanship is meticulous as he records observations from today's visit to the canal: the footprint discovery and his interaction with the townsfolk.

Determined to explore every possible avenue, De Vries sketches out an initial plan for tomorrow's inquiries. He will delve into archives for records that might shed light on Willem's ancestors—documents untouched by time's forgetful dust might hold keys to understanding present mysteries.

And Willem himself—De Vries resolves to learn more about him beyond town gossip and tragic lineage. There must be threads within Willem's own story that could lead to either exoneration or damning proof; threads that need careful unraveling by hands unshaken by superstition or haste.

As patrons laugh and converse around him, oblivious to his solitary quest within their midst, Inspector Gerard De Vries continues writing late into the night. Each word committed to paper reaffirms his commitment: he will chase this elusive truth down every shadowed alley and into every whispering canal until justice emerges clear and unsullied from Brugge's murky depths.

A Reluctant Ally

The University of Brugge's dimly lit library is a second home for Helena De Baere. She sits at her desk, hunched over, surrounded by towering stacks of leather-bound books. She pores over a series of documents with meticulous care, each page bursting with her meticulous annotations and cross-references. The rich, musty scent of aged paper fills the air, mingling with the faint aroma of herbs clinging to her apron. Her morning spent at the apothecary lingers, a reminder of her passion for knowledge and her dedication to her studies.

The peaceful hush of the library is suddenly interrupted by a soft knock at the door. Helena's intense focus is shattered as she turns to see a timid-looking page from the town hall standing in the doorway, nervously twisting his cap in his hands.

"Miss De Baere," he begins, voice tinged with urgency. "There's news you must hear."

With a nod, she motions him inside. The boy steps forward, unfolding a crisp sheet of newsprint and laying it before her. The headline screams of tragedy: another body found in the canals of Brugge. Helena's brow furrows as she absorbs the grim details—the town gripped by fear, a shadow cast upon one Willem Van Aarden.

Helena's heart twinges with a familiar pang—compassion. Willem, a man she knows only through whispered rumors and sidelong glances, now stands accused because of his family's blemished history.

"Thank you for bringing this to me," she says, her voice steady despite the turmoil brewing within.

The page nods and slips away as silently as he arrives, leaving Helena alone with her thoughts and the ink-black print staring back at her. She pushes aside her research notes; this new puzzle demands her attention.

Helena rises from her chair and walks to the window, peering out at the university courtyard below where students traverse cobblestone paths in earnest discussion. Her mind races—not just with scientific curiosity but with an innate sense of justice that cannot be quelled.

It is clear to her that this case calls for more than what local gossip and superstition can offer—it demands forensic insight. An insight that Helena knows she possesses in abundance.

She turns back to her desk, fingers tracing the edge of the newspaper as she considers the implications of involving herself in this matter. Her father would caution against it, reminding her of their duty to their patrons at the apothecary.

Yet as she stands there amidst whispers of academia and knowledge centuries old, Helena feels a pull stronger than duty—an unshakeable resolve to apply her skills where they are most needed.

Her decision crystallizes with every beat of her heart: she will involve herself in the investigation. She must offer a voice for reason and science where there is none.

Helena gathers her belongings—a notebook filled with observations, a magnifying glass often used to examine botanical specimens, and an assortment of pens. She tucks them into her satchel with determined care.

Exiting the library, Helena makes her way through the labyrinthine halls of the university towards Professor Leclercq's office—the head of forensic studies and an old family friend who has always encouraged her scientific endeavors.

The door creaks open to reveal Professor Leclercq hunched over his workbench littered with all manner of scientific instruments. He looks up from his microscope as Helena enters.

"Helena," he greets warmly but with a note of surprise. "What brings you here at this hour?"

"There's been another drowning," she says succinctly. "I intend to assist Inspector De Vries in his investigation."

Leclercq raises an eyebrow—a mix of admiration and concern etched into his features. "That's quite a departure from your usual botanical studies."

Helena nods firmly. "It is necessary. The man they suspect... I believe he may be innocent."

Professor Leclercq leans back in his chair, steepling his fingers as he regards Helena intently. "And what makes you think you can make a difference?"

Helena meets his gaze unflinchingly. "I have knowledge that could prove vital—a perspective grounded in science that could cut through superstition."

Leclercq nods slowly; understanding dawns on him like sunlight creeping across his cluttered desk. "Very well," he says at last. "You have my support."

As Helena expresses her thanks and briskly departs down the hallway, warmth spreads through her heart. The stone walls, steeped in centuries of academic endeavors, seem to echo her footsteps. Yet, her current pursuit is far from scholarly. Rather, it is a quest for justice on behalf of a fisherman shunned by society, who may just be a victim of unimaginable circumstances.

Emerging onto the winding streets of Brugge, Helena is greeted by the transition from day to dusk. The city's iconic medieval facades stretch out, casting long shadows across the cobbled streets. As she makes her way, lanterns flicker to life, signaling the imminent arrival of night.

With each step towards Inspector De Vries's office, Helena rehearses how she will present herself—not just as an apothecary's daughter but as a woman driven by logic and empathy—a woman determined to bring clarity to chaos.

Her resolve does not waver even as she reaches his door and lifts a hand to knock. For within Helena De Baere beats the heart not only of an amateur sleuth but also a beacon for truth amidst Brugge's whispering canals.

***

As the sun begins to set, the Brugge police station stands tall and watchful, its hard exterior unwavering. With determined steps, Helena makes her way towards the entrance, her composure a stark contrast to the chaos of the bustling evening streets. She climbs the steps leading up to the station, her fingers tracing the cold, unyielding iron railing.

Stepping inside, the station hums with energy. Officers move swiftly, their footsteps and voices blending in a focused symphony. Taking a brief moment to absorb the organized chaos of law enforcement, Helena finally makes her way to the front desk.

As the sergeant on duty looks up from his ledger, his face conveys a sense of inquiry mixed with fatigue. His words ring out with a subtle hint of exhaustion as he asks, "Is there something I can assist you with?"

Undaunted, Helena meets his gaze with a poised confidence. She announces firmly, "I am here to speak with Inspector Gerard De Vries. My name is Helena De Baere."

Recognition sparks in the sergeant's eyes. He's heard her name whispered in corridors, synonymous with intellect and unwavering logic.

"One moment," he says, rising from his chair to disappear through a door marked 'Private.'

As Helena waits in the room, her eyes scan the surroundings with intensity. The peeling paint on the walls seems to hold secrets, whispering of the many silent confessions and resolved fates it has witnessed over the years. And as her thoughts drift to Willem Van Aarden, the man who brought her to this place, she tightens her grip on her satchel as a silent vow to uncover the truth, where others may only see guilt.

The door swings open and Inspector De Vries emerges—a tall figure cutting through the station's din with an air of command that resonates with Helena's sense of purpose.

"Miss De Baere," he greets her with a courteous nod. "I'm told you have matters to discuss?"

"Indeed, Inspector," Helena replies, stepping forward. "May we speak privately?"

De Vries leads her down a narrow hallway lined with closed doors until they reach his office—a spartan room furnished with little more than a desk and two chairs.

"Please," he gestures towards a seat as he takes his own behind the desk.

Helena settles into the chair, placing her satchel beside her. She observes De Vries—the lines etched into his face telling tales of sleepless nights and battles against time.

"Inspector," she begins without preamble, "you are aware of my background as an apothecary's daughter—my familiarity with medicine and science."

De Vries nods; this much he knows.

"I have followed your career with interest," Helena continues. "Your reputation for thoroughness precedes you."

A hint of surprise flickers across De Vries's features; praise is seldom directed his way in such straightforward terms.

"Thank you," he replies. "And your interest in this case?"

Helena leans forward slightly. "The canal murders have cast a shadow over Brugge—a city already steeped in too many whispers and not enough facts."

De Vries watches her intently now; she has his full attention.

"I believe my knowledge could be invaluable in your investigation," she states plainly. "The reliance on circumstantial evidence and superstition is not only unjust but unscientific."

"And what exactly are you proposing?" De Vries asks, his skepticism softened by curiosity.

Helena reaches into her satchel and retrieves a small stack of papers—her research notes and findings meticulously documented.

"I propose a collaboration where science aids law enforcement—where we examine evidence through a lens of logic and fact rather than conjecture."

She spreads the documents before him, each page brimming with potential insights—a testament to her dedication and expertise.

De Vries picks up one of the papers, scanning its contents—a detailed analysis of botanical substances that could prove pivotal in determining the cause of death.

"You've done considerable work already," he remarks, impressed despite himself.

Helena meets his gaze squarely. "There is more at stake here than solving crimes. There is truth—and I intend to unearth it."

Silence settles between them as De Vries considers her words—the weight of responsibility heavy upon his shoulders.

As De Vries carefully arranges the disordered papers before him, the air in the room grows heavy with thoughtful silence. Helena gazes at him intently, her pulse quickening with a blend of eager anticipation and unwavering determination. Her fingers lightly graze the surface of the desk, a quiet symbol of her preparedness to delve deeply into the center of the inquiry.

"Civilians," he begins, voice laced with the caution of experience, "typically lack the... stomach for this sort of work."

Helena remains undeterred, her eyes steady upon his. "I assure you, Inspector, my constitution is quite resilient."

A trace of a smile touches De Vries's lips, fleeting as a shadow. "And what of your time? Your studies, the apothecary..."

"My professor and my father understand my need to pursue this," Helena interjects smoothly. "They support my endeavors."

Relaxing in his seat, De Vries studies Helena with a penetrating look, one that has skillfully untangled countless complicated truths. "Having a love for science is all well and good," he remarks, "but this particular investigation is rife with danger and emotional turmoil."

Helena acknowledges his warning with a nod, yet her voice carries a firmness that echoes off the bare walls. "The pursuit of truth often is."

The inspector's doubt appears to fade as he watches her poised demeanor. She is not just another resident of Brugge swept up in the hysteria surrounding the killings; she is a partner in rationality—a fellow soldier in the fight against baseless beliefs and unquestioned assumptions. With a gesture, he draws her attention to the pile of papers on his desk. "These are the official autopsy reports for the victims discovered in the canals," he informs her.

Helena reaches out with a measured hand and draws the topmost report towards herself. The parchment feels cold under her fingertips as she carefully unfolds it to reveal its grim contents.

As her eyes move across the text, Helena's mind begins to construct a clearer image of each victim—details overlooked by others now starkly apparent to her trained eye.

"Inspector," she starts, tapping a finger on a line in the report, "these marks on the victims' wrists—do you see? They suggest bindings, but no rope or cord was found at any scene."

De Vries leans forward to peer at where she points. His eyes narrow slightly as he processes her observation—a detail that had been filed away as inconsequential by others.

"And here," Helena continues, moving to another section, "the presence of certain plant residues within their nails." She retrieves a small magnifying glass from her satchel and offers it to him.

De Vries accepts it and examines the detailed sketches accompanying the report—the remnants beneath fingernails magnified through Helena's lens become evidence calling for explanation.

"The residue is from a plant not native to Brugge's environs," she explains. "It grows only in well-tended gardens or conservatories."

Her revelation dangles between them like ripe fruit—information begging to be plucked and examined further.

Helena does not miss De Vries's subtle shift—a straightening of posture, an alertness creeping into his expression.

"You've given this much thought," he remarks after a moment, placing the magnifying glass down with newfound respect for its bearer.

"Not just thought," Helena clarifies. "I've begun mapping out where these plants might be found around Brugge."

De Vries regards her anew—as if seeing past Helena De Baere, apothecary's daughter, and glimpsing something more—a mind as sharp and discerning as any detective's badge could bestow.

He pulls another report towards him and flips through its pages until he finds what he's looking for—an account of bruising patterns that had stumped him since their discovery.

"These bruises here," he says, pointing them out. "What do you make of them?"

Helena leans over for a closer look, studying each bruise's shape and location before speaking. "Their distribution suggests restraint—but not during their time in the water." Her finger traces an invisible line across an illustration of limbs marred by violence. "This was done pre-mortem."

De Vries' brow furrows as he absorbs her analysis—another piece sliding into place within the complex puzzle laid out before them.

"Remarkable," he mutters almost to himself before raising his eyes to meet hers again. "Your insight is... invaluable."

Helena acknowledges his praise with a humble tilt of her head but remains focused on their shared goal—the unraveling mystery that has brought them together in this spartan room where facts mingle with uncertainty.

***

A bit later, as they make their way through the winding streets of Brugge, Helena De Baere trails after Inspector Gerard De Vries with eager strides. The soft glow of lanterns guides their path, eventually leading them to the latest site of a brutal canal murder. Weeping willows stretch out their delicate fronds to caress the water's surface, lending an air of melancholy to the secluded spot.

Anticipation tingles in the air as they reach the cordoned-off area. A solemn officer offers a nod of recognition to De Vries before lifting the tape for them to pass under. Stepping onto the scene, Helena's eyes sharpen, taking in every minuscule detail: the curve of the canal's edge, the arrangement of pebbles on the bank, and the foliage surrounding the crime scene.

"This is where they found him," De Vries says quietly, gesturing to a patch of ground near the water's edge.

Helena nods, taking in the space with an analytical gaze. "The ground here," she begins, kneeling to examine it closely, "it's been disturbed. Recently."

De Vries crouches beside her, observing as she points out subtle impressions in the soil. "Footprints," she murmurs, "but not deep enough to have been made by someone carrying a body."

Her keen observational skills are at work, dissecting each nuance of the scene before them. She rises and moves closer to the canal's edge, where reeds sway in a gentle dance with the evening breeze.

"Inspector," she calls softly over her shoulder. "May I?"

De Vries nods, understanding her request without the need for further words. Helena carefully collects a sample of water from the canal in a small vial she produces from her satchel.

"What do you hope to find?" De Vries inquires as she seals the vial meticulously.

"Traces," she replies succinctly. "Residues or substances that shouldn't naturally be present."

Her mind races with possibilities—chemicals, toxins—each potential clue another step towards understanding.

"And here," Helena gestures towards a cluster of reeds partially trampled by past activity, "there may be fibers caught from clothing or ropes used to bind."

She retrieves tweezers and small evidence bags from her satchel, each movement deliberate and practiced as she collects samples with utmost care.

De Vries watches her work with growing respect. Helena moves with an ease that belies her amateur status—a testament to her intelligence and meticulous nature.

"Have you considered employing advanced forensic techniques more broadly?" he asks after a moment.

Helena stands straight, turning to face him. Her eyes shine with an eagerness that is infectious. "Absolutely," she confirms. "For instance, water sample analysis could reveal much about what transpired here."

She elaborates on potential findings—changes in pH levels, foreign substances indicative of struggle or disposal methods—each point punctuated by her gesturing hand.

"Fiber collection," she continues seamlessly, "could provide us with information on contact between victim and assailant."

De Vries listens intently as Helena discusses modern forensic methods—techniques not yet widely accepted or understood by many within his profession.

"We could look for trace elements," Helena adds, "minute details that escape casual observation but scream volumes under scrutiny."

The inspector nods thoughtfully at this barrage of knowledge. "You're proposing a more scientific approach than we're accustomed to," he admits.

Helena meets his gaze squarely. "Science doesn't cloud its judgment with emotion or bias—it seeks only facts."

De Vries' expression softens slightly—a smile flickering at the corners of his mouth. "And you believe these methods will yield results?"

"With certainty," Helena affirms. Her confidence is not born of arrogance but of trust in empirical evidence and its ability to illuminate truth.

"Then we shall proceed as you suggest," De Vries decides. The authority in his voice does not waver—it carries instead a note of partnership.

Together they survey the scene once more—a pair united by purpose if not by experience. The air grows chill as night asserts itself upon Brugge, but neither seems to notice—their focus remains unwaveringly fixed upon unraveling this dark tapestry woven by an unseen hand.

As they collect their findings and prepare to leave, Helena glances back at the water once more—a mirror reflecting both light and shadow much like this case that has captured her intellect and resolve.

***

The police station's buzz dims as Helena strides through its halls the following morning, her head held high with the bearing of someone who knows their worth. She carries with her the promise of a new approach, one that could revolutionize the investigation. Officers pause in their tasks, stealing glances at her as she passes—a mixture of skepticism and intrigue marking their faces.

Inspector De Vries's office door stands ajar. Helena knocks lightly before entering, finding him poring over a map of Brugge marked with the locations of the recent tragedies. He looks up, a hint of relief crossing his features as she approaches.

"Good morning, Inspector," Helena greets him, placing her satchel on his desk and withdrawing several neatly labeled vials.

"Miss De Baere," he replies with a nod. "Your findings?"

Helena doesn't miss the subtle shift in his tone—the undercurrent of anticipation. "I've analyzed the water samples from last night," she explains.

"There are traces of a substance that should not naturally be present in canal water."

De Vries leans forward, interest piqued. "And this substance is?"

"Barium sulfate," Helena reveals. "It's often used in medical imaging but can be toxic in certain forms."

A murmur ripples through the office as officers nearby overhear the exchange. Their expressions turn thoughtful, considering Helena's words.

"Could this have contributed to the victims' deaths?" De Vries inquires.

"Possibly," Helena admits. "But it is more likely a clue to where they were before they entered the water."

De Vries nods slowly, absorbing her insight. He gestures to his officer standing near the doorway—Constable Hendrik De Jong, eager and attentive.

"Constable, please gather the team in the briefing room," he instructs. "Miss De Baere will share her findings."

As De Jong hurries off to comply, De Vries turns back to Helena with a level gaze. "Are you prepared to present your methods to my team?"

Helena straightens, meeting his gaze unflinchingly. "I am."

In the briefing room, skeptical eyes follow Helena as she takes her place at the front beside De Vries. She arranges her notes and samples before her—a display of evidence that cannot be ignored.

"Gentlemen," De Vries begins, commanding attention with ease. "Miss De Baere has been working closely with me on this case. Her expertise in scientific analysis has already proven invaluable."

Heads turn as murmurs fill the room—some voices carry doubt while others express curiosity.

Helena clears her throat and begins, confident yet measured in her delivery. "Science offers us tools that can illuminate details invisible to even the most trained eye."

She details each step of her process—how she collected samples, what tests she performed—and then shares what each finding might signify for their investigation.

The room grows silent as officers lean forward, captivated by her words. The initial air of skepticism fades like mist before sunlight—dissolving under the weight of her compelling evidence and clear expertise.

Constable De Jong raises his hand tentatively—a question burning behind his eyes.

"Yes?" Helena acknowledges him.

"How did you manage to identify barium sulfate?" he asks, voice laced with genuine interest.

Helena smiles faintly at his inquiry—a welcome sign of engagement from one so young and earnest.

"I used reagents that react specifically with barium ions," she explains patiently. "The resulting precipitate confirmed its presence."

Hendrik De Jong nods thoughtfully while others exchange impressed glances—a chorus of whispers acknowledging her skillful handling of forensic techniques unfamiliar to them.

As questions continue, each answer Helena provides cement her role not merely as an outsider but as an integral part of their team—a catalyst for progress within an investigation mired in uncertainty.

De Vries watches on—a quiet pride settling over him at having brought Helena into their fold. Her ability to articulate complex scientific concepts in understandable terms bridges gaps between old methods and new possibilities.

Sergeant Brouwer—a man known for his staunch adherence to traditional policing—speaks up from where he stands against the wall, arms folded across his chest.

"Miss De Baere," he begins gruffly, "how certain can we be that these techniques will lead us to our killer?"

Helena meets his challenging gaze without hesitation. "Science does not deal in certainties but probabilities," she replies firmly. "What I offer is a way to narrow down our search—to focus our efforts based on tangible evidence rather than conjecture."

Brouwer grunts—an acknowledgment that while he may not fully understand or agree with her methods, he cannot dispute their potential value.

As the briefing concludes and officers disperse back to their duties, several pauses by Helena's side—offering nods or words of thanks for shedding new light on their grim task.

Inspector De Vries remains behind as well—his presence a silent bastion of support for Helena's continued involvement.

"You have given them much to consider," he comments once they are alone again.

Helena gathers her notes together—a small smile touching her lips at his understated praise. "I hope only to contribute to justice being served."

"And you have," De Vries assures her warmly. "Your clarity and professionalism have earned you their respect—as it has mine."

With those words lingering between them like a shared secret promise, they set about charting their next course—a course guided by science's unwavering compass toward truth amidst Brugge's murky waters.

***

The soft, tranquil evening has settled over the university campus like a warm shawl, as Helena De Baere sits alone in her humble office. The shelves that surround her are lined with well-loved medical texts and botanical encyclopedias, standing guard like faithful sentinels. The flickering light from a lone oil lamp illuminates the pages of her journal, as she seeks solace and clarity in this haven of books and quiet reflection. Here, Helena grapples with the events of the day and her moral compass, finding sanctuary in the sanctuary of knowledge and introspection.

As her pen glides across the page, it is not guided by the meticulousness of her scientific research, but rather the contemplative nature of her thoughts. Her words delve into matters of ethics and equality, not the composition of chemical compounds or remedies. It is in these pages, marked with the indelible ink of her thoughts, that Helena grapples with the choice to stray from traditional norms and plunge fearlessly into the murky depths of criminal inquiry.

Helena pauses, her gaze drifting to the window where Brugge's spires pierce the twilight sky. She reflects on Willem Van Aarden—the man whose life has become inextricably linked with her quest for truth. His solitude, marked by society's cruel branding, is a constant reminder to Helena of the fragility of reputation and how quickly one can be ostracized by fear and ignorance.

She considers Willem's plight—a scapegoat for a town's buried guilt and simmering superstitions. In him, she sees not just a fellow victim of circumstance but a reflection of humanity's darker tendencies to shun those who differ or who bear undeserved shame. Helena feels a surge of empathy for Willem; his isolation resonates with her sense of being an outsider within academic circles that often regard women with condescension.

Returning her focus to the journal, Helena contemplates her initial hesitation to involve herself in Inspector De Vries's investigation. Her father's expectations for her to continue their familial legacy within the apothecary trade had been clear, as were society's unwritten rules that sought to confine her intellect and curiosity within prescribed boundaries.

Yet there is a fire within Helena—a spark ignited by injustice and fanned by the pursuit of knowledge—that refuses to be quenched by convention or caution. She recalls her first encounter with De Vries, how his mixture of skepticism and intrigue mirrored her internal conflict—her scientific mind urging her forward while self-doubt whispered words of restraint.

Helena dips her pen back into the inkwell, its tip grazing against the glass before emerging darkened once more. She writes about her choice to push through that veil of uncertainty—to reach out to De Vries with findings she knew could alter the course of his inquiry. It was a moment when science became more than just an occupation; it became a calling.

The room around Helena fades as she loses herself in memories—the initial chill of rejection from some officers at the station melting away under the warmth of their eventual respect. She had entered their world as an outsider but now stood among them as an ally—a testament to their shared commitment to uncovering truths hidden deep within Brugge's shadowed heart.

She sets aside her pen momentarily, fingers tracing lines across the wood grain on her desk—a desk that has borne witness to countless hours of study and discovery. Her thoughts turn to Willem once more—to his haunted eyes that hold stories untold and sorrows unshared.

Helena recognizes a kinship with Willem in their mutual pursuit: he seeks redemption; she seeks answers—both are driven by an inherent need for resolution that transcends personal risk or societal judgment.

The clock tower bell tolls in the distance—a measured count that resonates through Brugge's cobblestone streets and into Helena's contemplative silence. Time presses onward, indifferent to human endeavors or desires.

Yet it is this very passage of time that fuels Helena's urgency—an understanding that each moment wasted is another where injustice remains unchallenged. The thought propels her forward; it reinforces her resolve to use every skill at her disposal to ensure justice is not just served but served fairly.

She resumes writing in her journal, each word a pledge—an oath etched in ink—to stand against bias and misconception. She writes for those like Willem who have been pushed to society's periphery—whose voices are drowned out by fear-mongering whispers.

As Helena approaches the conclusion of her entry, she radiates a newfound lucidity - a powerful clarity that has been carefully nurtured through introspection and action. She acknowledges that the journey she has embarked on is a treacherous one, full of challenges and heartache, but also teeming with opportunities for transformation.

As she gazes down at her words, each sentence speaks volumes about her growth and bravery - a poignant record not only of what has been but what could be if one dares to confront the shadows with hope.

A deep breath steadies her resolve as she closes her journal—the leather cover pressing against parchment like a protective embrace. The lamp's flame flickers gently as if affirming Helena's conviction in its silent dance.

Rising from her chair, Helena extinguishes the light—plunging the room into darkness save for slivers of moonlight casting silver streaks upon floorboards worn smooth by time.

A Confrontation

Mist curls around my boat like a shroud, the dawn breaking over Brugge with a reluctant whisper. I push off from the canal's edge, the gentle lapping of water against the hull a familiar comfort. The city sleeps, but I find no rest; my nets and lines are my only companions in these solitary hours before the town stirs.

My fingers, tough as old rope, work mechanically, casting nets with a precision born of countless mornings just like this one. The world is reduced to the rhythm of the sea, the pull of the tide, and the silver flash of fish beneath the surface. The worries that plague me—whispers of witchcraft, murmurs of murder—dissolve in the briny air. Here on the water, I am just Willem the fisherman, not Willem Van Aarden, a descendant of alleged witches.

I steer my boat through the fog, navigating by memory and instinct. The soft glow of dawn filters through, painting everything in hues of gold and grey. I'm no stranger to being alone; it's a mantle I've worn since childhood after that terrible blaze consumed my family's legacy. But out here, solitude is a balm rather than a burden.

As the sun climbs higher, dispelling the last remnants of mist, I turn back toward Brugge. My catch is modest—enough to sell but not enough to draw attention or envy. The last thing I need is more eyes on me.

The city awakens as I moor my boat and haul my catch to the market. My arrival does not go unnoticed; eyes follow me with suspicion etched deep within their gaze. I keep my head down as I walk through cobbled streets that once welcomed me.

The fish market bustles with life—the call of vendors hawking their wares, the clatter of carts on stone, the sharp scent of salt and seaweed. My stall stands at the edge of it all, a space begrudgingly given to me by those who fear what association might bring them.

I lay out my fish on crushed ice—a glistening array that should be enough to draw in customers despite their reservations about their source. But today, even those who once greeted me with a nod and a smile pass by with barely a glance at my catch.

Their whispers slither through the air like eels in shallow water. "They say he's cursed," one woman murmurs to another, not bothering to lower her voice enough.

"Aye," her companion agrees with a shudder. "They say those Van Aardens have darkness in their blood."

I resist the urge to confront them; it would only serve to stoke the fires of their fear and suspicion further. Instead, I focus on arranging mackerel and herring in neat rows, my movements sharp and practiced.

A man approaches—a regular customer whose name I've never learned—and pauses before my stall. He doesn't look at me as he points at some haddock.

"How much?" His voice is gruff; his eyes never meet mine.

"For you? Two stuivers," I reply quietly.

He nods and tosses me the coins without another word. Our hands brush during the exchange—his warm and soft from less weathered work than mine—and for an instant, there's an unspoken acknowledgment between us: he knows these whispers are nothing but shadows, yet he steps back quickly as if burned by our fleeting contact.

I wrap his purchase in brown paper with swift movements while others pass by with nary a glance at my wares or a word spoken in my direction—except for sharp intakes of breath or quiet clucks of disapproval.

This town was once home; now it feels like an alien landscape where every familiar face hides suspicion or worse—hatred for what they believe me to be. The air grows thick with unspoken accusations; every cold stare another brick in an invisible wall separates me from them.

I slide a knife beneath the scales of a cod, my motions steady despite the roiling in my gut. Amidst the bustling marketplace, alive with the hum of busy vendors and eager customers, I remained in solitude. My stall, resembling a lone rock jutting out from the sea, was avoided by wary sailors.

A shadow falls across my fish-laden table. I glance up to find Pieter De Vos, his portly frame wedged between me and the morning sun. His eyes are narrow slits of suspicion.

"Van Aarden," he sneers, his voice oily as the eels he peddles from the stall down the way. "Seems your catch is as foul as your bloodline."

I keep my grip on the knife steady, refusing to let it tremble. "My fish are fresh, De Vos. Fresher than your manners."

A cruel smirk curls his lip as he leans closer. "Fresh enough to wash away the stink of death you carry?"

I set the knife down with deliberate care, meeting his gaze. "You speak boldly for a man who knows little."

His chuckle is a dark rumble. "Oh, I know plenty. We all do." He gestures broadly at the market-goers, who steal glances our way while pretending to haggle over vegetables and bread. "Whispers travel fast in Brugge, and they all say the same—Willem Van Aarden's cursed hands pull more than fish from these waters."

Heat floods my cheeks, but I battle it back with a deep breath. "Lies spread by cowards are no concern of mine."

De Vos snorts. "Cowards? Is that what you call those poor souls found drowned? Is that what you call justice for their families seeking answers?"

"I've drowned no one," I say through gritted teeth. The accusation claws at me, raw and unjust.

He steps closer still, his bulk casting a chill despite the warmth of daybreak. "Then how come every body pulled from the canal lays heavy on your conscience? How come every whisper of witchcraft finds its way back to you?"

The words sting like salt in an open wound; my hands ball into fists at my sides. Before I can trust myself to speak again, a firm hand lands on De Vos's shoulder.

"That's enough, Pieter," comes Constable Hendrik De Jong's steady voice.

De Vos flinches under Hendrik's touch but recovers quickly, puffing out his chest like a bantam rooster ready for a fight.

"And what business is it of yours?" De Vos demands.

Hendrik's grip tightens ever so slightly on De Vos's shoulder—a silent command that carries more weight than any words could.

"It's my business when peace is being disturbed," Hendrik says evenly.

De Vos shakes off Hendrik's hand with a grunt and turns to face him fully. His bravado wanes under Hendrik's sharp blue gaze.

Hendrik turns his attention to me then, his eyes softening just enough for me to read the sympathy within them—an unspoken solidarity that offers a brief respite from my isolation.

"Willem," Hendrik begins, his voice low enough that only I can hear it over the din of market chatter. "You'd do well to keep your head down these days."

I nod once, curtly—a silent acknowledgment of his counsel.

Hendrik gives me a final nod before turning back to De Vos. "Pieter, return to your stall. This isn't helping anyone."

De Vos looks as if he wants to argue further but seems to think better of it under Hendrik's watchful eye. With one last glare in my direction—one that promises this isn't over—he retreats into the crowd.

The constable remains for a moment longer; his presence is like a shield against the stares that continue to pierce me from all sides.

"Thank you," I murmur as I pick up my knife again and return to gutting the cod before me.

Hendrik offers me another sympathetic look before he speaks again. "Just looking out for Brugge's peace," he says simply.

He pats my shoulder—a fleeting touch that speaks volumes—and walks away, leaving me with my thoughts and the fish that lie cold and still upon my table.

I take a moment to steady myself before resuming my work with renewed focus—each slice of my knife through flesh and bone an effort to carve out some semblance of normalcy in this world that seems bent on seeing me undone.

As customers trickle by—some stopping briefly out of necessity more than desire—I exchange pleasantries through lips that feel numb and distant from their own words. Each interaction is laced with an undercurrent of tension that never quite eases.

But even as I sell my catch piece by piece, wrapping them carefully for those few who dare purchase them from me, I cannot shake off Pieter De Vos's words or the cloud they cast over this day that had begun with such simple clarity upon the water.

I am surrounded by a thick fog of whispered rumors. Suspicion weaves its way around me, tightening its grip with each covert conversation. The superstitious townsfolk have always been wary, but today their glances are sharp as knives, piercing through me. I can almost hear the ground beneath my feet murmuring accusations, the very stones of Brugge's streets singling me out by name. I am tainted by a past I played no part in, and it seems like the whole city knows it.

I pack up my stall early. The sun still hangs high, but the shadows that cling to me are long and dark. The ice that cradles my unsold fish has begun to melt, water pooling around the crates like blood from an unseen wound. My movements are mechanical, devoid of the care I usually take in preserving my livelihood. Today, it feels futile.

As I fold away my tarp and secure the ropes around my unsold catch, the murmur around me grows louder. A part of me wants to stand up to them, to shout at the top of my lungs that their suspicions are unfounded. But what would be the use? Instead, I retreat into myself further with each knot I tie.

"You leaving us so soon, Van Aarden?" The voice comes from Joris, who sells bread two stalls down. His tone carries a feigned concern that doesn't reach his eyes.

I glance up briefly, meeting his gaze. "It seems today's not a day for fish," I reply flatly.

Joris chuckles—a sound as hollow as the empty barrels behind him. "Or perhaps it's not a day for fishermen with murky pasts."

I say nothing more, shouldering my way through the crowd that parts reluctantly before me. Their disdainful looks follow me like shadows clinging to my back. Every step away from the market is heavy; each one is a reminder of how far I've fallen in their eyes.

***

The walk home takes me past familiar haunts—places where laughter once found me easily and friendship was a simple thing. As if drawn by these memories, I find myself on a path where youth was spent under softer skies. There on a stone bench sit Karel and his brothers—boys who became men alongside me—engaged in animated conversation.

Their voices carry across the square, easy and free until they catch sight of me approaching. Silence falls like a sudden frost; smiles fade from their faces as if they've seen a ghost rather than an old friend.

"Willem," Karel greets first, but it's cautious and strained.

"Karel," I nod in return. The weight of their stares is something tangible; it presses against me with an almost physical force.

"We didn't expect to see you out here," says Lukas, the middle brother, shuffling his feet uneasily on the cobblestones.

"I was just passing through," I say quietly.

Their nods are stiff; their eyes dart between each other like sparrows ready for flight. They wish for nothing more than for this encounter to end—to retreat into their comfortable lives untouched by scandal or suspicion.

"We were just leaving," says Henrik—the youngest—standing abruptly.

They mumble excuses—chores that need doing, errands that can't wait—and yet there's no conviction behind their words. It's fear that moves them; fear of what being seen with Willem Van Aarden might bring upon them.

I watch as they hurry away without looking back—a trio of backs turned against me. A cold emptiness settles in my chest where warmth used to reside when camaraderie was not yet spoiled by whispers of witchcraft and death.

Their departure leaves an echo in its wake—an echo that reverberates through the empty square and lodges itself within my heart. Once again, Brugge reminds me of my place within its walls—a place carved out by suspicion and superstition.

As their footsteps fade into silence, I turn towards the canal with only shadows for company—the shadows cast by friends who can no longer bear to look at me, by a town that sees only what it fears rather than what is true.

***

I settle on the weathered bench by the canal, my lunch a modest parcel of bread and cheese. The water's surface mirrors the sky, a canvas of grey upon grey, broken only by the occasional leaf drifting past. It's here, by these silent waters, that I choose to eat—here where the town's whispers turn into roars in my head.

The bread is tough and the cheese tasteless; I chew mechanically, my thoughts far from the meal. This canal, once a source of life and livelihood, has become a watery grave for unknown souls and the stage for my supposed guilt. The faces of those pulled from its depths haunt me—not because I am responsible, but because I know their fate could so easily have been mine if not for mere chance.

I glance at the passing townsfolk on the far side of the canal. Their eyes flicker in my direction before skittering away, as if even a moment's contact could condemn them. Once I was Willem the fisherman; now I am Willem the whispered-about, Willem the watched.

A mother pulls her child closer as they pass by, her hand quick to cover his eyes. "Don't look at him," she hisses. "He brings bad luck."

Her words cut deeper than she knows. To be seen as an omen of ill fortune rather than a man—how did it come to this? My heart grows heavy with each bite of food, and by the time my lunch is done, it feels like I've swallowed stones.

I fold the paper wrapping carefully, more out of habit than any real care for orderliness. The bench feels colder now, less inviting. It's time to leave this place of judgment and sorrow behind, if only for a moment.

As I stand and stretch my legs stiff from sitting too long, I notice a small group of children playing on the opposite bank. Their laughter carries across the water—a reminder of simpler times when laughter was part of my own life. But even their joy is tainted; as one boy spots me watching them, he points and shouts something that's lost in distance but clear enough in intent.

The others look over, their play forgotten as they join in a chorus of jeers directed at me. The boy who first noticed me cups his hands around his mouth and yells louder: "Murderer!"

His word echoes off the water like a stone skipping across its surface before sinking into its depths—and into me.

I turn away sharply, walking briskly back toward my boat tied up further along the bank. Each step feels like an escape attempt—an effort to outrun their taunts and my own growing despair.

When I finally reach my boat—a small vessel that has weathered storms both literal and figurative—I stop short. My breath catches in my throat as if snagged by an invisible hook.

Scrawled across her side in jagged letters is a single word: "MURDERER."

The paint is still fresh; droplets cling to the letters like blood from an open wound. It stands out against the worn wood like a brand—a mark that cannot be unseen or easily removed.

For a moment I stand frozen, unable to tear my eyes away from this new assault on my name—on my very being. Then anger surges within me, hot and fierce as a gale-force wind.

With shaking hands, I yank a bucket from inside the boat and plunge it into the canal's murky waters. The liquid sloshes over its rim as I haul it up and set it down with more force than necessary.

The letters blur under my furious rubbing but do not fade away completely; they cling stubbornly to the woodgrain like leeches feasting on its lifeblood.

Passersby stop to watch—silent spectators to this spectacle of desperation. Their eyes are wide with curiosity or perhaps fear; it's hard to tell when you're on your knees trying to erase accusations from your only refuge in this world.

"Serves him right," someone mutters loud enough for me to hear over my frantic scrubbing.

"He should be locked up," another agrees with venomous satisfaction.

Their words are daggers thrown from afar; each one finds its mark with unerring accuracy even as I continue my futile task.

My arms ache from exertion but still I persist—the rag now more water than fabric in my hands as it drips onto already soaked trousers clinging coldly to my skin.

"Let them talk," I whisper to myself between gritted teeth—a mantra against their condemnation—but even as I say it, doubt creeps into my voice like water seeping through cracks in an old dam ready to burst at any moment under pressure too great to hold back any longer.

This boat—my sanctuary—is tainted now just like everything else connected with me: tainted by suspicion born out of fear rather than fact; tainted by ignorance that refuses enlightenment; tainted by history that won't stay buried beneath Brugge's cobbled streets or its placid canals where dark secrets lie waiting just below calm surfaces ready to pull us all under if given half a chance...

The water of the canals holds a stillness that seems to mock me. It reflects a world turned upside down, where the innocent are marked and the guilty walk free. I can't scrub away the stain on my boat any more than I can wash away the town's suspicions. The word 'murderer' clings to me, a shadow I cannot shake.

***

As dusk approaches, I make my way to the local cemetery. The stones here are old friends, silent and steady. They stand in rows like soldiers guarding memories long passed. My family's plot lies at the far end, under the shade of an ancient oak tree. Its leaves whisper secrets to the wind, secrets of lives that were and could have been.

I kneel before the gravestones, their edges softened by time and moss. "Mother, Father," I begin, my voice barely above a whisper. "It's been another day." The words feel heavy in my mouth, like stones sinking into the canal bed. "The town still whispers your names in fear, just as they do mine."

I trace the engraved letters with my fingertips, feeling their grooves as if trying to connect with those who lie beneath. "They think I'm following in our family's footsteps—that I've brought death to Brugge." A bitter laugh escapes me, hollow in the quiet of the graveyard. "If only they knew how much I've strived to live a life you'd be proud of."

The air grows colder as night takes hold. Shadows stretch across the graves, dark fingers reaching out as if trying to pull me into their embrace. "I miss you," I admit to the stones and myself. "Your guidance, your warmth... Now there's only cold suspicion and loneliness."

I stand and take a moment to look around at all the other graves—each one holding someone's story, someone's sorrow. "But here, with you, there's a peace I can't find anywhere else." My heart clenches with a mix of grief and longing for understanding that never comes.

The sky darkens further as I make my way home—home to a small house on the outskirts of town where no neighbor ever calls. Inside, it's quiet except for the crackling of firewood in the fireplace. The flames dance with a life all their own—a stark contrast to the stillness within me.

I sit heavily in an old armchair that creaks under my weight—a familiar sound in an otherwise silent room. The day replays in my mind: Pieter De Vos's sneer at the market; Karel and his brothers turning their backs; children calling out 'murderer' as if it were nothing but a game.

Each memory is like a coal added to the fire—glowing hot with injustice and pain. Yet no matter how much they burn me up inside, there's nothing I can do but endure.

My hands are rough from years of fishing—calloused and scarred—but today they seem foreign to me as they rest on my knees. These hands have never harmed another soul, yet they're seen as instruments of death by those who don't bother to look beyond rumors.

I close my eyes and lean back in the chair, letting out a weary sigh that feels like it carries the weight of all Brugge upon it. The wood pops and hisses behind me—a small battle against darkness that even fire must fight.

In this quiet room, where every shadow flickers with flame's touch, despair creeps closer like fog rolling in from the sea. Will there ever be an end to this? Can truth ever emerge victorious when lies have taken root so deeply?

A tear traces its way down my cheek—an intruder in this place where I've fought so hard to keep emotions at bay. It feels hot against my skin—a single drop of truth in a sea of deception.

"I'm tired," I confess aloud though there's no one here but shadows for company. "Tired of fighting against ghosts of the past that refuse to die."

The fire crackles on unabated; its light fights against encroaching darkness but offers no answers—only more questions that burn in my mind without respite.

How long must I bear this curse? How long before they see me for who I truly am rather than what fear tells them? How long before I can walk through Brugge without feeling like every eye is upon me—judging me guilty without trial?

Unlikely Companions

As soon as you step into the Brugge police station, a chill immediately permeates the air, emanating from the very essence of the ancient stones. In his office, Inspector Gerard De Vries is surrounded by a stillness broken only by the solitary glow of a single lamp. As the light casts long shadows across his face, he pours over the files before him - a complex web of testimonies and evidence, each one concealing a hidden secret within the city's murky waterways. With a sharpness honed by years of discerning between deception and truth, his eyes scan the pages once more, determined to uncover the elusive truth within.

The inspector leans back in his chair, temples throbbing with the weight of unsolved riddles. The room is silent but for the ticking of the clock and the distant hum of voices from the station's corridors. He knows this case calls for more than routine police work; it requires an unorthodox alliance.

He rises, straightens his jacket, and strides through the labyrinthine corridors of the station with purposeful steps. The time has come to bring together those who might see what he cannot, those whose very lives have become entwined with the mystery itself.

Helena De Baere's shop smells of herbs and dried flowers—a stark contrast to the stale air of De Vries's office. She looks up from her meticulous work as he enters, her intelligent eyes reflecting a blend of surprise and caution.

"Inspector De Vries," she greets him with a nod, wiping her hands on her apron.

"Miss De Baere," he acknowledges. "I trust you're aware of why I'm here."

Helena nods, her expression serious. "The canal murders," she says simply.

"Indeed." De Vries pauses, measuring his words. "I've been considering our predicament and your unique position within this community. Your knowledge of medicine and science could prove invaluable. How about you and Willem join me to find the murderer?"

She clasps her hands together, her expression betraying a hint of concern. "I understand the urgency of these drownings but I must admit I have reservations about working alongside Mr. Van Aarden."

De Vries nods, his expression solemn. "Your concerns are not unfounded given the town's sentiments. But let me assure you, our interest is in the truth—wherever that may lead."

Helena's eyes lowered for a moment before meeting his gaze once more. "I fear that my involvement might stoke further rumors—about me and Willem."

"Rumors are like shadows," De Vries replies calmly. "They grow long and distorted at dusk but vanish at noon when faced with the light of truth. You can help bring that light, Ms. De Baere."

She considers this quietly, the inspector's metaphor lingering in her thoughts like mist over morning water.

"I'm not blind to what people whisper about Willem," she continues softly. "His past... my reputation as an unwed woman consorting with him... it's delicate."

De Vries gives a slow nod of understanding. "Discretion will be paramount, Helena. Your role can remain confined to analysis and insight—I will ensure it does not compromise your standing."

Her fingers trace the wood grain of the armrest as she contemplates her next words carefully. "My father always says that to remain silent in times of injustice is to side with the oppressor."

A flicker of admiration crosses De Vries's face at her resolve. "A wise man indeed."

Helena lets out a slow breath, feeling the weight of history pressing upon them both—the legacy of witch hunts and persecution that has long haunted Brugge's cobbled streets.

"I will help you," she declares finally, determination settling over her features like armor. "But Willem must understand I am here for science and truth alone."

"Understood," De Vries assures her with a nod.

Helena rises from her seat as if buoyed by newfound purpose. Her skirts swish softly against the floorboards as she moves towards the door.

"I'll need access to all your findings—reports, witness accounts, anything that might hold a scientific clue," she says over her shoulder.

De Vries offers a nod, solemn yet hopeful. "Together, we'll cut through superstition with reason."

***

The evening's quietude shatters with the persistent knock at the door, a sound too deliberate to be anyone but him—Inspector De Vries. Even before I see him, there's a certainty that cloaks the moment, a prelude to the inevitable intrusion. As he stands in the doorway, the day's last light throws his shadow forward, an elongated specter that breaches the threshold of my home, carrying with it a sense of foreboding.

His eyes, those sharp sentinels, sweep across the room, pausing only when they find mine. "May I come in?" he asks, his voice laced with a politeness that doesn't quite mask the resolve beneath. It's a dance we've performed before, his presence here a familiar yet unwelcome ritual. Reluctantly, I step back, allowing him entry, not out of welcome but resignation. The door closes with a definitive thud, a sound that seems to resonate with judgment.

"Willem," he starts, his hat removed in a gesture that straddles the line between respect and tactic, "I'm here because we need your help." The words float in the space between us, imbued with an irony that doesn't escape me. Help, from me, the man already judged by many eyes.

"I'm no detective," I retort, the bitterness tangible in my voice, a defense against the role they've thrust upon me.

"No," he agrees, his movements measured as he places his hat aside, acknowledging my point yet pressing on. "But you know these canals better than anyone. And you have a vested interest in seeing this matter resolved." His words are a mirror, reflecting a truth I cannot deny. The whispers of nature that have always been my solace now seem to echo with accusations, urging me towards a path I'm reluctant to tread.

The prospect of aligning with the law, of inviting further scrutiny, weighs heavily on me. Yet, De Vries's acknowledgment of my unique insight, paired with the mention of Helena De Baere and her forensic acumen, ignites a sliver of hope—or perhaps a resurgence of something deeper, a connection I thought lost.

"Fine," I concede after a moment heavy with unspoken thoughts. "But not for you—for me." It's a declaration more to myself than to him, a reaffirmation of my stake in this tangled narrative.

De Vries's nod is one of understanding, perhaps even expectation as if my acquiescence was never in doubt. In this shared silence, our alliance is formed—not of trust, but of necessity, each of us driven by our ghosts and the search for a truth that might yet clear my name and restore a semblance of peace to these troubled waters.

***

The police station looms before us as we approach—a beacon of supposed safety and order amidst whispers of chaos and death. De Vries leads the way inside, his steps echoing through the hall like marching orders.

In an austere room with walls that seem to absorb light rather than reflect it, she waits—Helena De Baere. Her presence is both commanding and subtle; her eyes hold a depth that suggests she's seen more than her fair share of humanity's darkness.

Helena stands as we enter, her gaze flitting between De Vries and me with clinical precision. She offers her hand first to him then to me; her grip is firm, betraying no hint of hesitation or fear.

"We have much to discuss," De Vries states plainly, directing us to sit at a table scarred by time and burdened with paperwork—the detritus of countless cases past.

The chair groans under my weight as I take my seat across from Helena. Her tools are spread out before her: papers, photographs... items dredged from dark waters.

"Willem," she begins, her voice clear and devoid of any judgment that has been my constant companion these past weeks. "Your knowledge of the canals is crucial. We need to understand the currents, hidden alcoves... anything that might help us find who is responsible for these deaths."

I nod slowly; she speaks my language—the language of water and tides—and in that moment, our purpose aligns like stars over Brugge's night sky.

De Vries clears his throat, drawing our attention back to him.

"We believe there may be patterns to these drownings," he says while unfolding a map across the table—Brugge's veins laid bare for all to see.

Patterns... The word resonates within me; patterns are what separate randomness from intention—from guilt.

"We'll need your eyes," De Vries continues his finger tracing lines on the map—routes known only to those who give their lives to the canals.

I lean forward then, drawn despite myself into their world of clues and conjectures—a world where perhaps I can rewrite my own story.

Our meeting unfolds like an intricate dance; we circle theories and possibilities—each step tentative yet purposeful. De Vries leads with questions sharpened by years of seeking truth in lies; Helena follows with insights born from science and observation.

And me? I am the local guide through murky waters—the reluctant navigator charting a course through suspicion and fear toward some semblance of justice.

We are an unlikely trio: the inspector whose life is law; the scientist whose domain is death; and the fisherman haunted by whispers both real and imagined. Together we form an alliance shaped by necessity and driven by desperation—an alliance fragile as glass yet strong as iron bonds forged in adversity's fires.

De Vries eyes us both, a steel edge to his gaze that seems to cut through the fog of uncertainty that's settled over Brugge. "We're stepping into a quagmire," he says, voice firm. "The townsfolk are on edge, quick to point fingers, quicker still to stoke the fires of fear. We can't afford missteps."

He leans back in his chair, the creak of wood punctuating his words like a period at the end of a sentence. "I've been down this road before—suspicion can turn into conviction in the blink of an eye in these close-knit communities."

Helena nods, her expression somber yet resolute. I find myself doing the same, feeling an unexpected surge of solidarity.

"We need to establish some ground rules," De Vries continues, tapping a finger against the grainy surface of the table. "Firstly, respect for each other's expertise and opinions. We might not always agree, but every perspective is valuable."

I shift in my seat, my mind grappling with this notion of respect—a commodity rarely afforded to me in this town.

"Open communication," he adds. "No secrets among us. If you find something, no matter how trivial it may seem, bring it to the table."

Helena pulls a small notebook from her apron pocket, ready to jot down thoughts that might arise. I've no notebook to speak of—my memories and knowledge are etched in the calluses of my hands and the lines on my face.

"And finally," De Vries says with emphasis, "a focus on facts. Conjecture has its place in building theories but facts will lead us to the truth."

"Agreed," Helena replies promptly.

I nod again; facts are anchors in the shifting sands of rumor and superstition that have plagued my life.

"Now," De Vries gestures towards Helena with an open palm. "Miss De Baere, please share your forensic insights with us."

Helena straightens up, her hands deftly arranging papers like a card player about to reveal a winning hand. "The autopsy reports," she begins, "they're inconsistent." She points to a series of notes she's made in the margins. "Bruising patterns on some of the victims suggest struggle before death—not consistent with accidental drowning."

De Vries leans forward, interest piqued as he examines her notes closely.

"The water temperature and rate of decomposition don't align with the time of death listed for two of the victims either," she continues. "It's possible they were kept somewhere else before being placed in the canals."

Her words hang in the air—a chilling possibility that adds another layer to an already complex puzzle.

"Kept somewhere else?" I echo her statement, my mind racing with implications.

"Yes," she confirms with a nod. "If we reexamine where each victim was found relative to water flow and tides..." Her voice trails off as she consults another chart filled with meticulous handwriting.

"We might determine where they entered the water—or were placed there," De Vries finishes her thought.

Helena's gaze meets mine across the table—a silent acknowledgment that my intimate knowledge of these waters could be key to unlocking this part of the mystery.

"Exactly," she says.

The room is quiet for a moment as we each consider this new avenue of investigation. The sound of quill scratching paper as Helena annotates her findings becomes a steady rhythm—an auditory anchor amidst our collective contemplation.

"What else have you noticed?" De Vries asks after a time.

"There are trace elements under the victims' fingernails—soil and plant matter not native to where they were found." She hands him a small glass vial containing a sample.

De Vries examines it against the light filtering through grimy windows before setting it down carefully. "This suggests they were somewhere completely different before ending up in our canals."

Helena nods again; her demeanor suggests she's far from finished.

"And one more thing," she adds, pulling out a photograph—one that makes my heart skip as I recognize Pieter De Smet his pale face staring back at me from beneath a veil of deathly stillness.

"The last victim... Pieter." Her voice softens as she speaks the name—a mark of respect for one who will speak no more. "There's something about how he was found—his positioning—it doesn't match up with post-mortem lividity or rigor mortis patterns."

De Vries studies the photograph closely while I look away; some truths are too stark when captured in shades of black and white.

"This could indicate staging post-mortem," Helena posits—a theory that feels like cold water down my spine.

"Staging?" The word tastes bitter on my tongue; someone is playing games with death as their chessboard.

"It means someone positioned his body after death for some reason—possibly to send a message or mislead investigators." De Vries's eyes flicker to me then back to Helena as he considers this latest revelation.

My hands clenched into fists beneath the table; Pieter was more than just another victim—he was someone who looked beyond my tainted legacy with genuine kindness in his eyes.

As I sit, I am enveloped by the weight of generations, their presence bearing down on me. The whispers of my ancestors are as tangible as the chill seeping through the stone walls. The inspector and Helena diligently examine the documents, but my attention is drawn to the map spread out before me. I recognize my home, Brugge, with all its secrets exposed - the veins of its canals, known to me like the back of my weathered hand.

Helena's words about Pieter echo in my head, haunting and sharp. Pieter, with his soft eyes that saw through the murk of my family's history, now another silent shadow beneath the water's surface. It's personal now, more than ever.

De Vries finally looks up from the photograph. "Willem, we could use your knowledge of these waters. Any insight you have could be crucial."

The room waits for me—waits for the man who knows these canals not just as pathways through the city but as lifelines that pulse with secrets. I clear my throat and lean over the map.

"The currents," I begin, tracing a path with a finger roughened by nets and ropes. "They're tricky here. Can drag a man under before he knows he's in trouble." I point to a bend where two canals meet—a spot notorious among us fisherfolk. "Victims could've been dumped upstream."

Helena leans in, her interest evident as she follows my movements. "You think they were placed in the water at night?"

"Likely," I reply. "Fewer eyes to see, and the moonlight plays tricks on the water."

De Vries scribbles notes furiously as I speak. "And what of local customs? Are there any events or celebrations that could've provided cover for these crimes?"

I nod, recalling festivals where masks hide more than just faces. "The Feast of St. Boniface was three nights before Pieter was found. The whole town was ablaze with lanterns and revelry."

"An ideal time for misdeeds," De Vries mutters.

We talk then of patterns—of tides and time; Helena's scientific mind intertwining with my lived experience to weave a tapestry of possibility.

De Vries straightens up, his eyes meeting mine squarely—a silent acknowledgment of value given and received.

"We need to re-examine each site where they were found," he decides. "Willem, you'll guide us through the canals."

I nod; it's an honor and a burden to serve as Charon in my tragic tale.

"And we must talk to those who knew them," Helena adds. "Friends, family... anyone who might shed light on their last days."

"I'll arrange it," De Vries says with an assertive nod. His authority is unspoken yet understood—a captain setting course in uncharted waters.

"What about historical records?" Helena suggests. "The town archives might hold clues—patterns from past crimes or events that mirror what we're seeing now."

De Vries taps his chin thoughtfully. "Good thinking," he concedes.

As the meeting inches towards its end, the once spacious room seems to shrink, burdened by the weight of our daunting task. The looming responsibility descends upon us like the warm wool blankets that protect against Brugge's cold. With a determined air, Inspector De Vries rises from his chair, its scraping reverberating with the same authority that he holds over the room. His gaze briefly connects with mine before he confidently declares, "We have our plan. Let us not waste any more time."

Helena rises with a grace that seems at odds with the grimness of our discussion. She collects her papers with practiced hands, tucking them into a satchel that's seen better days. There's a determination in her movements, a sense of purpose that I can't help but admire.

I stand too, slower, feeling every year of my weathered life in my bones. The chair beneath me groans its relief, and I'm reminded once again of how out of place I feel amid these walls—walls that have likely heard more confessions than the local priest.

"Willem," De Vries says, extending a hand towards me. His grip is firm, unyielding—like his gaze. "Your help is invaluable."

The words sit awkwardly within me; praise is a stranger to my ears. "Just doing my part," I mumble, unsure of where to look.

Helena steps forward then, her hand finding mine in a gesture that's equal parts thanks and solidarity. Her touch is warm—a stark contrast to the cold suspicion I've grown accustomed to.

"We'll see this through," she assures me, and I believe her.

There's a moment then—a suspended slice of time where we stand in a circle, hands clasped in unity. It's fragile and fleeting and speaks to something like hope or perhaps just shared resolve.

"We'll start tomorrow at first light," De Vries declares, breaking the silence. "Meet at the docks."

I nod; it's where I'm most at home—where the water whispers secrets for those patient enough to listen.

"Goodnight," Helena offers with a small smile as she shoulders her satchel.

"Goodnight," I echo back, and there it is—that awkwardness as we each grapple with the roles we've been thrust into.

De Vries gives us both a curt nod before he turns on his heel and strides towards the door, his coat billowing behind him like a sail catching wind.

The door shuts with a definitive click, leaving Helena and me alone in the quiet aftermath. We share an uncertain glance—two people caught in the currents of something much larger than ourselves.

"I should go too," Helena says after a moment. "Preparations for tomorrow."

"Yeah," I reply, stuffing my hands into my pockets—the universal sign of unease. "Tomorrow."

She hesitates at the door, looking back at me with those perceptive eyes of hers. "Willem?"

"Yeah?"

"This is... it's good what we're doing."

It takes me a second too long to find words—words that don't come easy at the best of times. "Yeah... it is."

She nods then, as if confirming something to herself more than to me, and slips out into the corridor beyond.

I'm left alone in the room where shadows cling to corners like old friends. The map remains spread out on the table—a tangle of blue lines that hold more than just geography.

I fold it carefully, feeling each crease under my fingers—a tactile memory of paths yet to be navigated. My thoughts drift to tomorrow—to Helena's steadfastness and De Vries's sharp intellect—and for an instant, I allow myself to believe that maybe we can dredge truth from these dark waters after all.

The station is quiet as I make my way out—the kind of quiet that's thick with thoughts left unspoken. My footsteps are soft against stone floors worn smooth by countless soles before mine.

As I step outside, night has fully descended upon Brugge—the sky above is a tapestry woven from darkness and stars. The air carries whispers from the canals—whispers that now feel less like accusations and more like conversations waiting to be had.

I walk slowly towards home—the path familiar but now laden with new purpose. Each step is measured; each breath drawn deep against lingering doubts.

The night envelopes me—a shroud or perhaps a cloak—and in its embrace, I find myself straddling two worlds: one rooted in history's pain and another seeking tomorrow's absolution.

An odd trio we make—De Vries with his steadfast adherence to law; Helena with her bright mind wrapped in compassion; and myself—a man more accustomed to silent waters than human intricacies.

***

Inspector Gerard De Vries reclines in his chair, the leather protesting under his considerable frame as his gaze wanders through the makeshift office. A beam of moonlight sneaks past the window, creating a luminous glow over the rugged wooden surface of his desk. With the precinct commotion muted by distance, he's left alone to ruminate in the quiet atmosphere. Here in this secluded sanctuary, he delves into his thoughts, carefully retracing the twists and turns of the day's happenings.

He'd entered that meeting with Willem and Helena with a well of skepticism deep enough to drown any hope. Yet, as he sits in the quiet, an unfamiliar sense of cautious optimism bubbles to the surface. They are an unlikely trio: a fisherman scarred by legacy, a forensic mind sharp as broken glass, and himself, an inspector whose life is stitched together with unsolved puzzles and unspoken truths.

De Vries runs his fingers through his hair, flecks of gray stark against the dark strands. Helena De Baere had been an unexpected ally; her forensic expertise could very well be the compass they needed to navigate through the murky waters of this case. Her insights had already shed new light on areas he had thought dimmed by dead ends.

Willem Van Aarden is another matter entirely. The man carries a heaviness around him like an old sea cloak, woven with threads of suspicion and isolation. Yet there is something in Willem's steadfast gaze that convinces De Vries of his innocence—a flicker of truth that belies the darkness of his lineage.

De Vries rises from his chair and begins to pace, the rhythmic thud of his footsteps grounding him in thought. He recognizes strength in their diversity; where he sees patterns and shadows, Helena sees evidence and certainty. Where he questions motives, Willem understands silence and sorrow.

The inspector pauses by the window again, watching as a lone boat drifts silently along the canal below. It's a haunting reminder of why they've come together—this alliance formed not out of friendship but necessity. Their differing personalities and backgrounds are challenges indeed, yet in them lies their collective power.

A sigh escapes him as he contemplates their task ahead. The path to unmasking a killer is fraught with danger and deception. De Vries knows this all too well; each case carves its mark upon his soul, a permanent reminder of justice sought—and sometimes justice denied.

Yet tonight there is something akin to resolve to settle in his chest—a silent oath that this time will be different. With Helena's analytical prowess and Willem's intimate knowledge of Brugge's secrets, they might just have a fighting chance.

The Guild's Secrets

The magnificent Brugge Central Library stands before me, a treasure trove of historical secrets waiting to be whispered to those who enter its doors. As I step inside, the majestic Gothic windows shower the dimly lit room with ethereal rays, illuminating the ancient floors covered in a layer of dust. Never did I think I would have the privilege of exploring this scholarly sanctuary, where the hushed tranquility is only broken by the musty aroma of old books, merging with the salty scent from the nearby canals. Inspector De Vries, strides with confidence, leading the way with determination. Right behind him, Helena matches his quick pace, her eyes gleaming with anticipation at the thought of uncovering new knowledge.

We huddle in a secluded corner, the librarian Mr. Dubois eyeing us with a mix of curiosity and suspicion. I feel out of place, like a rough-hewn stone among polished gems. The shelves surrounding us seem to hold endless mysteries, and it's those very secrets that have drawn us here.

Helena's fingers dance over spines and parchment as she whispers about the witchcraft history that once ensnared my family. "The answers might be sleeping in these records," she murmurs, more to herself than us.

De Vries nods, his eyes narrowed in thought. "If we're to understand what's happening now, we must dive into Brugge's darker days."

A forgotten section calls to us. Cobwebs cling to oak shelves laden with ledgers so old their leather covers crackle under Helena's careful touch. Her eyes shine with excitement as she opens a book to reveal meticulous entries of medieval guild activities. "This could be it," she breathes out.

My throat tightens as memories stir within me—whispered tales from my youth about shadowy ceremonies and cruel retributions doled out by those very guilds whose secrets now lay exposed on the table before us. I can almost hear the hushed voices of old widows recounting rumors of strange rituals and masked figures stealing through alleyways at night. There were stories of those who dared speak against the guilds later found floating in the canal, or of skilled craftsmen who lost the use of their hands under mysterious circumstances when their work drew too much acclaim.

I recount these chilling stories to De Vries and Helena, my voice low and steady despite the chill that creeps up my spine. "The guilds weren't just about trade and business," I explain, meeting their eyes gravely. "They had other rites...other duties. There were punishments for those who crossed them or threatened their power." My companions listen raptly as I speak of clandestine gatherings in candlelit rooms far from prying eyes, where fates were decided and penalties were meted out by figures cloaked in authority and secrecy. Though vague, the rumors hinted at a brutal system of justice, self-preservation, and control that lurked beneath the guilds' public face.

"To uphold their monopolies, they resorted to shadowy means," I continue, a heaviness in my chest as I unearth long-buried memories of my hometown's darker heart.

Helena flips through another tome, the dusty pages crackling beneath her fingers, and gasps softly as she comes across a startling discovery. We lean in, crowding around the aged book to see what she's found—a record of a secret tribunal that operated in the shadows, hidden within the guilds' hierarchy. "They used to call themselves 'The Judicators'," she says, her voice hushed. "According to this, they passed judgment on anyone they deemed a threat, meting out punishments without mercy."

I feel a chill run down my spine at her words. The Judicators—how had we never heard of them before? What kinds of terrible deeds had they carried out, cloaked in anonymity? Helena's eyes reflect the flickering candlelight as she scans the page. "Listen to this," she murmurs. "'Let it be known, we are the guardians of order. Those who defy our authority will be made examples of, so that all may know the cost of defiance.'" She looks up, her expression grave. "It seems they acted as judge, jury, and executioner. All in secret."

My companions exchange uneasy glances as we absorb this disturbing revelation. What else don't we know about our town's past? How many more secrets lie buried beneath the surface, echoing faintly through the canals? I shake my head slowly. "The more we uncover, the less we truly understand this place and its history," I say ruefully. Helena nods, carefully closing the book. One thing is clear—there are hidden depths yet to be revealed, and disentangling truth from legend will be no easy task.

Inspector De Vries removes his small leatherbound notebook from the inner pocket of his overcoat, opening it to a fresh page. I notice his normally steady surgeon's hand shaking ever so slightly as the pieces begin falling into place. He takes out a sharpened graphite pencil and starts scribbling notes furiously, his eyes alight.

"If such a secret tribunal truly existed back then," he muses aloud, his voice echoing in the cavernous archives, "could it be possible that remnants of it persist, somewhere in the shadows?"

He looks up, his gaze piercing. "Could they be the ones responsible for these canal drownings?"

His chilling question hangs heavy in the dusty air between us. We continue rifling through the aged parchment records, our search revealed just how deeply the medieval guilds had once threaded themselves through every facet of Brugge's lifeblood—politically, economically—like veins of iron through the stone.

"It stands to reason," De Vries continues, his voice now laced with certainty—the growing conviction of a seasoned detective meticulously piecing together a puzzle from scattered shards of history. "Old power structures and feuds have a way of persisting, even when those who instigated them are long gone. Like ripples expanding slowly across the surface of a lake, eventually reaching even the most distant shores."

Helena looks up from her research, her expression one of resolve mixed with trepidation. "If we're right about this," she starts but doesn't finish.

We don't need her to; the implication is clear enough.

In this library steeped in silence and shadow, surrounded by ancient history, we stand on the cusp of a truth that might just unravel Brugge's present mystery—or entangle us further in its ominous tangle.

The dust swirls and twirls in the gentle rays of light, as Helena delves into the pages of an age-old manuscript. Her expression knitted with intense focus, I stand beside her in the sacred stillness of the library, an unsettling feeling creeping over me. It's as though we are invading secrets that were purposely kept hidden.

She pauses and reaches for a magnifying glass, examining a faded illustration of a guild ritual. The room is silent save for the faint creak of leather-bound tomes and the distant tolling of a church bell.

"These symbols," Helena says, tracing the outline of an intricate emblem on the page, "they're eerily similar to the markings we found on the victims' skin."

My pulse quickens at her words. I lean closer to see what she sees—a series of angular marks that form a pattern both strange and familiar. "But those marks could be anything," I counter, hoping to stem my rising alarm. "Surely there's another explanation."

Helena shakes her head, her fingers skimming over other illustrations depicting hooded figures gathered around a ceremonial table. "These rituals were deeply significant to the guilds," she explains, her voice low but steady. "They were about more than just tradition—they were a show of power, unity... control."

She flips through more pages, stopping at an image that makes my heart sink—a figure laid out on a table, arms crossed over their chest, with similar markings adorning their skin.

"The rituals were sometimes used as punishment," Helena continues, her gaze fixed on the drawing. "A way to enforce obedience within their ranks or to warn off those who might threaten their interests."

I feel a cold knot forming in my stomach as I take in the implications. The idea that these ancient practices could be linked to the canal drownings is unthinkable.

Inspector De Vries steps closer, his eyes scanning the text over Helena's shoulder. "It's like they branded their own," he muses, his voice tinged with both fascination and revulsion.

The inspector looks up at me, his sharp eyes seeking confirmation or perhaps reassurance. But what can I offer? The waters of my understanding are as murky as those of our canals.

"I've heard whispers," I admit reluctantly, memories of old tales surfacing unbidden. "Tales passed down through generations about those who crossed the guilds and paid dearly for it."

De Vries nods slowly as if this new information is another piece slotting into place within his mental puzzle.

"We need more than old stories and similarities," he says with resolve. "We need concrete evidence."

Helena turns another page and points to a paragraph written in elegant script. "Here," she says, "it describes how they would mark traitors before casting them out or... worse." She doesn't finish her sentence; she doesn't need to.

I look away from the book and focus on my hands—they're trembling slightly. All my life I've felt like an outsider in Brugge, my family's history setting us apart from everyone else. Now it seems that history might be repeating itself in ways I never could have imagined.

Helena's voice draws me back from my spiraling thoughts. "Willem," she says softly but with urgency, "did your family keep any records? Anything that might shed light on these practices?"

I shake my head slowly. Our past was something we rarely spoke of; it brought only pain and ostracism.

"We never kept such things," I say quietly. "My family wanted to forget... to move on."

"But perhaps not everyone wanted to forget," De Vries interjects thoughtfully.

Helena nods in agreement before returning her attention to the book before us. She reads aloud from another passage detailing a specific ritual—one involving water as both a purifier and a weapon.

"As water cleanses, so shall it judge," she recites solemnly.

The library's heavy air weighs on me, thick with dust and the hint of long-forgotten treasures. The rows of timeworn books seem to loom closer, almost beckoning us to uncover their sinister stories. As Helena and Inspector De Vries delve into the ancient guild records, my hands quiver with anticipation. Every revelation peels back a layer of my personal history.

Helena's fingers trace the faded ink on a page, her touch gentle as if she fears the words might crumble under too firm a grip. "The guilds were powerful... influential," she says, not looking up from the book. "They held the city in their grasp, molding it to their will."

The inspector nods, his eyes not leaving the text. "And they were ruthless in maintaining that power," he adds, his voice a low rumble in the quiet of the library.

My throat tightens as I listen to them. The stories my grandmother used to tell me echo in my mind—warnings really, about how our family once held a place of respect before the guilds turned on us. I always thought they were just that—stories. But standing here now, with evidence of such darkness within these very walls, I'm not so sure.

"I never wanted any of this," I whisper, my voice barely carrying across the table. Helena looks up at me, her expression softening with empathy.

"We know," she replies gently. "But understanding this might help clear your name."

I want to believe her, yet there's a gnawing fear in my gut that tells me some truths are better left buried. The thought that my ancestors might have been entangled in these grim rituals is more than unsettling—it's terrifying.

De Vries leans back in his chair, rubbing his chin thoughtfully. "Willem," he begins, "do you recall any specific tales or... legends from your family that might be relevant?"

I hesitate before answering; these are memories I've fought hard to suppress. "There were whispers," I start slowly, feeling their attention fixed on me. "About a betrayal within the guilds—one that led to a brutal reprisal against those deemed responsible."

The inspector raises an eyebrow, interest piqued. "Go on," he urges.

"My great-great-grandfather was part of the guilds—a man of some standing." I can hear my voice shaking as I dredge up the painful history. "He discovered corruption among the ranks... tried to expose it."

Helena's eyes widen as she connects the dots. "And they silenced him for it?"

I nod grimly. "They branded him a traitor and... executed him publicly." Saying it aloud feels like tearing open an old wound.

The inspector reaches out and places a reassuring hand on my shoulder—a surprising gesture from a man usually guarded by his professionalism. "We'll get to the bottom of this," he says firmly.

As we delve deeper into the archives, each page turn feels like peeling back layers of Brugge's facade to reveal its rotting core. We find accounts of secretive meetings held under cover of night; coded messages passed between cloaked figures; and punishments dealt out swiftly and without mercy.

Helena pauses at an entry detailing a ritualistic drowning—a punishment reserved for those who threatened to expose guild secrets or sought to escape their clutches. She reads aloud, her voice steady despite the horror etched into every word.

My hands clench into fists at my sides as I listen. Could it be that these ancient practices are being revived? Is someone out there meting out twisted justice according to long-forgotten laws?

Inspector De Vries stands abruptly, his chair scraping against the stone floor—a jarring sound in this place of quiet study. He begins pacing back and forth like a caged animal seeking an escape from its confines.

"Think about it," he says with a fervor I haven't seen in him before. "The drownings today... they could be imitating these old rituals—someone using history as a blueprint for murder."

***

As we step into the study of Professor Jan Van Eck, the smell of aged parchment and dust engulfs us. It's as if we have entered a sanctuary of knowledge, with every inch of the wall adorned with shelves overflowing with books that hold untold stories of the past. And there, standing amidst the literary treasures, is the historian himself, a timeless fixture in this place, just like the ancient tomes he diligently protects.

"We seek understanding, Professor," De Vries begins, his voice echoing slightly in the hallowed space. "The guilds of Brugge... there are whispers of their past, things left unsaid. We believe they may hold the key to the drownings."

Van Eck peers at us from behind his spectacles, a hint of intrigue lighting up his eyes. "Ah, the guilds," he muses, steepling his fingers. "Powerful entities they were, each a kingdom unto itself. They did not tolerate insubordination. To maintain their grip on trade, they'd go to great lengths.

Sometimes," he pauses, allowing the weight of his words to sink in, "to chilling extremes."

Helena leans forward, her interest piqued. "Chilling? How so?"

"The canals were their veins, commerce their blood. But when blood clots," Van Eck taps a finger against his temple, "measures are taken to clear the passage."

I shuffle uncomfortably; his metaphor feels too close to our grim reality.

"Are you suggesting the guilds would... dispose of troublemakers?" De Vries probes.

Van Eck nods solemnly. "Historical accounts are often sanitized narratives penned by victors. Yet delve deeper and you find... aberrations. Members who crossed lines drawn in silence would vanish."

De Vries exchanges a glance with Helena before turning back to me. I can tell he's thinking what I'm thinking: we're onto something here.

"But why now?" I ask. "The guilds' power has waned over centuries."

Van Eck rises from his seat and walks over to a cabinet, retrieving a worn leather-bound journal. He blows dust off its cover before opening it to a marked page.

"This journal," he says, "belonged to Pieter Van Brussel, a guild master who lived two centuries ago." His finger traces lines of faded ink. "Here he speaks of a covenant among the guilds—a pact that transcends time, sworn upon the Brotherhood of the Silver Swan."

Helena's breath catches at the mention of the Brotherhood—a legend she's been chasing since her first foray into forensics.

"What was this pact?" De Vries asks.

"To uphold their legacy," Van Eck replies. "A legacy they believed was worth protecting at all costs."

De Vries rubs his chin thoughtfully while Helena scribbles notes feverishly.

"And how does this tie into our current plight?" I press on.

Van Eck closes the journal with a soft thud and returns it to its resting place.

"The answer lies in what your city values above all else—history," he states flatly. "Perhaps someone believes that by resurrecting old ways, they can restore Brugge to its former glory."

***

The tavern's cozy warmth is a comforting contrast to the harsh cold of the night. The dim light from the fireplace creates a mesmerizing spectacle on the weathered tables, conjuring a sense of companionship and confidentiality among the close-knit group of patrons. As someone who typically shies away from crowds, I find myself tucked into a corner booth with Inspector De Vries and Helena, savoring the rare chance for some semblance of privacy.

I nurse my ale, its bitter tang grounding me as we delve into conversations better suited for hushed tones and locked rooms. De Vries leans forward, his eyes scanning the room before settling on us, "We need to talk about what we're up against."

As our eyes lock, Helena's spark reveals a blend of anticipation and uncertainty, mirroring my own emotions. "The guild's past is very interesting," she shares. "But many of their stories are trying to remain hidden in the past."

De Vries nods, his fingers drumming on the table's surface. "Which means we're tugging at something that doesn't want to be unraveled."

The air thickens with the gravity of our undertaking. The tavern's joviality seems distant now as if we're in a world apart from the laughter and clinking glasses around us.

"We need names," De Vries states, pulling out a small notebook from his coat pocket. "Descendants of those guild members who might still hold sway over Brugge's darker corners."

Helena pulls a pen from her hair, her brow furrowing as she considers this. "We'll have to cross-reference the historical records with current archives. It won't be easy or quick."

"And it won't be safe," I add, my voice low. The room feels smaller suddenly, the walls closing in with each syllable spoken.

De Vries meets my eyes, his expression is solemn. "I know you've borne the brunt of suspicion, Willem. But we can't let fear dictate our steps—not when there's a chance to end this."

I look at them both—De Vries with his unwavering sense of duty and Helena with her fierce intelligence—and feel a resolve steeling within me. We are an unlikely trio, bound by our search for truth amidst whispers of the past.

"We should start by listing prominent families," Helena suggests, her pen poised above a blank page in De Vries's notebook.

De Vries nods in agreement, pulling up a chair closer to us. The tavern's din recedes as we hunch over our task, murmuring names and connections like incantations against the darkness we seek to dispel.

The evening wears on as we fill pages with potential leads—names linked across centuries by bloodline and influence. Our list grows longer and more daunting with each addition.

Helena pauses mid-sentence, rubbing her temples. "This is like navigating a labyrinth without a map."

De Vries gives her an encouraging nod. "But we've got the next best thing—a historian with insight into this labyrinth's construction."

I can't help but smirk at that. Professor Van Eck's passion for Brugge's history had seemed excessive at first, but now it's proving invaluable.

The tension in the room mounts as we acknowledge what lies ahead: confronting descendants who may harbor secrets akin to those kept by their ancestors—secrets they may go to great lengths to protect.

A silence falls upon our table, each of us lost in thought over our list of names—each one a doorway that might lead us closer to understanding or deeper into peril.

As hours slip into the night outside the tavern windows, we finish our drinks in contemplative silence—the weight of our findings pressing down upon us like heavy stones in deep water.

We rise together—a pact sealed not just by necessity but by an understanding that what we seek could change everything or cost us dearly.

A Glimmer of Truth

Lucas Rombouts strides through the hushed streets of Brugge, the first light of dawn casting long shadows on the cobbles. He approaches his gallery, a sanctuary for his unconventional art nestled between aged brick facades. The crisp morning air carries the promise of a new day, a stark contrast to the turmoil churning within him.

He fumbles for the keys in his pocket, anticipation mixed with a touch of dread. Today, he unveils his latest collection—a series of haunting canvases that reflect the city's recent tragedies. Pushing the door open, Lucas steps into the dim interior, flicking on the lights.

The sight that greets him severs his breath.

Canvases lie shredded on the floor, thick streaks of red paint smeared across their remnants. Frames hang askew, glass shattered like frozen raindrops beneath them. His once meticulously arranged exhibit is now a grotesque mockery, mirroring the violence of the canal murders more closely than any brushstroke could.

"No..." Lucas whispers, heart hammering against his ribs. He stumbles forward, hands trembling as he lifts a piece of canvas—his vision of Brugge's dark underbelly now defaced with violent abandon.

His mind races as he pulls out his phone with shaking hands and dials the police. The gallery echoes with the distant ring before a click signals an answer.

"Police station, how can I assist?"

Lucas' voice cracks as he reports the devastation before him. "My exhibit... someone has destroyed it—completely vandalized."

Within minutes, Constable Hendrik De Jong arrives at Lucas' gallery. He steps over the threshold with measured calmness that belies his concern for this new development.

Hendrik scans the chaos, his keen eyes cataloging every detail—the jagged tears in canvas, the chaotic splatters of paint, and broken frames. His mind pieces together a silent narrative of destruction.

"Lucas Rombouts?" Hendrik's voice grounds Lucas back to reality.

"Yes," Lucas responds, anguish lining his features. "It's all ruined."

Hendrik nods solemnly. "We'll need to document everything before anything is touched." He pulls out a notebook and starts jotting down notes.

Lucas watches Hendrik move through his space with professional detachment. The constable crouches to inspect a half-torn portrait—a woman's face peering out from a web of cuts.

"This one... it's as if they wanted her to watch," Hendrik muses aloud, then turns to Lucas. "Your work—it has always stirred conversation. Did anyone express particular disdain?"

Lucas rakes a hand through his hair, frustration etched in his furrowed brow. "Critics have been harsh, but nothing like this... nothing violent."

Hendrik straightens up and continues his examination of the room. He pauses by a splash of red so vibrant it seems fresh blood oozes from the wall.

"The choice of red," Hendrik begins, fingertips hovering just above the stain without touching it. "Symbolic?"

"It's not just color—it's emotion," Lucas says with conviction despite his distress. "But this—" he gestures at the vandalized red "—this is not my doing."

Hendrik takes note of Lucas' reaction; an artist's passion can often ignite others' fury—or fanaticism.

The constable moves methodically through the gallery space, leaving no corner unscrutinized. Each piece tells its own story: an anguished whisper from Brugge's darkest corners; now silenced by an act just as dark.

Lucas watches Hendrik work and feels a surge of helplessness wash over him. His creations are more than art; they are fragments of himself—now violated and exposed in their destruction.

Hendrik finally stands back and takes in the scene as a whole once again. "I'll need you to compile a list of anyone who might hold a grudge against you or your art," he says.

"Will they be suspects?" Lucas asks, voice edged with anxiety.

"Potentially," Hendrik replies without committing further. "For now we gather information; motives will reveal themselves in time."

Lucas nods mutely and retreats to his desk amidst the ruins to begin writing names—critics who scoffed at him, rivals who envied him, strangers who lingered too long in front of certain pieces.

As Hendrik watches Lucas jot down potential leads with fervent strokes, he reflects on how art and life have collided with violent force in this quiet city where secrets run as deep as its canals.

***

The damp cobblestones glisten under the moonlight as I follow Inspector De Vries and Helena down the narrow alley that leads to Lucas Rombouts' gallery. The evening air carries a chill that settles into my bones, but it's the weight of the guilds' secrets we've uncovered that chills me more. We're a strange trio, bound by necessity: an inspector, an apothecary's daughter, and a fisherman with a family history darker than the canals at midnight.

De Vries's coat flaps behind him as he strides forward, a lantern swinging in Helena's grip, casting long shadows on the walls. The inspector's phone call had been brief, his expression growing taut as he listened to the voice on the other end. When he snapped the device shut, his eyes met mine with a spark of urgency.

"Lucas' gallery," he'd said, voice low. "We need to go now."

Helena had been quick to gather her things, curiosity lighting up her eyes like the flame she now carries. As for me, I'm not sure what help I'll be among paintings and sculptures. My hands are more familiar with nets and ropes than delicate works of art. But this isn't just about art anymore; it's about finding answers, and clearing my name.

We round the corner and there it is—Lucas' place of pride and struggle. The door hangs off its hinges, a gaping maw leading into darkness. The inspector wastes no time stepping inside, and we follow.

The smell of turpentine assaults my nostrils as we enter the gallery. It's chaos—a violent storm passed through here, leaving canvases slashed and sculptures decapitated. De Vries moves from piece to piece, his brow furrowed as he examines each act of destruction.

"Lucas has always been... unconventional with his art," Helena says softly, approaching a canvas where paint still drips like fresh wounds. "But someone wanted to hurt more than just canvas and clay."

She's right. There's intent here in the ruins—a message scrawled in jagged lines and shattered frames. De Vries crouches beside a bronze figure twisted grotesquely on the floor.

"This wasn't just mindless vandalism," he murmurs more to himself than to us. "It was targeted."

Helena nods in agreement, her gaze analytical as she surveys the room. "Look at this," she calls us over to where she stands before a wall lined with portraits.

I join them, squinting in the dim light as Helena points out the defaced paintings. Each one is a historical figure from Brugge's past—members of those same guilds we've been investigating.

"Their faces," she says, her voice barely above a whisper, "they've been scratched out—obliterated."

De Vries runs a hand over his beard, deep in thought. "A statement against the past... or against those who carry its legacy?"

It's a question none of us can answer yet.

I stand shoulder to shoulder with De Vries and Helena, our shadows mingling on the gallery walls. The air is thick with the scent of destruction. Lucas hunches over a ruined canvas, his hands buried in his hair, his frame shuddering with silent sobs.

De Vries steps forward, his voice a calm anchor amid the chaos. "Lucas, tell us about your work."

Lucas lifts his head, his eyes red-rimmed and haunted. He waves a hand at the carnage surrounding us. "It's my life's blood," he chokes out. "Each piece is a chapter of Brugge's past—its myths, its legends."

Helena kneels beside a sculpture, its features marred beyond recognition. "Your pieces," she starts gently, "they resonate with the history we've been uncovering."

Lucas nods, dragging himself to his feet. He walks over to a painting spared by the vandals, one depicting a lone figure standing by the canal's edge, a shrouded form floating in the water beside him.

"This one," he says, voice cracking. "It's inspired by an old tale—The Mourner of Minnewater. A ghostly figure that roams the lake searching for her lost love, her tears keeping him just beneath the surface."

De Vries frowns, exchanging a glance with me. The parallel to the recent drownings doesn't escape any of us.

"I never meant..." Lucas swallows hard, "I didn't know."

Helena touches his arm. "You couldn't have known," she assures him.

"But I did," Lucas insists. "On some level, I felt it—the undercurrent of something dark stirring in these waters."

De Vries leans against a table strewn with sketches. "Could someone have taken inspiration from your art?"

Lucas shakes his head vehemently. "Art is meant to provoke thought, not action like this!"

I can't help but wonder if Lucas's work has become a self-fulfilling prophecy—a dark echo from history surfacing in brush strokes and spilled paint.

The lantern's glow dances off the walls, casting a golden sheen over the gallery's chaos. Helena moves through the room, her presence a calm force amid the disarray. I watch her closely, admiring how her mind works, dissecting the scene before us with a meticulous eye.

She pauses by a painting, its canvas slashed, dark streaks of paint bleeding down like open wounds. Helena crouches, peering at the jagged tears with an intensity that seems to draw the shadows closer. I can't help but move closer myself, drawn to her focus.

"What do you see?" I ask quietly, not wanting to break her concentration.

Helena glances up at me, and for a moment, her eyes are like those of an owl I'd once seen perched on a tree by the canals—a silent observer of the night.

"Something's not right," she murmurs and points to the edge of the tear. "This paint here—it's still tacky. It's been added after the original piece was completed."

Inspector De Vries joins us, his tall figure looming as he bends down to follow Helena's gaze.

"An addition by Lucas?" he asks, his voice low and even.

"No," Lucas interjects from behind us, his voice strained. "I would never deface my work."

Helena nods in agreement. "And there's more." She pulls out a small magnifying glass from her apron pocket and inspects the fresh paint. "This isn't just any paint—it's an uncommon composition used in textile dyes."

I frown, confused. "Textile dyes? Here?"

She stands up and looks around the gallery with new eyes. "And there are fibers," she adds, gesturing to where fine threads cling to the edge of the frame—barely visible but there nonetheless.

De Vries steps closer. "Could these be from the vandal?"

"It's possible," Helena says as she delicately picks off a fiber with tweezers and slips it into a small vial. "These don't match anything in Lucas' studio. And if my guess about this dye is correct, it might lead us back to someone connected to Brugge's textile guilds."

The inspector's sharp eyes catch mine for a brief moment before returning to Helena. "Textile guilds? That aligns with our line of inquiry into Brugge's old guild members."

Lucas watches us talk, his arms wrapped around himself as if holding in his anguish. His gallery was more than just walls and art; it was an extension of his very soul.

Helena steps over to him and places a comforting hand on his shoulder. "We'll find who did this," she assures him.

I nod in agreement but feel a surge of helplessness mixed with anger. Someone out there is using our past—our history—as a weapon, turning Brugge into their stage for some twisted performance.

"We should document everything here," De Vries says decisively. "Every piece of evidence could be crucial."

Helena and I nod in unison and get to work—she collects fibers and samples while I make notes and sketches of their placement around the room.

Hours pass as we catalog every detail—the size of footprints left in spilled paint, the pattern of destruction among Lucas' art pieces, any object out of place that could tell us more about our intruder.

The inspector's decision doesn't surprise me. He's a man who sees patterns where others see chaos and connections where others see coincidence. "Lucas, we're putting you under police protection," De Vries announces, his voice echoing slightly in the stillness of the ravaged gallery.

Lucas, who's been lost in a silent reverie since we arrived, snaps to attention. "Protection? But why? I'm just an artist."

De Vries rests a hand on his shoulder, firm and reassuring. "Exactly," he says. "An artist whose work has become intertwined with a killer's design. You might be at risk."

I watch Lucas' face shift from confusion to fear, the reality of the situation dawning on him. He nods slowly, reluctantly accepting the shield of the law around him.

I turn away from them, scanning the room once more. There's a tension here now, a silent alarm that buzzes in my ears. I need air—I need to think. Stepping outside into the cool night, I pull my jacket tighter around me and look around at the scattered clusters of people that linger near the gallery.

Artists and patrons alike stand huddled in small groups, their murmurs floating on the breeze like leaves in an autumn gust. I drift closer to one cluster, where a young woman with paint-stained fingers gestures animatedly.

"I heard someone was lurking around here last night," she says to her companions, her voice tinged with unease.

Her words pique my interest and I lean in closer under the pretense of lighting my pipe.

"A shadowy figure," another adds, pulling his scarf up over his mouth as if to ward off more than just the cold. "Just standing there, watching."

I draw on my pipe and let out a plume of smoke that mingles with my breath in the chill air. A watcher—or perhaps more aptly, a sentinel guarding some dark secret.

"Did anyone see his face?" I ask casually, injecting myself into their conversation.

They turn to me—a stranger among them—but my weather-beaten face and fisherman's garb seem to put them at ease.

"No," says the woman with a shake of her head. "He was cloaked in darkness. But it felt... ominous."

I nod thoughtfully and thank them before moving on to another group. The story is the same—a shadow among shadows; a presence that's felt rather than seen.

My mind churns as I weave through more conversations, gathering threads of rumor and fear. It seems this figure was more ghost than man—seen by few but sensed by many.

Returning inside, I find De Vries coordinating with his officers while Helena assists Lucas with gathering what remains of his art.

"Inspector," I say quietly as I approach him. "There are whispers of someone watching the gallery last night."

De Vries's eyes flicker with interest as he listens intently to my recounting of the rumors.

"A potential witness—or suspect." His voice is contemplative as he mulls over this new piece of information.

"We need to ," he decides after a moment. "See if anyone else saw this figure or can provide a better description."

He dispatches two officers immediately before turning back to me with an appraising look.

"Willem," he begins in a tone that tells me he values my opinion more than he lets on, "what do you make of all this?"

I weigh his question carefully before answering. "Fear makes people see shadows where there are none," I say slowly. "But this feels different—like someone is stirring up these waters deliberately."

De Vries nods solemnly. "Agreed."

A hushed conversation snags my attention. It's coming from behind a partition where damaged sculptures stand like silent mourners. Helena is closer; I see her pause, her head tilting ever so slightly toward the voices. The light from her lantern flickers across her face, revealing a frown of concentration. She is listening, I realize, and not to the inspector or Lucas.

My gaze shifts to De Vries, who is speaking with an officer near the entrance. He hasn't noticed Helena's distraction—or the low murmur that has drawn her in. I move closer to her under the guise of inspecting a twisted piece of metal that once might have been part of a grander work.

The voices grow clearer as I approach.

"...shouldn't have happened this way," one hisses—a man by the timbre.

"Quiet!" The other voice is sharper, laced with fear. "Do you want to be caught?"

I glance at Helena; her eyes meet mine, wide with alarm. She steps away from the partition just as I pretend to stumble against it, drawing their attention away from their illicit exchange.

The voices fall silent as two figures emerge—a man and a woman cloaked in heavy garments that do little to hide their agitation.

"Is everything alright?" Helena asks them innocently enough.

The man clears his throat, his eyes darting between us. "Yes," he says quickly. "We were just... discussing the tragedy of it all."

The woman nods vigorously but says nothing, her hands clenched together tightly.

Helena offers them a small smile before moving toward De Vries with purpose in her step. The pair watch her go before slipping away into the night outside.

I follow Helena at a distance, watching as she pulls De Vries aside. Her voice is too low for me to hear over the murmurs of officers and onlookers that fill the gallery now turned crime scene. But I see De Vries's posture stiffen; his gaze sharpens as he looks toward where the couple stood moments ago.

"Willem," he calls me over, his expression grave.

I join them, my curiosity piqued by their seriousness.

"Helena overheard something," De Vries informs me quietly. "A conversation about tonight's events—potentially linked to the guild."

My heart hammers against my ribcage at his words. It seems every discovery we make ties back to those damned societies—the keepers of Brugge's deepest and darkest truths.

"What did they say?" I ask Helena directly.

She glances around before speaking in a hushed tone. "They mentioned something going wrong—that it wasn't supposed to happen like this."

"And they mentioned the guild?" De Vries presses.

"Yes," she confirms with a nod. "They spoke as if they were part of it—or knew who was."

De Vries rubs his chin thoughtfully before turning his attention back to me. "Willem, keep an eye on Helena while I handle this."

He doesn't wait for my response; he trusts I'll do it without question—and he's right.

Helena meets my gaze with an unspoken agreement as we watch De Vries weave through the crowd and disappear beyond the door.

We're alone now in our corner of chaos—her with her knowledge of science and medicine, me with my history and instincts honed by years on unforgiving seas.

"Should we follow them?" she asks quietly.

"No," I reply after considering for a moment. "We might spook them further away into hiding."

She nods in understanding but frustration flickers across her face—the same frustration I feel gnawing at my gut. We're close to something; I can sense it like a storm brewing on the horizon—inevitable and dangerous.

We resume our pretense of examining the ruined art pieces while keeping our senses attuned to any further whispers or suspicious behavior among those who linger here out of curiosity or perhaps guilt.

***

Lucas sat on the cold stone floor of the gallery, surrounded by the wreckage of his latest exhibit. Torn canvases and shattered frames lay strewn around him, the once provocative and meticulously crafted artworks now reduced to refuse. He ran his fingers over a gash in one of the paintings, the oils smeared and blended into a chaotic mess.

Looking at the destruction, Lucas was overwhelmed by a storm of emotions. There was sadness at seeing his creations so callously ruined, anger at the small-minded vandals who had done this, and fear about what it meant for his future as an artist in Brugge. But beneath it all, simmering strongest of all, was a defiant resolve not to be silenced or intimidated.

Lucas thought back to the reactions when he had first displayed this controversial new collection. Many had been shocked and even outraged at the dark, macabre nature of the paintings. Whispers had followed him as he walked the streets of Brugge in the days after the show opened. The locals saw the eerie parallels between his art and the recent canal murders as an ill omen, a ghoulish glorification of horrific deeds.

He had staunchly defended his work, trying to explain that his intention was not to glorify at all, but to artistically explore the shadows that lurk within men's souls. Lucas had no way of knowing his confronting images would turn out to mirror disturbing reality so closely. That was the alchemy of his art, not malevolence. But the authorities had begun scrutinizing him nonetheless, and the locals had only grown more suspicious.

And now this. Lucas realized he had underestimated just how much hostility his singular vision could provoke. He should have known better. After all, he was no stranger to having his work misunderstood. Even his mentors at the Academy had warned him that his aesthetic was too challenging, too uncomfortable for most. They had encouraged him to soften the jagged edges, tone down the darkness, and paint pretty portraits that would sell.

But Lucas could never bring himself to compromise his vision that way. Just like these vandals could not compromise it by destroying it. He slowly rose to his feet, a spark of resolve flickering inside him. As he looked around at the chaos, Lucas knew he could not allow this act of intimidation to succeed. He would salvage what he could, repair the damage, and reopen the exhibit.

Even if he must stand guard night and day, he would not retreat or hide his art away in shame or fear. These creations were his truth, dredged up from the depths of his soul. He had to share them with any who cared to see. If that meant facing incomprehension, anger, or even danger - so be it.

The Artist's Plight

Lucas Rombouts stares at the disarray in his studio, the morning light barely piercing through the grimy windows. Canvases lean against the walls, some face down as if ashamed of their own shadows. Paint tubes litter the floor, their caps missing, like a cry for closure that never comes. Lucas's fingers twitch, yearning for the brush, but his mind is a tempest, thoughts colliding with the force of a brutal spring storm.

The door creaks open, heralding the arrival of Inspector Gerard De Vries and Helena De Baere. Lucas doesn't turn; he knows who it is by the measured steps and the subtle scent of lavender that always seems to trail after Helena.

"Mr. Rombouts?" De Vries's voice is a low rumble in the cramped space.

Lucas faces them, his gaze piercing through the dimness. "Inspector. Miss De Baere." His words are brittle, like dry leaves underfoot.

De Vries surveys the chaos, his eyes lingering on a canvas depicting a figure draped over a canal bridge, lifeless and limp. "Your work is... provocative."

Lucas scoffs, a hollow sound. "Provocative enough to have someone tear through my exhibit."

Helena steps forward, her eyes not on Lucas but on the art surrounding them. "Your paintings are speaking to someone," she says softly. "Perhaps too loudly."

"Or perhaps they're just paintings," Lucas counters, his tone defensive yet weary.

De Vries pulls out a notepad from his coat pocket. "You understand why we're here then?"

Lucas nods, runs a hand through his unkempt hair. "Because some fool thinks my brush is predicting deaths."

Helena approaches a canvas smeared with dark hues swirling into an abyss. "It's more than that," she murmurs. "There's an undercurrent of truth in your work that's hard to ignore."

Lucas watches her examine his art and something akin to relief washes over him—someone sees beyond the grotesque.

De Vries clears his throat. "We need to understand your process, Mr. Rombouts. Where you draw your inspiration from."

Lucas gestures vaguely around the room. "From here," he says cryptically.

"Here?" De Vries presses.

"The city," Lucas expands with a flourish of his arm as if to embrace all of Brugge within his studio walls. "Its history, its secrets..."

Lucas regards the two of them pensively, as if deciding how much of himself to reveal. Finally, he steps towards a half-finished canvas propped against the wall.

"Let me show you something," he says, beckoning them over.

The background of the painting depicts the façade of a medieval building, all sharp angles and arched windows. In the foreground, a faceless figure cowers before a shadowy, sinister form.

"I was reading about the old guilds when this image came to me," Lucas explains. "Their secrecy, the way they dominated so much of life here centuries ago."

He points to the indistinct shape looming over the cowering figure. "The guilds inspired fear to maintain control. Many were said to have used violent means to protect their interests."

De Vries studies the painting intently, saying nothing. Helena's eyes widen slightly at Lucas's words.

Lucas moves deeper into the studio, the floorboards creaking underfoot. He stops before a painting splattered with shades of deep crimson. "And this...I learned about the witch hunts. How many were drowned in the canals."

Helena shivers visibly. Lucas pauses, seeming to retreat into himself for a moment. "Violence leaves traces, even if the blood gets washed away."

"Is that why you depict it in your work?" De Vries asks.

Lucas shrugs. "I paint what I see, Inspector. Both the beauty and the darkness in this city's legacy."

He gestures to a cluster of serene landscapes hanging under a grimy skylight. "Brugge captures the imagination. I can't resist putting brush to canvas to capture its spell."

De Vries walks over to examine a painting depicting a hanged woman, her face a grimacing mask of anguish. "And this?" he questions. "Where did you see this?"

Lucas stiffens almost imperceptibly. "Nowhere. That came from...within."

"It bears an uncanny resemblance to the second victim," De Vries points out quietly.

Lucas looks away. "An unfortunate coincidence."

Helena touches De Vries's arm lightly. "Inspector, many artists explore humanity's darker facets. It needn't be more than that."

De Vries nods reluctantly, pocketing his notepad. Lucas exhales, seeming to deflate slightly.

"You have a gift, Mr. Rombouts," Helena says gently. "But also a responsibility in how you use it."

Lucas turns his piercing gaze on her. "I don't take that lightly, Miss De Baere. My art comes from within, but also from this city. I can't change what I see."

Helena moves slowly around the studio, studying each painting intently. Lucas watches her carefully, his body tense like a cornered animal. Inspector De Vries hangs back near the doorway, giving Helena space for her examination.

She pauses before a painting of a canal scene, depicted at night. The surface of the water is obsidian black, swallowing the meager light of a slivered moon. In the foreground, a slender hand breaches the water's edge, pale fingers splayed as if clawing for purchase.

"You capture the mood of each setting so vividly," Helena murmurs. She leans closer, noticing nearly imperceptible ripples surrounding the ghostly hand.

"The water distorts things, doesn't it?" Helena continues. "Reality becomes fluid, deceptive. Much like memory."

She turns to Lucas. "When did you paint this?"

He rubs his unshaven jaw, thinking. "A few weeks before the first drowning."

Helena's gaze sharpens. She moves to the next painting, depicting the silhouette of a hooded figure on a bridge. The figure's cloak blends with the night, making it seem one with the darkness.

"You conceal as much as you reveal," Helena observes. "The facelessness of the killer, the ambiguity of his purpose."

She scans the rest of the paintings, looking for any hidden patterns or similarities. Many feature watery backgrounds or cloaked figures barely distinguishable from the shadows.

Turning back to Lucas, Helena asks, "Have you noticed any strangers around your exhibits? Anyone paying particular attention to certain paintings?"

Lucas shrugs. "I don't pay much mind to gawkers. The work matters more than who is looking."

Helena presses further. "And have any of your paintings gone missing before?"

"No, never." Lucas's tone grows impatient.

Helena gestures to the vandalized canvases. "Clearly someone was inspired by your work. Perhaps too literally."

Lucas rakes a hand through his hair in agitation. "What are you suggesting?"

"Only that the parallels are unsettling," Helena says gently. "That perhaps your paintings are being used as a perverse template."

Lucas shakes his head vehemently. "No. I don't accept that."

Inspector De Vries steps forward, interjecting softly, "We aren't accusing you, Mr. Rombouts. Only exploring all possibilities."

Lucas's shoulders sag slightly. He turns away, staring at a half-finished seascape. "My only crime is seeing too much," he mutters.

Sensing Lucas's growing distress, Helena changes course. "Tell me about this recent period of creativity. Have you been working more furiously than usual?"

Lucas presses his palms against his eyes, exhaling slowly. When he looks up, his expression is pained.

"It hasn't been a creative period at all," he confesses. "I've been blocked for months, grasping at images that feel just out of reach."

He gestures around the studio. "You're looking at nearly a year's worth of work. Pathetic, really."

Helena blinks, surprised by this admission. "What broke the block?" she asks gently.

Lucas thinks for a moment, glancing unconsciously at the painting of the canal victim. "Inspiration comes in strange ways. A walk along the canals at night, a scrap of overheard conversation..."

His voice trails off. After a heavy silence, he continues, "The failures have been piling up. No sales, no patrons." He laughs mirthlessly. "I should be grateful my work is getting attention now, even if for the wrong reasons."

Helena feels a pang of sadness at Lucas's despair. "Attention can be a fickle friend. What matters is staying true to your gift."

She touches his arm lightly. "You have a rare talent. Trust it, even through the darkness. It will see you through."

Lucas leans against a paint-splattered easel, the light from the lone window casting shadows across his face. His eyes are distant as he recalls his encounters with the mysterious patron.

"There was someone," he starts, hesitance lacing his voice. "A patron who appeared a few months ago took a peculiar interest in the more... morose pieces."

De Vries leans in, intrigued. "Can you describe this patron?"

Lucas runs a hand through his hair, struggling to remember. "Details are foggy. Always came cloaked, face half-hidden beneath a wide-brimmed hat. Spoke with an accent I couldn't place."

Helena interjects, "Did he ever mention why he was drawn to those specific paintings?"

Shaking his head, Lucas frowns. "No, but there was a fervor in his eyes... like a collector seeking out prized oddities."

Inspector De Vries pulls out a small notebook and pencil from his coat pocket. "Anything else? Height, build?"

Lucas scrunches his brows in concentration. "Tallish, slender. Moved with a certain... deliberation." He gestures with his hands, mimicking the patron's precise movements.

"And he purchased your work?" De Vries probes further.

"Just one piece." Lucas points to an empty space on the wall where dust outlines a missing painting's frame. "A scene of the old Saint Anne's district on a foggy night. More shadows than shapes."

Helena moves closer to the outlined dust on the wall. "Why that one?"

Lucas shrugs. "He didn't say. Paid handsomely though—cash in an unmarked envelope."

De Vries scribbles in his notebook before looking up sharply. "You still have that envelope?"

Lucas shakes his head regretfully. "No, spent it on supplies." He gestures to the tubes of paint scattered around.

The inspector's eyes narrow slightly as he processes this information.

"Think carefully," Helena urges softly. "Was there anything else about this person that stood out?"

Lucas hesitates before speaking again, each word measured and deliberate. "He had a scent—faint but distinct—like old books or dried ink."

De Vries makes another note before glancing up at Helena who nods thoughtfully.

"Did you ever meet outside of these walls?" she asks.

"Just once," Lucas admits reluctantly. "He wanted to discuss art over coffee at The Golden Swan."

"The Golden Swan?" De Vries echoes, recognition flashing in his eyes.

"Yes," Lucas confirms, scratching at an old paint stain on his sleeve. "It was odd; he spoke about art but seemed more interested in Brugge's history... and my interpretation of it."

De Vries and Helena exchange a look; The Golden Swan was well-known for its patronage by locals with an interest in Brugge's past.

"Do you remember anything specific from your conversation?" De Vries asks.

Lucas shakes his head slowly. "Just vague talk about darkness in art reflecting society's shadows."

The inspector pauses before asking another question. "And nothing else? No names mentioned or personal details shared?"

Lucas exhales deeply before responding, his gaze fixed on the inspector's intent expression.

"Only a first name—Emile." Lucas rubs at his temple as if trying to summon more details from memory.

"Emile," De Vries repeats thoughtfully, etching the name into his notebook alongside the sketchy description Lucas provided.

"And did Emile show any interest in your upcoming exhibits or particular pieces you were working on?" Helena probes further.

"He asked what I was planning next," Lucas says with a nod. "I mentioned I was exploring themes of life and death—more out of discomfort than anything else."

"Life and death," Helena murmurs, her voice low but sharp with insight.

Lucas glances at her keenly before turning back to De Vries. "I got the sense that Emile was searching for something in my work—or maybe through it."

Inspector De Vries caps his pen and slips the notebook back into his pocket. He steps closer to Lucas, lowering his voice to ensure only he can hear him.

"Mr. Rombouts," he begins carefully, "this is crucial information for our investigation."

Lucas meets the inspector's gaze squarely now, any previous defensiveness replaced by solemnity.

"I understand," he replies earnestly.

De Vries holds Lucas's gaze for a moment longer before speaking again.

"We may need to speak with you further as things progress," he says with a firmness that brooks no argument.

"Of course." Lucas nods stiffly; it's clear he understands the gravity of their situation now.

Helena steps forward once more, her tone gentle yet unwavering.

"Lucas," she begins, capturing his attention fully with her use of his first name, "you've been thrust into this without choice but know that we appreciate your cooperation."

She offers him a small smile—a glimmer of warmth amidst the cold reality of their predicament—and Lucas can't help but return it faintly.

"We should let you get back to your work," De Vries says finally, indicating their intent to leave with a subtle nod towards the door.

As they turn to exit the studio, Lucas calls out after them tentatively.

"If I think of anything else..."

"We'll be in touch," De Vries assures him without looking back as he and Helena step out into the cobbled street bathed in diffused morning light.

Eva's Discovery

Eva Van Der Meer leans over a large, ancient tome that sprawls across the mahogany table in the hushed sanctuary of the Brugge Central Library. Dust motes dance in the slanting beams of light piercing the tall, stained-glass windows, each a silent witness to her diligent search. The pages before her crinkle under her careful touch, their edges worn by time and the hands of those who sought knowledge before her.

She scans the genealogy records, names, and dates blurring into one another as she hunts for a connection to the locket that rests heavily around her neck. It's a piece of her grandmother's past, an enigma wrapped in metal and mystery. Eva feels the weight of history pressing upon her as she flips through another page.

A librarian passes by, offering a sympathetic smile before resuming his quiet vigil over the domain of books and whispers. Eva nods in acknowledgment, barely lifting her gaze from the records. She's close; she can feel it in her bones, an almost electric tingle that tells her she's on the verge of uncovering something monumental.

She pauses, squinting at a faded inscription on one of the pages. There it is — a name that resonates with a frequency that makes her heart skip: Van der Asten. Eva's fingers trace the letters as if to coax more secrets from them. This prominent family name, etched into Brugge's very foundation, now appears linked to her lineage.

With trembling hands, she opens the locket once more and angles it toward the light. The inscription inside had always been difficult to read, its letters worn down by time and touch. But now, with this new piece of information fueling her resolve, Eva peers closer, employing a magnifying glass to bring the faded script into focus.

The characters slowly reveal themselves to her persistent gaze: "Adeline Van der Asten." The revelation sends a shiver through Eva's spine as she absorbs the implications of this discovery. Her grandmother had never mentioned any ties to such an illustrious line — why would she have kept this hidden?

Eva leans back in her chair, feeling both elation at the breakthrough and unease at its potential meaning. The Van der Asten family was deeply entwined with Brugge's guilds — powerful entities with long memories and shadowy influences.

As Eva sits in contemplation amid the silent archives, oblivious to time passing outside these walls, she understands that this locket is more than just a family heirloom; it is a piece of history itself, one that might very well be intertwined with the dark events unfolding around the canal murders.

She needs to know more about the Van der Asten family and their connection to both her grandmother and possibly to whatever forces now shake Brugge to its core.

***

Eva stands at the wrought-iron gates of the Van der Asten estate, her heart drumming a nervous beat. The sprawling grounds before her bear the scars of time, once-pristine gardens now surrendering to the wild embrace of nature. The mansion, an imposing structure of faded grandeur, looms against the gray sky, its windows like watchful eyes.

She opens the gate, its hinges groaning in protest, and walks up the gravel path. Eva rehearses her introduction, each word carefully chosen to convey respect and a shared lineage. Her fingers toy with the locket around her neck, drawing strength from its presence.

The door of the estate creaks open before she can knock. A man stands in the shadowed doorway, his posture rigid. His hair is white as the lilies that once might have graced this place, his face etched with lines like a map of memories long past.

"Can I help you?" His voice is guarded, eyes narrowing with suspicion as they fall upon Eva.

"I'm Eva Van Der Meer." She offers a small smile, hoping to disarm any hostility. "I believe we may be related through my grandmother's side. I've come seeking information about our family."

Frederik Van der Asten studies her for a long moment, then steps aside with a reluctant nod. "Come in," he says, his voice a whisper of silk over stone.

The interior of the mansion is a reflection of its exterior — grandeur faded to a genteel shabbiness. Dust lies heavy on furniture that must have been opulent once, and tapestries hang in silent testament to glory days gone by.

"Please forgive the state of things," Frederik begins as he leads Eva through a hallway lined with portraits of stern-looking ancestors. "The estate has seen better days."

Eva follows him into a sitting room where time seems to stand still amidst antique furnishings and heavy drapes that block out the light. She sits on the edge of an embroidered chair as Frederik settles into one opposite her.

"I must admit your visit is unexpected," he says, steepling his fingers together. "The Van der Asten name does not invite casual inquiry."

Eva nods understandingly. "I discovered something that suggested a connection I was unaware of," she explains, revealing the locket and watching for any flicker of recognition in Frederik's eyes.

He leans forward slightly, inspecting it from afar. "That locket... I remember it faintly. It belonged to Ellen — my aunt." Surprise softens his features for an instant before they settle back into their usual reserve.

"She was my grandmother," Eva reveals, holding his gaze.

A shadow crosses Frederik's face. "Ellen left under... difficult circumstances," he admits after a pause heavy with unspoken history.

Eva leans in earnestly. "Anything you can tell me about her would mean so much."

Frederik sighs, his eyes drifting towards the window where ivy claws at the glass from outside. "Ellen was willful — too much so for her time." He hesitates but continues under Eva's attentive gaze. "She fell in love with someone beneath our station. Caused quite the scandal."

"And the locket?" Eva prompts gently.

"A gift from her lover," Frederik says with a note of disapproval lingering in his tone. "When she chose to leave with him, it broke my father's heart — and in some ways sealed the fate of this family."

Eva absorbs this new chapter of her grandmother's life with awe and sympathy; Ellen's choice to follow love over duty resonates deeply within her own heart.

"What happened to them?" she asks quietly.

Frederik shrugs helplessly. "They disappeared into history. Some say they left for America; others believe they met a darker end." He fixes Eva with a serious look.

Eva senses the weight of history in Frederik's words, a history entangled with the grandeur of the room around them. The air is thick with the scent of aged wood and wax, and as Frederik begins to speak again, his voice seems to pull from the very walls, a rich tapestry of nostalgia and regret.

"This estate," he gestures with an open hand, "was once the heart of our influence. The Van der Asten family thrived through its connections with Brugge's guilds." He pauses, lost for a moment in memories that dance behind his eyes. "We were cloth merchants, influential in trade and politics."

Eva leans forward, her interest piqued. The locket feels heavy against her chest, a symbol of her connection to this storied past.

"The guilds were more than just commercial alliances," Frederik continues, his voice lowering as if sharing a confidential truth. "They held power that stretched beyond mere commerce; they could make or break a man's destiny."

His eyes darken slightly. "And with power came conflict." He stares into the middle distance, as if watching scenes from the past unfold before him.

"Jealousies brewed like storms, and grudges ran as deep as the canals that vein our city."

Eva nods, absorbing his words. She imagines the figures in the old portraits eyeing them with disapproval or perhaps understanding. The tales of power struggles resonate with her search for answers — perhaps these family conflicts had reverberations that reached even into her present.

"Was there an Adeline involved in these... conflicts?" Eva asks tentatively, remembering the name she'd seen associated with her locket.

Frederik stiffens at the mention of Adeline, and for a moment, he seems to debate with himself whether to reveal more. Finally, he exhales slowly.

"Adeline," he begins carefully, "was different from others in our family. She had a mind for the esoteric, a curiosity for what lay beyond the seen." He shifts uncomfortably. "Some say she dabbled in practices best left alone."

Eva feels a shiver at his words — practices best left alone. It is an echo of something dangerous and forbidden; it ties to whispers she'd heard about Brugge's darker histories.

"Do you have anything of hers? Any... artifacts?" Eva ventures.

Frederik regards her with newfound scrutiny before rising from his chair. "Come with me," he says abruptly.

They traverse through hallways lined with more silent portraits until they reach an area of the estate less touched by time's hand — where velvet drapes still hold their color and the carpets are less worn.

Frederik stops before an ornate tapestry depicting Brugge's iconic skyline — spires piercing the heavens above stoic stone buildings. With practiced ease, he pulls it aside to reveal a door hidden within the wall.

He produces a key from his pocket — old and ornate — and fits it into the lock. The door creaks open on reluctant hinges to reveal a small room bathed in dusky light filtered through heavy curtains.

The walls are lined with shelves filled with curios: strange sculptures, dusty books bound in leather, and objects whose use is not immediately apparent. Eva's eyes roam over these relics of another age until they settle on something unexpected: a portrait hanging alone on the far wall.

It depicts a woman of striking beauty — her features almost identical to those captured within Eva's locket. She has an enigmatic smile that suggests secrets held close to her heart.

"That's Adeline," Frederik says softly behind her.

Eva steps closer to the painting. Adeline's eyes seem alive, holding within them stories untold — tales of rituals whispered beneath moonlit skies alongside Brugge's silent canals.

"She was beautiful," Eva murmurs, unable to tear her gaze away from those compelling eyes.

"And dangerous," Frederik adds grimly. "Her involvement with certain guild rituals... it brought us under scrutiny we could ill afford."

"What kind of rituals?" Eva asks without looking away from Adeline's portrait.

Eva feels the chill of the room's secrets wrap around her as she watches Frederik, waiting for him to continue. The man's face, usually so composed, flickers with the struggle of a conscience caught between duty and truth.

"The guilds," he begins, his voice a reluctant whisper, "they were not just commercial enterprises. They were brotherhoods, wielding influence over life and death in Brugge. The Van der Asten family... we played our part."

Eva watches as Frederik paces slowly, his hand running along the spines of ancient books as if seeking solace in their leathery touch. "Our ancestors sat on secret tribunals," he confesses, "judging those they deemed a threat to their power."

Her heart quickens. "And what happened to those they judged?"

"They were... dealt with." Frederik's words are heavy with implication. "Sometimes, exile or fines. Other times..." He doesn't finish, but he doesn't need to.

The silence stretches between them like the dark waters of the canals at midnight. Eva imagines shadowy figures cloaked in secrecy, delivering verdicts that could upend lives or send them spiraling into the abyss.

Frederik halts his pacing and faces her. "Adeline was part of this world," he admits. "She was fascinated by the rituals, the power they held. She may have even... expanded on them."

Eva's mind races. Rituals expanded upon — could these be connected to what's happening now? The recent murders? She needs more than just stories; she needs evidence.

"Is there anything written down? Records of these tribunals or rituals?" Eva asks, her voice steadier than she feels.

Frederik hesitates, then nods towards a large chest in the corner of the room, bound in iron straps. "There is a ledger," he says slowly. "It was meant to be destroyed long ago."

He walks over and lifts the heavy lid with care that borders on reverence. Inside, amidst various artifacts, lies a book bound in dark leather, its edges charred as if someone had indeed tried to burn it away from memory.

Frederik retrieves it and hands it to Eva with a solemnity that makes her hands tremble as she takes it. The ledger is old; its pages are yellowed and brittle. She opens it carefully and begins to read.

The entries are meticulous — dates and names alongside descriptions of ceremonies conducted under cover of night. As Eva reads further, a cold realization dawns upon her: these rituals described in archaic language eerily align with the recent canal murders.

There are drawings too — symbols that match those found at the crime scenes, figures cloaked and masked engaged in acts meant to be unseen by any outside their order.

Eva feels her pulse hammering in her ears as she turns page after page. This ledger is more than history; it's a blueprint for horror being replicated on Brugge's canals today.

Eva clutches the locket, its metal warm against her skin, as if it pulses with the life of its former owner. She feels an intimate kinship with Adeline, whose portrait watches over the room with a gaze that speaks of shared secrets across time. The locket is no longer just an heirloom; it is a silent testament to a woman who dared to defy convention, who might have been misunderstood, even maligned, for her boldness.

As Eva runs her thumb over the intricate filigree of the locket, she senses Adeline's spirit urging her forward, compelling her to unravel the tightly wound threads of history. This connection transcends mere blood; it is a mingling of souls bound by the pursuit of hidden truths. Eva knows that she cannot turn away from this path now — Adeline's legacy and her quest for understanding are inextricably linked.

She carefully places the ledger on the table beside her, its pages open to a particularly chilling entry. Her eyes linger on the words, each one etched with a gravity that pulls at her core. This book holds answers but also poses questions about how far one should delve into shadows not meant for the light.

"Adeline," Eva whispers, as if confiding in an old friend. "What were you seeking? What did you find?"

Frederik watches Eva with a gaze that has seen much and reveals little. He steps closer, his voice barely above a murmur when he finally speaks. "You must tread carefully, Eva. The past has claws that can tear at the present."

Eva looks up from the ledger to meet his solemn eyes. "I understand there are risks," she admits, her voice steady despite the tremor she feels within.

"The guilds are long disbanded," Frederik says as he retrieves the ledger from beside her and closes it with a soft thud. "But their descendants remain — influential men and women who value their ancestors' legacies above all else."

He places the ledger back into the chest and locks it away once more. "They would not take kindly to someone unearthing old sins," he continues, his words laced with an ominous undertone.

Eva nods slowly, absorbing his warning while weighing it against her need to discover what ties these ancient practices have to recent events — and her bloodline.

"I'm not seeking to expose anyone," she assures him. "I just need to understand."

Frederik offers a thin smile that does not reach his eyes. "Understanding can be a dangerous thing." He moves towards the curtains and draws them back slightly, letting in a shaft of light that cuts through the dimness of the room.

"You've seen what happened to Lucas Rombouts," he says pointedly. "His art provoked someone enough to bring violence into his world."

Eva remembers Lucas sitting amidst his ruined canvases, a mix of fear and defiance etched on his face. She feels a pang of sympathy for him — another soul caught in this web of secrets.

"But I'm not making public accusations or creating provocative art," Eva argues gently. "I just want answers."

Frederik sighs and looks out of the window where Brugge lies beyond, its rooftops huddled together like whispered confidences against an overcast sky.

"There are those who believe some stones are best left unturned," he tells her cryptically.

Eva stands up from her chair, emboldened by Frederik's caution rather than deterred by it. "And there are those who believe that light should be shed on darkness," she counters softly.

Frederik turns back from the window and regards Eva for a long moment before speaking again. "If you must continue on this path," he begins reluctantly, "be discreet."

He walks over to one of the bookshelves and retrieves a small journal bound in faded blue velvet. "This belonged to Adeline," he says as he hands it to Eva.

She accepts it with reverence; it feels like receiving a baton in an age-old relay race against time and secrecy.

"Thank you," Eva says sincerely.

"Just remember," Frederik adds gravely as he escorts her back through the maze-like hallways towards the front door of the estate, "the truth can be liberating or it can be a noose."

As they reach the door, Frederik pauses before opening it for her. He looks down at Eva with an expression that is both stern and compassionate.

"You carry more than your grandmother's locket," he says softly. "You carry her courage — and perhaps her fate."

***

Eva steps out of the Van der Asten estate, the ancient door closing behind her with a sound that echoes finality. The air is crisp, a contrast to the dust and stillness of the room she's left behind. She pauses at the top of the steps, her hand clasping the locket, feeling its weight and warmth as if it pulses with life — a life entwined with secrets that reach deep into the fabric of Brugge.

The estate recedes behind her as she walks down the path, her mind teeming with revelations and warnings. Frederik's words, intended to dissuade, only fuel her resolve. The locket feels like a talisman against the encroaching doubts — doubts that would have her abandon her quest for truth.

Eva considers Frederik's parting words. The truth is liberation or a noose — she cannot deny the risk. Yet, to turn back now would be to forsake the stirring within her, the same stirring that must have driven her grandmother in her pursuit of knowledge and passion.

She reaches the gate and looks back once more at the Van der Asten mansion, its façade both imposing and weary under the weight of its history. Eva's determination does not waver; if anything, it is solidified by the very atmosphere of Brugge that surrounds her — an atmosphere where every stone speaks of centuries past, where every whispering canal holds a reflection of life and death.

The path before Eva stretches onward, leading back into the heart of Brugge. The city awaits with its cobbled streets and shadowed alleys, each corner a potential clue, each face a possible ally or adversary. The locket against her chest is a reminder of her grandmother's defiance — a defiance Eva now embraces as her own.

As she moves through the streets, she notes how ordinary life continues around her: vendors hawk their wares with boisterous calls; children play games that echo through time; couples walk arm in arm, lost in each other rather than in the city's darker mysteries. Yet beneath this veneer of normalcy runs an undercurrent of fear — fear birthed from recent horrors found in still waters.

Eva reaches into her bag and pulls out Adeline's journal. Its cover is worn from touch and time, yet it remains a beacon to guide her forward. She opens it carefully, mindful of its fragility. Inside are entries in elegant script, some pages marked with pressed flowers whose colors have long since faded.

The entries speak of daily life but also hint at something more: coded messages about meetings and rituals. Adeline's world was one where society's rules were both adhered to and subverted in secret gatherings that defied explanation.

Eva turns page after page as she walks, absorbing each word. She knows these words are keys to understanding not just Adeline but also herself — for what are they but reflections across generations?

The city whispers around her as she delves deeper into Adeline's thoughts. The journal speaks of love — a forbidden love that defied status and expectation. It speaks of art — art that was both celebrated and feared for its power to reveal truths society wished hidden.

Eva stops at an intersection where ancient buildings lean toward one another like old friends sharing confidences. She raises her head to look at them and feels their history seep into her bones.

Brugge has always been more than stone and water; it is a living tapestry woven from human endeavor and emotion. Eva senses that Adeline understood this intimately — understood that to affect change one must engage with the essence of place and people.

The journal leads Eva next to an account of an evening when Adeline felt both exhilaration and terror — emotions born from dabbling in matters not meant for public consumption. It was an evening that changed everything for Adeline, an evening when love clashed with duty, when curiosity brushed against danger.

Eva reads about symbols used in those secretive rites: symbols meant to bind participants to one another and their cause; symbols meant to invoke protection or power depending on need or desire.

These same symbols now mark sites along Brugge's canals where lives have been lost under mysterious circumstances. Eva's heart races as she connects past with present — this cannot be mere coincidence.

As dusk begins to fall over Brugge, casting long shadows across its squares and lanes, Eva knows time is both an ally and an enemy. She needs answers before another body surfaces in those silent waters or before those who wish these secrets buried turn their attention toward her.

Her walk becomes more purposeful now; each step takes her closer to Father Emile's parish — a man whose knowledge of Brugge's past could prove invaluable. If anyone can help decipher Adeline's journal entries within the context of local lore, it is Father Emile.

Eva feels anticipation mixed with anxiety as she approaches the church. The steeple pierces the sky like an accusation or perhaps a beckoning finger calling forth seekers of truth.

She pushes the heavy wooden door open; it groans in protest or maybe warning. Inside is hushed reverence punctuated by candlelight flickering like distant stars fallen from heaven.

Father Emile stands near the altar, his silhouette framed by stained glass scenes depicting saints who witnessed humanity's breadth — from its benevolence to its brutality.

"Father," Eva calls softly as she enters his domain fully.

He turns toward her voice; his expression holds both welcome and weariness — weariness from knowing too much yet never enough.

"I need your help," Eva begins without preamble as she walks toward him holding out Adeline's journal like an offering or perhaps armor against what might come next.

Father Emile takes it gently into his hands; they are hands that have blessed infants and comforted dying elders; they are hands accustomed to bearing burdens not entirely his own.

He looks up at Eva and then back down at Adeline's words captured on paper yellowed by age but vibrant with intent. "What is it you seek?" he asks in a voice that carries through nave and transept like sacred melody or somber dirge depending on the ear that hears it.

"The connection between my family's past..." Eva starts then pauses collecting herself before continuing "...and these canal murders." Her eyes lock onto Father Emile's searching for understanding seeking alliance seeking hope amidst despair wrapped in an enigma shrouded by history's cloak woven from threads darkened by blood spilled innocent or otherwise across centuries across continents across hearts seeking solace seeking salvation seeking...

"Truth," Father Emile finishes for her knowing full well what haunts spaces between words left unsaid what haunts minds when night falls heavy what haunts souls when questions outnumber answers when past collides with present leaving the future uncertain leaving legacy questioned leaving...

The determined resolution was written upon her brave face not unlike Adeline's whose portrait watches over secrets held within the walls whispers.

Whispers Eva Van Der Meer refuses to let lie silent refuses unchallenged despite warnings, despite risks, despite...

The Locket

The next day, while wandering through the cobblestone streets of Brugge, Eva stumbled upon an eclectic shop nestled between two imposing Gothic buildings. The sign above the door read "Hendrik Bosch - Antiques and Curiosities." Intrigued by the name, Eva decided to venture inside.

The shop was a treasure trove of historical relics and artifacts, each with its own fascinating story to tell. As Eva browsed through the collection, she felt drawn to an antique display case at the back of the store. Inside it lay a collection of ancient books bound in leather and adorned with intricate gold embellishments. She recognized them as grimoires - books containing spells and incantations from various magical traditions.

Eva approached the display case cautiously, feeling a strange mixture of excitement and apprehension. She reached out tentatively to touch one of the books, and as her fingers brushed against its cover, she felt a shiver run down her spine. It was as if the book itself was calling out to her, urging her to unlock its secrets.

Just then, a voice behind her made her jump. "Can I help you find something?" It was Hendrik Bosch himself - a tall man with silver hair tied back in a ponytail and piercing blue eyes that seemed to see right through her. He wore an old-fashioned waistcoat adorned with brass buttons and carried a walking stick decorated with intricate carvings.

Eva hesitated for a moment before responding. "I'm looking for information about my family's history," she admitted sheepishly. "Specifically, I have this locket that belonged to my grandmother." She held up the ornate piece of jewelry for him to see. "I want to know more about its origin and what it might mean."

Hendrik clears a space on a cluttered oak table, its surface etched with the patina of age and gestures for her to lay down the locket. As Eva places it carefully on the wood, she watches Hendrik don a pair of delicate white gloves. His movements are precise, and reverent as he lifts the piece for closer inspection.

Under the warm glow of an oil lamp, he turns the locket over in his hands. Eva leans in, her curiosity a tangible thing between them. She watches his eyes—those sharp blue irises that seem to dissect layers not visible to her untrained eye.

"This is exquisite work," Hendrik murmurs, tracing the filigree with a gloved fingertip. "See here? These engravings are not just decorative. They speak of a time when craftsmanship was steeped in symbolism."

Eva nods, absorbing his every word. Her heart quickens as he continues.

"The style is unmistakably late 17th century Brugge." His voice is soft yet carries an excitement she feels echoing in her chest. "And if I'm not mistaken," he adds with growing enthusiasm, "this belonged to the Van der Asten family."

"Yes," Hendrik confirms. "A prominent family deeply entwined with Brugge's most powerful guilds at that time."

Eva watches him delve deeper into the examination, holding her breath as if afraid to disturb the past that's slowly unraveling before her.

With a small tool akin to a surgeon's scalpel, Hendrik eases open a hidden compartment within the locket—a secret place that might have gone unnoticed by less discerning eyes. Inside is a space just large enough for something like a portrait or... an emblem.

"There!" Hendrik exclaims softly, pointing to an indentation that Eva had mistaken for wear. It's faint but deliberate—the mark of skilled hands from centuries past.

As Hendrik holds the locket up to the light, angles playing off its surface reveal an emblem etched so subtly it seems part of the metal itself—a sigil hiding in plain sight.

Hendrik's breath catches; he knows this symbol well.

"The guild," he breathes out in awe. "This is their mark."

Eva leans closer, peering at the barely-there emblem—their discovery casting ripples through her understanding of her family's past.

"This guild... were they like merchants or craftsmen?" Eva asks tentatively.

"More than that," Hendrik replies, locking eyes with hers. "They were among Brugge's elite—guardians of knowledge and power who shaped much of our city's history through secret rituals and covert gatherings."

Her mind races as she processes his words. Her grandmother had never spoken of such connections—never hinted at a legacy shrouded in mystery and shadowed corridors of influence.

Hendrik carefully places the locket on the table, treating it with a delicate touch as if it holds great importance and power. As their eyes meet, they both recognize the significance of this discovery. It is a mere glimpse into a vast network of hidden tales, intricately woven through the ages. It is the first step towards unlocking the secrets within the serene canals and strong, unyielding buildings of Brugge.

"These are not just relics," he starts, his voice barely above a hush. "They're the legacy of lives lived... and lives lost." He pauses, considering his next words carefully. "The witch trials here were not like those you might have read about in other places. They were orchestrated, systematic, and the guild... the guild played its part."

Eva feels a chill despite the warmth of the shop. She watches him intently, hanging on every word.

"The trials were a tool," Hendrik continues, "used to eliminate threats or dissenters under the guise of purging evil." He walks around the counter, coming closer. "Anyone could be accused—competitors, rivals... women who knew too much."

Eva's hands tighten around the locket as if to protect it from the dark history it signifies.

"Your locket," Hendrik says, his gaze fixed on the piece still lying open on the table, "may very well have been a symbol of resistance. A quiet rebellion against tyranny."

Her heart pounds at the implication. Could Adeline have been part of this rebellion? A woman defying a secret society that wielded power over life and death?

Hendrik seems to read her thoughts. "I suspect whoever wore this was brave... or desperate." His eyes meet Eva's again. "Sometimes both are necessary when facing such oppression."

Eva swallows hard, absorbing his words. She's aware of her breathing now—shallow and quick—as if fear itself lingers in the air around these ancient artifacts.

"Imagine," Hendrik says as he gestures around him, "a city where whispers carry more weight than truth. Where a simple locket could be a shield in a silent war fought in alleys and behind closed doors."

The idea terrifies her—the notion that beauty and craftsmanship could serve as armor in such a clandestine conflict.

Hendrik moves to a shelf laden with yellowed papers and bound manuscripts. He selects one bound in dark leather with corners worn soft from use. "Here," he offers it to Eva, "read about them yourself."

The book feels heavy in Eva's hands, laden with more than just its physical weight—a tome of tragedies and triumphs untold.

As she flips through pages scribed by hand, Hendrik narrates snippets of history—tales of those who stood accused: herbalists who understood healing too well; widows who inherited wealth; young women whose beauty sparked envy or desire.

"With each trial," Hendrik says solemnly, "the guild solidified its hold over Brugge."

"But how?" Eva's voice is but a whisper. "How did they maintain such control?"

"Through fear," Hendrik replies without hesitation. "And through something far more insidious—secrets."

She senses there is more he wishes to say but holds back—a hesitation born of caution or perhaps respect for the gravity of what they discuss.

They stand together amidst whispers of centuries past—Eva clutching her grandmother's locket, Hendrik with one hand resting atop the aged tome. Both feel the weight of histories untold pressing upon them—a shared silence that speaks volumes.

It is then that Eva realizes this journey into her family's past is no longer just about satisfying curiosity—it's about understanding sacrifice and secrets woven into the very fabric of Brugge itself.

"Did they... did my ancestors survive these trials?" The question slips from Eva's lips before she can hold it back.

Hendrik regards her for a moment before answering. "Some did." His voice is steady but not without empathy for what such survival entails. "They endured by adapting—hiding their truths beneath layers of conformity... or symbols like your locket."

Eva holds the locket in her palm, its cool metal offering a stark contrast to the warmth bubbling within her. She can almost hear her grandmother's voice, a gentle hum from decades past, guiding her through the mists of time. The shop, with its ancient artifacts and dusty shelves, fades into the background as she focuses on the intricate designs etched into the locket's surface. They're more than mere decoration; they're whispers of defiance, a silent language of resistance passed down through generations.

She traces the hidden emblem with her fingertip, feeling a connection to her grandmother that transcends time and blood—a kinship of spirit. It dawns on her that this small piece of jewelry represents much more than a family heirloom; it symbolizes an unyielding will to stand against oppression. Her grandmother had not just been a keeper of traditions and tales; she had been a guardian of secrets, a silent warrior in a covert battle for autonomy.

A surge of pride swells in Eva's chest, mingling with sorrow for the struggles endured by those who came before her. She pictures Adeline, young and determined, clasping the locket for courage as she navigates a world rife with hidden dangers and veiled threats. It's no longer just an accessory; it's an artifact imbued with the strength and resilience of its bearer—a talisman against the tyranny of the guild.

Hendrik watches Eva with an understanding gaze, recognizing the depth of her emotions as they wash over her features. "You carry their legacy within you," he says softly, his voice echoing in the quiet shop.

Eva lifts her eyes to meet his. In them is reflected not only her newfound resolve but also Hendrik's profound respect for the past and its enduring impact on the present.

"It feels like such a burden," she admits, the weight of centuries bearing down on her shoulders.

"But also an honor," Hendrik adds quickly. "To be entrusted with such a legacy is no small thing."

Eva nods slowly, absorbing his words like a balm to soothe the ache in her heart. The locket isn't just a link to her grandmother—it's a bridge to all those who fought in silence, their bravery echoing through time.

As Eva continues to examine the locket, she realizes that this is not just about understanding history—it's about honoring it. She feels compelled to learn more about these secret rebels and their clandestine struggles. There's an urgency within her now, a need to uncover their stories and give voice to their silenced sacrifices.

Hendrik can see this newfound determination etched on Eva's face. He steps back, giving her space to process this connection that now binds her irrevocably to Brugge's shadowed past.

"You're part of something much larger than yourself," he tells her gently. "The past lives on through you."

Eva closes her fingers around the locket, feeling its presence as both a shield and a reminder. It represents generations of courage—her heritage—and now she holds it in her hands.

"Will you help me?" she asks Hendrik earnestly. "Will you help me uncover more about my family's role in all this?"

Hendrik nods without hesitation. "Of course," he responds warmly. "This is what I live for—to bring history into the light."

Together they pore over old documents and faded letters that Hendrik has collected over years of meticulous research—each paper holding fragments of stories long buried by time and fear.

Hendrik pauses, his finger tracing a passage in a brittle ledger. "Here," he says, his voice steady despite the revelation. "The guild had a particular method of dealing with those they deemed traitors or threats."

Eva leans in, squinting at the faded ink. The script is archaic, looping and flowing like the canals themselves.

"They would be bound and cast into the water," Hendrik reads aloud, "left to the mercy of the depths."

A shiver runs down Eva's spine, an icy finger tracing her vertebrae. She pictures the dark waters of Brugge's canals, now a sinister grave for those unjustly condemned.

"Do you think," she starts, hesitating as she formulates her thoughts, "the murders... could they be mirroring these punishments?"

Hendrik removes his glasses, polishing them with a cloth as he considers her question. He looks not at her but at some unseen point in the distance where past and present might converge.

"It's a chilling thought," he admits. "But it's possible that someone is using the guild's old methods to send a message or to continue a legacy."

The very idea that someone could twist historical retribution into a modern vendetta sends cold tendrils of fear coiling around Eva's heart. The locket in her hand suddenly feels like a piece of a puzzle—a macabre clue to understanding a murderer's motives.

"But why?" Eva asks, her voice barely above a whisper. "Why replicate such horrors now?"

Hendrik replaces his glasses, looking back at Eva with eyes that have seen too much of humanity's capacity for darkness.

"History is cyclical," he says. "Patterns repeat themselves when we fail to learn from them. And there are always those who cling to the past—whether out of nostalgia or malice."

Eva reflects on his words, thinking about how the locket—a symbol of resistance—could be tied to these grisly reenactments.

"Could it be that whoever is behind this believes they're carrying out some form of justice?" she muses aloud. "Or perhaps they're making a statement?"

Hendrik nods slowly. "It could be either—or both." He sighs deeply, replacing the ledger on its shelf with care. "What worries me is that this locket and your family's history might not just be keys to understanding the motives... but also potential targets."

Targets. The word echoes ominously in Eva's mind. Her family—a lineage of silent rebels—could now be marked by an unseen hand guided by vengeance or twisted honor.

"Then we must proceed with caution," Eva says, more to herself than Hendrik. Her resolve hardens like steel tempered by fire.

Hendrik watches her closely, his expression one of admiration and concern.

"You're brave," he tells her softly. "But bravery alone won't protect you from those who lurk in shadows."

Eva nods, acknowledging his warning but unwilling to let fear dictate her actions. She tucks the locket safely within her dress pocket—a small act of defiance against the looming threat.

Together they continue their search through Hendrik's archives, uncovering more about Brugge's shadowy history with each document they examine. Eva can't shake the feeling that every piece of information brings them closer to danger—as if they're unraveling a tapestry that should have remained intact.

As evening approaches and lamplighters ignite flames along Brugge's streets outside, Hendrik suggests they take a break from their research.

"You need rest," he insists gently. "We both do."

Eva reluctantly agrees, knowing that fatigue will only cloud her judgment.

As she steps out into the cobblestone streets bathed in twilight, Eva can't help but glance warily at the canals—those serene waterways now tainted by death and mystery. The gentle lapping of water against stone seems less peaceful now and more like whispers of warning.

She makes her way home through familiar lanes but feels an unfamiliar sense of disquiet shadowing her steps—an awareness that knowledge can be both a shield and a curse.

Once home, Eva sits by her window overlooking one of Brugge's quieter canals—a mirror reflecting both moonlight and memories. She takes out the locket once more, holding it up to catch the silver glow streaming through glass panes.

Her thoughts turn again to Hendrik's theory: Could these canal murders truly be emulating historical punishments? If so, what purpose does it serve? Retribution? Fear? A longing for days best left forgotten?

Eva's fingers curl around the locket, its cool metal a stark reminder of the weighty legacy she carries. In the quiet of her room, with the gentle murmur of the canal outside her window, she allows herself a moment to reflect on the day's revelations. The secrets nestled within the locket's intricate designs beckon her, promising answers yet warning of dangers untold.

She rises from her chair, pacing the small space as if movement could help order her thoughts. Her grandmother had been more than just a matriarch with tales and traditions; she had been a custodian of a history that now rested in Eva's hands. The locket wasn't merely a keepsake; it was a testament to a lineage of resilience, a symbol of silent battles fought against oppression.

A resolve settles within her—a determination not just to unearth the truths buried in Brugge's shadowed past but to honor those who stood against tyranny. The echoes of their defiance reverberate through time, calling out to Eva to join their ranks and bear witness to their struggles.

With each step across the wooden floorboards, Eva feels her purpose solidify. This quest is no longer solely about satiating personal curiosity; it has become a duty to those who came before her, an obligation to shine a light on injustices that have long lain dormant in the city's undercurrents.

The locket seems to pulse with an energy that matches her own—a silent encouragement spurring her on. She stops at the window, peering out at Brugge's night-shrouded streets. The soft glow from lampposts casts shadows that dance just out of sight, much like the history she seeks—present yet elusive.

Eva considers Hendrik Bosch's words about cycles and patterns repeating through history. She ponders how such cycles can be broken if not by bringing their darkest aspects into the light. Perhaps by understanding what transpired all those years ago, she can help prevent its repetition in today's Brugge.

She retrieves the leather-bound journal from her desk—a companion that has seen many late nights filled with sketches and dreams. Now it will hold her findings, theories, and fears as she delves into this investigation. With a steady hand, she begins to pen down everything Hendrik shared with her: the guild's role in historical punishments, their methods of maintaining control through fear and secrets, and how their symbol came to rest hidden within her grandmother's locket.

Eva pauses, ink pooling slightly on parchment as she contemplates what steps to take next. There are records to scour for names and connections—descendants of guild members who may still influence Brugge's societal threads—and documents that might hold more than just dates and events but motivations and alliances.

As much as she longs for solitude in this endeavor—fearful of drawing others into potential peril—she knows she cannot do this alone. Hendrik's knowledge is invaluable; his expertise will guide her through historical intricacies she cannot navigate by herself.

Eva takes one last look at the canal outside—the still waters hiding depths untold—and turns away from the window. She lights a small candle beside her bed, its flame flickering like a beacon in the encroaching darkness.

The candle burns lower as minutes turn into hours, and Eva's eyes grow heavy with fatigue. But sleep is an elusive companion tonight—her mind too fraught with possibilities and plans for rest to claim her easily.

Eventually, Eva rises once more and walks over to lock her door—an act less about physical security and more about sealing herself off from distractions that might dilute her focus or sway her path.

She returns to bed then but does not extinguish the candle just yet. Instead, she watches its flame—a sentinel against uncertainty—and lets its steady burn anchor her thoughts one final time before sleep finally comes.

Eva dreams of waterways winding like veins through Brugge—of whispers turned into shouts as secrets rise from their watery graves. In these dreamscape canals swims a determination undeterred by fear or doubt—a resolve mirrored in Eva's waking heart: To uncover truths hidden beneath ripples and reflections; to continue a legacy that thrums within her blood; to stand against shadows with nothing but light clasped firmly in hand—the light held within an old locket charged with silent strength.

Shadows of the Past

Father Emile stands in the sacred stillness of St. Michael's Church, a solitary figure enveloped by the immense stone columns and majestic Gothic arches. The air is cool and laden with a haunting stillness that seems to seep into his very being, almost like the whispers of phantoms from bygone eras. Multicolored rays stream in through the opulent stained glass, enveloping the aged floor in a stunning array of hues and casting a shadow of regret upon the priest.

He glances at the aged clock on the wall; its steady tick is a metronome to his racing heart as he anticipates their arrival. Father Emile smooths his cassock with trembling hands, an unconscious attempt to steady himself for what is to come.

The heavy wooden doors creak open, admitting Inspector Gerard De Vries and Helena De Baere into the church's embrace. The inspector's presence commands attention, a stark figure against the backdrop of holy serenity. Beside him, Helena moves with a grace that belies her determination, her eyes scanning the interior with quiet curiosity.

Father Emile greets them with a nod, gesturing towards the confessional. "I appreciate you coming," he says, voice barely above a whisper.

They follow him into the cloistered space reserved for unburdening souls. Helena's gaze lingers on the intricate carvings that frame the entrance to the confessional—a testament to secrets kept and sins forgiven.

Inside, they settle into their respective places; Father Emile behind the screen meant to offer anonymity, Helena and De Vries on the other side, where so many have sought absolution.

"Father," De Vries begins, "you mentioned having information about the guilds?"

Father Emile closes his eyes briefly. "Yes, Inspector. There are things I've carried within me for far too long." He takes a deep breath, feeling each word weigh heavily on his tongue. "As a young priest, I was... unwittingly drawn into circles I did not understand—circles of influence and power."

Helena leans forward slightly. "The guilds?"

"Yes," he replies. His fingers trace patterns on the worn wood as if to draw strength from it. "In those days, my eagerness to belong blinded me to their true nature."

"And what was their nature?" Helena's voice is gentle but insistent.

"They were guardians of tradition," Father Emile begins slowly, "but also... enforcers of silence." He pauses, haunted by memories that crawl from dark recesses. "Their justice was swift and often merciless."

De Vries's silhouette stiffens at these words. "And you were part of this?"

"Not in action," Father Emile hastens to clarify, "but in silence... which can be just as damning." A shiver runs through him as he admits his complicity for the first time aloud.

"Tell us more about it," Helena prompts softly.

Father Emile exhales sharply—a sound filled with decades of pent-up guilt. "I was young and naïve," he confesses. "They said it was divine work—purging sin from our midst."

"And you believed them?" There is no judgment in De Vries's tone, only a thirst for truth.

"I wanted to," Father Emile admits with difficulty. "But as I watched... as I saw what they did in God's name... doubt crept in."

"What did you see?" De Vries's question is like a key turning in a lock long sealed.

Father Emile senses the weight of the confessional booth, a microcosm of the church itself, heavy with history and secrets. The musty scent of old wood and the lingering incense remind him of a time when the guilds' whispers filled the halls, seeping into the very stones of St. Michael's.

"They held power," Father Emile begins, his voice barely audible above a hushed reverence. "Not just over markets and trades, but over beliefs. Their word could sway judgments, turn hearts... condemn the innocent."

Helena's voice comes through the lattice, sharp and clear. "How did they manipulate religious beliefs? Can you give us an example?"

Father Emile recalls a specific memory, as vivid now as it was then. "The Van Aardens," he says. "A family steeped in tragedy. Accusations of witchcraft were leveled against them already long ago... whispers turned to shouts in the streets."

"And the church?" Helena asks.

He hesitates, his hands clasped tightly together as if in prayer. "The church was... under pressure." He hates to admit it, even now. "The guilds' leaders were prominent parishioners; their donations filled our coffers, and their influence extended to our pulpit."

De Vries shifts in his seat, a silent sentinel awaiting truth. "So you're saying the church didn't resist?"

"Resistance meant risking everything," Father Emile replies with a sigh. "The rector at the time was a man more concerned with earthly power than spiritual guidance."

Helena's curiosity is unrelenting. "Did no one question the validity of these accusations?"

"There were doubts," Father Emile admits, recalling hushed conversations in shadowed corners of the church. "But to speak against the guilds was to invite ruin."

"What about evidence?" Helena presses on. "Was there any actual proof?"

Father Emile remembers how 'evidence' was often nothing more than superstition cloaked in piety—a sick cow here, a blighted crop there—all laid at the feet of those accused.

"Evidence," he says with a bitter chuckle, "was whatever they needed it to be."

Helena pauses for a moment before her next question comes softly but firmly through the screen. "What happened to those who were accused?"

"Most were executed," Father Emile responds, feeling each word like a stone in his mouth. "Burned at the stake or drowned... deemed guilty by ordeal."

"And Willem's ancestors?" De Vries interjects.

Father Emile closes his eyes as he remembers their faces—etched with fear as they stood accused before a jeering crowd.

"The Van Aardens were among them," he confirms solemnly. "They faced their end with a dignity that belied their supposed guilt."

Helena leans closer to the lattice, her voice steady but filled with emotion. "How did it come to this? How did fear gain such power?"

Father Emile thinks back on those dark times—the hysteria that gripped Brugge like a fever dream.

"Fear is a powerful tool," he explains. "It can turn neighbor against neighbor... make monsters out of men." He pauses, reflecting on how quickly panic spread through the town's narrow streets.

"And what role did you play?" De Vries's question is not an accusation but an invitation for confession.

"I was complicit in my silence," Father Emile answers, shame tinging his words. "By accident, I stumbled upon incriminating information and kept it hidden from the outside world." He swallows hard against the lump forming in his throat.

Helena's voice is softer now, almost empathetic. "But now you're speaking out—why?"

"Because silence is no longer an option," Father Emile states resolutely. "The past must be acknowledged if we are ever to heal."

De Vries nods from behind the screen, understanding perhaps more than anyone what it means to face one's complicity.

"And what of redemption?" Helena asks gently.

Father Emile considers this—the possibility of forgiveness for sins so long buried beneath layers of regret.

"Redemption is God's to give," he says at last, his voice tinged with hope. "But perhaps... through truth... we may find our way towards it."

Father Emile's heart pounds as he gazes upon the expectant faces of Inspector De Vries and Helena. The dim light of the confessional throws their features into soft relief, casting long shadows that seem to stretch back through time. His voice, when it finally breaks the silence, carries the weight of years spent in quiet contemplation of a history most would rather forget.

"The Van Aardens," he begins, "were once much like any other family in Brugge—hardworking, devout, pillars of the community." His hands tremble as he fiddles with the edge of his cassock. "But envy is a poison that can seep into the hearts of men."

He recalls how the guilds eyed the Van Aarden's thriving business with covetous gazes, how whispers slithered through Brugge like serpents, seeking to destroy what they could not possess. "They were fishmongers," Father Emile continues, "respected for their trade. But prosperity breeds resentment."

Helena interjects softly, her voice a lifeline in a sea of memories threatening to pull him under. "What happened to them?"

The words catch in Father Emile's throat. He swallows hard against the pain that has never truly faded. "Accusations were made—baseless, vile accusations of witchcraft." His voice cracks as he envisions once more the faces of those who suffered under such claims—innocent and bewildered in their final moments.

"The guilds whispered into eager ears," Father Emile goes on, his eyes moistening as he speaks of bygone injustice. "A cow falls ill here; a child succumbs to fever there—all laid at the doorstep of the Van Aardens."

De Vries leans closer, his silhouette a dark shape against the flickering candlelight. "And none opposed this?"

"Some did," Father Emile admits, pride and sorrow mingling in his tone. "But fear is a silencer more potent than any blade." He pauses, reflecting on how quickly suspicion turned to conviction in the minds of the townsfolk.

"And so they were tried?" Helena asks, her eyes reflecting a fury at injustice that mirrors his own.

Father Emile nods solemnly. "A mockery of justice," he says bitterly. "Condemned by superstition and lies."

He pictures them—the Van Aardens—standing accused before a baying crowd whipped into a fervor by guild masters who watched with cold satisfaction as another obstacle was removed from their path to power.

"They were executed," Father Emile confesses, feeling each word as a lash upon his soul. "One by one, sent to meet their Maker on charges born from malice."

Helena reaches out instinctively towards Father Emile, though she cannot touch him through the screen—a gesture of shared humanity in the face of historical cruelty.

"And now?" De Vries's question pulls Father Emile back from the precipice of his emotions.

"Now," Father Emile says with newfound resolve, wiping away a stray tear with the back of his hand, "I must show you what I found years ago —a truth long concealed within these very walls."

They emerge from the confessional booth like souls reborn into a world that remains unchanged despite their transformation within. Father Emile leads them through the nave's silent expanse towards an area seldom frequented by parishioners—the church's old library.

Dust motes dance lazily in shafts of light as they enter; rows upon rows of ancient texts gaze down upon them like silent sentinels guarding forgotten knowledge. He moves towards a seemingly innocuous section where volumes on ecclesiastical law stand solemn and undisturbed.

"Behind these texts," he says with reverence, reaching out to trigger a mechanism hidden from untrained eyes.

A low groan emanates from the wall as it gives way to reveal a hidden compartment—a cavity within which lie bundles of documents bound in leather and string, their existence unknown to all but a few.

Helena steps forward with an apothecary's precision and curiosity burning bright in her gaze. She gently lifts one bundle from its resting place, setting off a cloud of dust that seems almost sacrilegious in its disturbance.

"These are records," Father Emile explains as Helena carefully unfurls one document to reveal an elegant script mired by time yet legible still. "Records kept by guild masters—minutes from meetings shrouded in secrecy."

De Vries watches over Helena's shoulder as she scans page after page—the handwriting changes but the content bears a sinister constancy.

"Here," she says quietly but with authority, pointing to a passage that makes her blood run cold. It details plans for accusing those who stand against them or pose a threat to their authority—a chilling blueprint for social assassination.

"They detail everything," De Vries murmurs incredulously as he reads over her shoulder. The manipulation of public opinion, strategies for disposing of 'problematic' individuals—it's all laid bare on aged parchment before them.

Helena looks up at Father Emile with respect tinged with sorrow for what he must have endured knowing these truths lay hidden beneath prayers and sermons. "Why keep these documents? Why not destroy them?"

Father Emile meets her gaze squarely. "Evidence," he says simply. "Proof against future corruption—against forgetting."

De Vries nods slowly as understanding dawns upon him—a policeman's mind grasping at implications both legal and moral.

"These documents could change everything," Helena breathes out softly.

"Yes," Father Emile agrees solemnly. "They could indeed."

Father Emile watches Helena, her fingers delicate as she sifts through the documents, each movement precise and measured. She pauses, her breath hitching ever so slightly as she uncovers a list—names scribed in a meticulous column, each one a story, each one a life upended by fear and power.

"Father," Helena whispers, holding the paper aloft as if it might crumble to dust at any moment. "These names... they were all targeted?"

He steps closer, peering over her shoulder at the damning litany. "Yes," he confirms with a nod. "These are families marked by the guilds—branded as outcasts, accused without cause."

Helena scans the list, eyes wide with the gravity of her find. "The Van Aardens," she murmurs, tracing the name with a trembling finger. "This could prove their innocence."

Father Emile feels a surge of something akin to hope, tempered by the knowledge of suffering these papers represent. He glances at Inspector De Vries, who has been poring over another set of documents with a furrowed brow.

"Inspector?" Father Emile prompts.

De Vries looks up, his eyes reflecting the fire of a mind piecing together a puzzle centuries in the making. "The methods," he begins slowly, "the systematic way in which these families were broken... It mirrors what we're seeing now."

Helena turns towards him, her mind racing to follow his train of thought. "You mean the canal murders?"

"Yes," De Vries nods sharply. "It's as if history is repeating itself—another purge disguised as justice."

Father Emile senses the weight of revelation settles upon them—a trio united by a quest for truth that now stretches across time. The church's vast silence envelops them as they stand among ghosts of the past, confronting shadows that have long darkened Brugge's streets.

Helena lays the list on a nearby table, her hands steady despite the tumult within her heart. She looks between Father Emile and Inspector De Vries—her allies in this strange dance with history.

"We need to go through these names," she says firmly. "Find connections to those recently lost."

De Vries moves beside her, his gaze intense as he scans the list. He nods in agreement—a silent pact forged between them.

Father Emile watches them work side by side—Helena with her keen eye for detail and De Vries with his analytical mind—and wonders at the courage it takes to unearth such buried truths.

They work well into the evening, candlelight flickering against stone walls as they cross-reference names from Father Emile's records with recent obituaries and town records. Patterns begin to emerge like constellations in a night sky—a web of connections that draw tighter around a central point.

Helena pauses occasionally to massage her temples or to share an insight that sends them down another avenue of inquiry. De Vries's determination is relentless; his focus does not waver even as shadows lengthen and merge into darkness.

"It's not just families," De Vries says at last, pushing back from the table and stretching his stiff limbs. "It's influence—positions within Brugge's society that could challenge the status quo."

Father Emile considers this—a hierarchy upended by strategic strikes against those who dare to rise too high or speak too freely.

"Like my family," Helena adds quietly, personalizing their discovery with a vulnerability that speaks volumes.

De Vries meets her gaze with respect and an understanding born from years of seeking justice amidst webs of corruption. "Exactly like your family," he confirms.

Helena returns to the list, her resolve redoubled by this new insight. She pores over each entry, seeking threads that might lead them forward or knots that might unravel to reveal deeper secrets.

Father Emile offers silent prayers for strength—for Helena who seeks vindication for Willem Van Aarden; for De Vries who chases justice like a hound on a scent; and for himself—a man caught between past sins and present redemption.

As midnight tolls from St. Michael's bell tower—a somber sound that reverberates through Brugge's silent streets—Helena leans back in her chair with an exhausted sigh.

"We've found something," she announces, voice laced with fatigue but underscored by triumph.

De Vries returns to her side swiftly, looking over her shoulder at the document she indicates—a page filled with annotations in Father Emile's steady hand.

"This," Helena points to an entry halfway down the page—an innocuous note that might have been overlooked if not for their meticulous scrutiny—"this could be our key."

Father Emile leans in closer to see what has captured their attention—a record of land disputes dating back decades; parcels of property passed down through generations until they became sites where bodies were found—each one a murder scene etched into Brugge's memory.

"It suggests premeditation," De Vries muses aloud, his voice echoing slightly off stone walls that have borne witness to centuries of whispered confessions.

"And revenge?" Helena adds thoughtfully.

"Perhaps." De Vries' reply is tinged with caution but not devoid of possibility.

They stand together in contemplative silence—the historian's daughter turned sleuth; the inspector whose moral compass never wavers; and Father Emile whose heart bears scars no confession can heal but whose resolve is bolstered by their presence in his church this night.

Father Emile stands in the muted glow of the church, his hands clasped before him, an embodiment of the remorse that has gnawed at his conscience for years. The weight of unspoken truths presses upon him, as heavy as the stone arches that loom above. He watches Helena and Inspector De Vries pore over the documents with fervor, their youthful energy a stark contrast to his weary soul.

"I have lived with this burden for too long," he begins, his voice barely above a whisper. The words come slowly, each one heavy with the weight of guilt. "The shadows of the past reach far and deep, entwining around the present like ivy on an ancient wall."

Helena pauses in her examination of the papers, her eyes lifting to meet Father Emile's gaze. The lines etched upon his face tell a story of inner turmoil and a battle with demons that have long resided within the hallowed walls of St. Michael's.

"I implore you both," Father Emile continues, his voice gaining strength as he steps forward into the light streaming through a stained glass window, "to bring these secrets into the light. It is only through truth that we can hope for justice—for redemption."

Inspector De Vries looks up from the records, his eyes locking with Father Emile's. In them, Father Emile sees not just a seeker of justice but a man who understands the complexity of human frailty and forgiveness.

"Father," De Vries replies solemnly, "we will do everything in our power to uncover what has been hidden. This city... these people deserve no less."

Father Emile nods gratefully, turning to Helena. Her presence in this sacred space—a woman whose intelligence and compassion shine as brightly as any candle—gives him hope that even the darkest histories can be illuminated.

"Helena," he says softly, "your pursuit of knowledge has led you here. Let it now lead us out of the darkness."

She nods resolutely, her eyes reflecting determination mixed with empathy. "We will not let these wrongs go unrighted," she promises.

A silence falls upon them—a shared understanding that transcends words. They stand united by a common goal: to piece together a tapestry woven from strands of pain and injustice.

The air in St. Michael's feels charged with purpose as Father Emile steps closer to the table laden with ancient records. His fingers brush against parchment yellowed by time, each touch a plea for absolution.

"Look at this city," he gestures towards an open window where Brugge lies spread beneath them—a view of rooftops and canals bathed in the waning light of day. "It has endured much—joy and sorrow, triumph and tragedy. Yet it remains beautiful, resilient."

Helena follows his gaze out towards Brugge, seeing it anew through Father Emile's eyes—a city that holds its history close to its heart.

"We are part of its story now," Father Emile says quietly. "We carry its past within us and shape its future through our actions."

Inspector De Vries joins them at the window, observing Brugge's silhouette against the dying light—a city whispering secrets that only they are poised to hear.

"We stand on the brink of revelation," De Vries states firmly. "We will face resistance; there are those who would keep these truths buried deep within Brugge's foundations."

"But we will not falter," Helena adds with conviction.

Father Emile looks between them—the inspector whose honor is as unwavering as Brugge's ancient belfry; Helena whose curiosity has blossomed into courageous pursuit—and feels a kindling warmth amidst his remorse.

"Together," he says slowly, allowing himself to believe in what seems an impossible dream—"together we will chase away the shadows cast by my silence."

They return to their task with renewed vigor; pages turn with whispers like rustling leaves in an autumn breeze as more connections come to light—names and dates aligning like stars destined to form constellations.

The evening wanes; candles flicker in their sconces casting elongated shadows across stone floors worn smooth by centuries of faithful footsteps.

As they work, Father Emile recounts tales from Brugge's history—a city both haunted and hallowed by its past.

Inspector De Vries listens intently to Father Emile's recollections, each story a thread weaving into their current tapestry of investigation. He scribbles notes feverishly—a map charting a course through history's labyrinthine passages.

Helena absorbs every word like rain into parched earth; her mind is alight with connections between past persecution and present violence—patterns emerging from chaos.

Time becomes fluid within St. Michael's walls—the outside world retreating until nothing exists but their quest for truth amid echoes of prayer and penitence.

As midnight approaches once more, they gather beneath stained glass windows where colors have faded from day's bright palette into twilight hues—a mosaic backdrop for their solemn vow.

"Let us make a promise here," Father Emile says gravely as they join hands beneath celestial depictions wrought in glass and lead—"a covenant bound by our shared humanity."

"We will uncover all that has been hidden," Inspector De Vries vows—"the full extent of historical injustices wrought by those who wielded power without mercy."

"And we will seek justice for all victims—past and present." Helena's voice rings clear within the sanctuary—a clarion call resonating against ancient stones.

They stand silent for a moment—three souls intertwined by fate in a city where every stone holds a secret; every canal reflects stories untold; every whisper carries weight beyond measure.

As they release their hands, their eyes meet—one last affirmation before stepping forth from St. Michael's embrace into Brugge's night—a triad resolved to right wrongs both old and new; three hearts beating as one against time's relentless tide; united in purpose beneath watchful eyes of saints immortalized in stained glass splendor.

With this pledge sealed within hallowed walls—their path laid out before them—they depart from St. Michael's into darkness pierced by stars; into silence broken only by whispers... whispers from The Canal Whisperer itself.

The Guild's Vendetta

The night hangs heavy over Brugge, a blanket of darkness punctuated by the occasional glimmer of a lamp through a window. My own reflection, cast in the rippling canal waters, seems like that of a stranger—haunted, hunted. The cold seeps into my bones as I pass by the police station, its windows dimly lit in the otherwise sleeping city.

There's a flicker of movement inside—one that I recognize. Inspector De Vries. His silhouette is bent over a desk piled with papers, illuminated by the tired glow of a lamp. The sight tugs at me, pulling me from my path and drawing me to the window to peer into his world of shadows and secrets.

Inside, De Vries is motionless but for the steady drumming of his fingers on the wooden surface. He's surrounded by ghosts of the past; old guild records sprawl before him like accusations. Recent case files lie open, their contents spilling out like so many spilled secrets.

He's searching for something. A connection that eludes him.

A chill runs down my spine as I watch him lean closer to a document, his eyes narrowing with what could only be recognition. He grabs his notes with renewed fervor, scribbling something quickly—a name, perhaps? Or a revelation?

It's clear he's found something. A pattern hidden within the chaos.

My heart races as I press closer to the glass, every fiber of my being straining to decipher what lies beyond it. Could this be it? The breakthrough that might clear my name or plunge me deeper into this nightmare?

A soft exhalation escapes my lips, fogging up the pane and obscuring my view for a moment. I wipe it away hastily, not wanting to miss a single gesture or glance that might betray his thoughts.

The inspector pauses and leans back in his chair, pinching the bridge of his nose in fatigue—or is it frustration? He looks older in this light, weighed down by the burden of truth-seeking.

The clock on the wall continues its relentless march, each tick a steady heartbeat counting the moments with an unwavering rhythm, indifferent to the world around it.

De Vries shakes off his weariness and dives back into the files. Page after page he turns, faster now. His body leans forward as if willing himself closer to understanding. His fingers pause on a page and he sits back abruptly as if struck by lightning.

It's as if I can hear the gears whirring in his mind, each thought clicking into place like precision machinery at work.

Suddenly he rises from his chair and strides to a filing cabinet in the corner. He returns with an even older tome—one that looks like it could crumble to dust if not handled with care.

I watch as he flips through it with reverence and purpose until he stops so abruptly that it's as if he's been physically halted by what he sees.

My breath catches in my throat when he retrieves one of the case files and places it beside the ancient record. Back and forth his gaze goes between them—a macabre dance of past and present intertwining.

What has he discovered? My hands clench into fists at my sides.

De Vries is suddenly animated, notes flying from beneath his pen as if trying to capture his thoughts before they escape him. He's onto something—a pattern emerging from the depths like some long-drowned truth finally coming up for air.

All victims descended from that tribunal... The very thought makes my blood run cold—the same tribunal responsible for condemning my ancestors with cries of witchcraft and malice.

I feel a kinship with De Vries then—a shared sense of purpose despite our different roles in this morbid play. He seeks justice; I seek redemption. Yet here we are—our fates entwined around the twisted roots of Brugge's dark history.

The inspector stands abruptly, knocking over his chair in haste. His eyes are alight with determination as he gathers up his findings—papers clutched close like protective talismans against uncertainty.

He reaches for his coat and hat, preparing to leave—I can tell by that set look on his face that there will be no rest for him tonight.

I step back from the window just as he turns off the lamp, plunging the room into darkness—a mirror of our ignorance until now. Only then do I realize how long I've been standing here, how cold I've become watching another man unravel my life's puzzle.

As De Vries exits the building and strides into Brugge's labyrinthine heart, I follow at a distance—not too close to draw attention but close enough to stay connected to this thread of hope he's unwittingly spun for me.

I trail behind Inspector De Vries, my heart a drumbeat of nerves in my chest. The cobblestones whisper beneath my boots as I keep to the shadows, not daring to close the gap between us. He's heading to Helena's lab, a sanctuary of science and solace amidst the chaos of our entwined lives.

When I arrive, the door stands ajar, and through it spills a slice of amber light. I hesitate on the threshold. Within that room are answers—answers that might weave my family's name back into the history of Brugge with honor or stain it further with blood and suspicion.

I push the door open.

Helena stands beside her workbench, her eyes wide with anticipation as De Vries unfurls his findings across the polished wood. Charts, maps of lineage, and names circled and connected by lines that create a web of historical intrigue. I can see in her gaze that she is already fitting pieces together in her mind's puzzle—a puzzle that has consumed us all.

"Willem," she greets me with a nod, her voice steady but not without warmth.

De Vries turns at the sound of my name, his eyes sharp as flint. "I've found something," he begins without a preamble. "It appears that all victims share a common thread—they're descendants of the guild tribunal members who passed judgment centuries ago."

The room falls silent as his words settle like dust in an abandoned hall.

I feel a twinge in my gut—a mix of dread and vindication. My family's past is no secret in Brugge; the Van Aarden name has been dragged through mud and blood for generations.

"The same tribunal," I echo, my voice hollow, "that condemned my ancestors for witchcraft."

Helena looks at me then, and there's something like sorrow in her eyes. She reaches out as if to offer comfort but hesitates. Her hand falls back to her side.

"Yes," De Vries confirms with a grave nod. "It seems we're looking at an act of historical retribution."

Anger surges within me like a gale-force wind, threatening to tear down the fragile walls I've built around my pain. The injustice inflicted upon my family—burned into our legacy like a brand—was it all for this? To be fodder for some vendetta spanning centuries?

I clench my fists until my nails dig into my palms, anchoring myself in the present through sheer force of will.

"My great-great-grandfather was a man of the sea," I start, words spilling forth like waves crashing against rock. "He provided for his family through storm and calm alike. But they said he consorted with devils, that his nets brimmed with fish because he traded souls for silver."

Helena steps closer now, her presence a balm to the rawness in my throat as I speak.

"They took everything from him—his livelihood, his dignity." My voice breaks like timber under strain. "And when they were done, they took his life too."

De Vries listens, his face etched with lines of concentration. This is more than just another detail to him; I can see that much. It's a glimpse into the heartache woven through every thread of Brugge's storied past.

"And now," I continue, feeling the weight of centuries bearing down upon me, "it seems they wish to finish what they started—to rid Brugge of what remains of us."

Helena's hand finds mine then—her touch gentle but firm. "We won't let that happen," she says with conviction.

"We'll put an end to this cycle," De Vries adds. "We owe it to your family and to those who've suffered because of these murders."

His assurance does little to ease the turmoil within me—a storm brewed from years of whispered slurs and sidelong glances—but it ignites something else: hope.

We pour over De Vries' findings together—the inspector explaining his deductions while Helena offers insights from her scientific mind. They discuss motive and opportunity with clinical precision while I stand between them—a bridge between past and present.

"The question remains," De Vries muses aloud, tapping on one name circled in red ink, "how deep does this vendetta run? And how far are they willing to go?"

We exchange looks then—three souls caught in a dance with death and history.

Helena leans over an old ledger, tracing her finger along lines written by hands long stilled by time. She pauses at an entry—a transaction or perhaps a decree—and looks up sharply.

"This could be important," she declares, tapping on the text. Her excitement is palpable—a spark in the gloom that surrounds us.

De Vries moves beside her, peering down at the ledger with renewed interest.

I watch them both—this unlikely alliance formed in shadow and suspicion—and feel a shift within me. For so long I've walked these streets alone, shrouded by my family's curse. But here with Helena and De Vries pouring over ancient records seeking justice for wrongs both fresh and faded—I dare to believe that perhaps redemption isn't just a fool's dream after all.

"Willem?" Helena's voice pulls me from my thoughts. She offers me a faint smile that doesn't quite reach her eyes but promises solidarity nonetheless.

"Yes?" My response is tentative—an ember glowing amid ash.

"Look at this." She points at another passage in the ledger—one that mentions my family name not with scorn but respect—a transaction made in good faith.

A piece of history untainted by tragedy—a rare thing indeed for someone like me.

It feels like grasping at straws in a tempest but it's something—a sign that perhaps there was more to us than whispers and witchcraft once upon a time.

De Vries meets my gaze then; his eyes are steady beacons cutting through the fog—through doubt and despair—and I realize he isn't just looking at me as another piece in this puzzle we're solving together—he sees me as Willem Van Aarden: fisherman, descendant... human being.

And for just a moment amidst this urgent meeting where we unravel threads of retribution—I feel anchored not by anger or sadness but by purpose and something resembling peace.

"I've found something," Helena says, breaking the silence that had settled like frost. Her voice is steady, but I can see a tremor in her hands as she points to the parchment before her.

I lean in closer, trying to make sense of the medical jargon and sketches that detail the fates of the victims. Helena taps a finger on a particular line in the report—a line that ties the present horror to an age-old cruelty.

"The methods," she begins, "they're not random acts of violence. They symbolically replicate the punishments once handed down by the tribunal."

My heart pounds against my ribs as if trying to escape the confines of my chest. The tribunal—my family's merciless judges—are they reaching from beyond their graves to exact further punishment?

"It's meticulous," Helena continues, her eyes never leaving the documents. "Drowning, weighted down in the canals—like those accused of witchcraft who were thrown into the water to test their innocence."

I can almost hear the echoes of history—the cries for mercy, the splash of bodies hitting the water, and the silent prayers for vindication that were never answered.

Inspector De Vries runs a hand over his chin, his face grim with understanding. "So we're dealing with a murderer who believes they're carrying out some twisted form of justice?"

Helena nods solemnly. "Exactly."

We sit in a triangle around Helena's findings—three minds grappling with a truth too chilling to bear. A murderer walks among us, cloaked in righteousness and wielding death as if it were divine providence.

The inspector breaks our shared trance with a sigh that seems to carry the weight of his badge. "We need to decide our next step carefully."

I glance between them both—Helena with her blend of compassion and intellect, De Vries with his unwavering dedication to justice—and feel an unfamiliar role settling upon my shoulders: protector.

"We have to warn them," I say, thinking of the descendants who walk unknowingly in the shadow of death. "The people who are at risk—they deserve to know."

De Vries nods slowly but there's caution in his eyes. "If we go public with this discovery, we risk causing widespread panic. And we might very well tip off our murderer."

"But what's our alternative?" Helena argues, her hands clenched into fists on the table. "Stay silent while more innocents die?"

***

I watch the dawn creep over Brugge like a cautious thief, its golden fingers prying into the night's embrace. The city stirs to life, unaware of the secrets that churn beneath its cobbled streets. Helena and Inspector De Vries have asked me to join them today—a revisitation of the crime scenes. They hope to find what was once missed, now that they see through the lens of history and vengeance.

We stand on the edge of the first canal, where the water holds memories that wish to remain submerged. De Vries kneels, his eyes scanning the embankment with a precision that reveals nothing escapes him.

"This is where they found Jan Verbeek," he says, more to himself than us. His finger traces a path along the ground as if he could still see the drag marks from that dreadful night.

Helena pulls out her notes, her face a mask of concentration. "Jan was a direct descendant of Pieter Verbeek, one of the tribunal's most fervent enforcers."

I can feel her gaze on me, full of unspoken apologies for dredging up such painful parallels. But I'm beyond resentment now; I only want to end this cycle of death that seems to orbit my existence.

"We should check under the bridge," I suggest, my voice steady despite the tremor I feel inside. "If this is an act of retribution, perhaps there's a symbol or sign left behind—a message from our murderer."

We move as one, Helena and De Vries flanking me as we make our way to the shadowed space beneath the arching stone. It's cooler here, the air thick with dampness and whispers of the past.

Helena runs her hands along the walls, her fingers searching for any indentations or markings that might betray a secret message. De Vries watches her closely before turning his attention to the water itself, peering into its murky depths.

"Look here," Helena calls out softly.

I join her side and see what she's found—an etching in the stone almost worn away by time and touch. It's a symbol: a swan with its wings spread wide in flight.

"The Silver Swan," I breathe out, recognizing the emblem of an old guild—one steeped in both prestige and darkness.

De Vries joins us, his eyes lighting up with recognition. "It's too coincidental for it not to be connected."

We document our findings with sketches and notes before moving on to the next site—another canal where another life was claimed. Here, too, we search for clues hidden in plain sight.

The day wears on as we traverse from one haunting site to another—each visit unearthing fragments of history and heartache. The victims were all different in life but now united in death by a common lineage—one that led back to those who once judged with iron fists and cold hearts.

As evening approaches and shadows grow long around us, we find ourselves at the last canal—a place where willows weep into waters that never forget. It's quieter here, farther from the bustle of town. A hush falls upon us as we approach.

"That's where they found Pieter," De Vries says quietly. His name hangs between us like a delicate shroud.

Helena crosses herself instinctively before setting down her bag and pulling out an old map—a web of family trees and their unfortunate connections.

"We need to be thorough," she insists as she unfolds it beside us. "Every detail could lead us closer."

I nod my agreement and crouch down beside her as De Vries keeps watch over our makeshift investigation site. We're so engrossed in our work that at first, we don't notice him—the figure standing on the opposite bank watching us with an intensity that feels like a physical touch against my skin.

When I finally sense his presence and look up, my heart lurches in my chest. There's something familiar about him—the way he stands motionless like a sentinel or perhaps an omen.

De Vries catches my gaze and follows it across the water to where our silent observer stands shrouded by twilight's embrace.

"Stay here," he commands in a low tone before striding toward our mysterious guest with determined steps.

But as quickly as he appeared, our watcher turned away—his form dissolving into shadows as if he were never there at all.

Helena looks at me with wide eyes—her fear reflecting my unease. "Who was that?"

I shake my head slowly; words fail me as an icy dread wraps around my spine—a premonition that whispers this is far from over.

De Vries returns empty-handed but not defeated; there's a fire kindled behind his eyes—a relentless drive that tells me he will not let this go easily.

"We'll increase patrols around these areas," he says more to himself than us. "If our friend decides to return…"

***

I watch as Inspector De Vries straightens his coat, a subtle but sure sign of his readiness for the task ahead. We're standing outside the ornate doors of the mayor's office, the heart of Brugge's governance, and I can't help but feel out of place. The polished brass and gleaming wood seem to whisper of power and decisions made far above the likes of a fisherman.

De Vries catches my eye, offering a curt nod that I've come to understand means 'It's time.' We enter together, Helena trailing just behind us, her presence a reassuring constant.

The mayor's office is grander than I expected, with walls lined with portraits of past leaders, their stern eyes surveying the room as if they could still influence the fate of our city. Mayor De Groote rises from behind a vast mahogany desk, her hand extended in greeting.

"Inspector De Vries," she begins, her voice smooth like the fine brandy I've seen others sip at the local tavern. "And this must be Willem Van Aarden and Helena De Baere. Please, have a seat."

We comply, and De Vries wastes no time in laying out our findings before the mayor—descendants targeted by someone with a twisted sense of justice, linked to an ancient vendetta born from Brugge's darkest days.

The mayor listens intently, her expression a carefully maintained mask of concern. When De Vries finishes, silence fills the room—a silence that carries the weight of history and the urgency of now.

"This is... most troubling," Mayor De Groote finally says, steepling her fingers beneath her chin. "Brugge cannot afford panic or scandal. Our reputation as a city of culture and tranquility must be preserved."

"But lives are at risk," Helena interjects, her voice firm despite the tremor that runs beneath it. "We need to act—discreetly but decisively."

The mayor nods slowly as if conceding to an unspoken argument. "Very well. I will provide additional resources for your investigation. Increased patrols in key areas and whatever else you might require."

De Vries leans forward, seizing upon the offered lifeline with a determination that borders on ferocity. "Thank you. We'll also need access to certain records—family histories and guild archives that aren't available to the public."

"Granted," Mayor De Groote agrees with a wave of his hand as if he could sweep away centuries of secrets with such a gesture.

"And protection for those who may still be targeted?" I ask before I can stop myself—the words tumbling from my lips unbidden.

The mayor fixes me with a gaze that would likely intimidate any other man. But I am Willem Van Aarden—I have faced worse than stern looks in my life.

"We will do what we can," she replies after a moment's pause. "But this must be handled with care—we cannot create hysteria."

I nod once, sharply—a fisherman agreeing to terms with those who navigate political currents rather than ocean tides.

As we leave the mayor's office, there's a new tension between us—an understanding that we've been granted both an opportunity and an immense responsibility.

***

The police station is quiet when we arrive—the calm before a storm perhaps or simply the lull of an evening where duty has given way to rest for most.

De Vries leads us to a back room lit by flickering gas lamps that cast long shadows against the walls—shadows that seem almost alive in their erratic dance.

"We need to compile our list—determine who else might be at risk," De Vries states as he unfurls maps and documents across an old table scarred with nicks and ink stains.

Helena joins him, her sleeves rolled up in readiness as she scans lineages and cross-references names with public records.

I stand by silently at first—what do I know of archives and genealogy? But then I realize that I am not just an observer here; this is my fight too.

"I'll go back through my family's records," I offer, my voice steady with newfound resolve. "There might be connections we've overlooked—names long forgotten."

Helena offers me an encouraging smile—one that speaks not just of gratitude but also belief—a belief in me that warms more than any lamp could.

De Vries looks up from his work—a silent nod acknowledging my contribution before he returns to his meticulous task.

Hours slip by as we delve deeper into Brugge's past—seeking out those who unknowingly walk in death's shadow. We compile names and addresses, histories intertwined so tightly they seem almost inseparable from the city itself.

But there is clarity too—in patterns recognized and strategies formed—a plan taking shape amidst chaos.

"Tomorrow," De Vries finally says, breaking our concentrated silence as midnight chimes echo from some distant tower. "We begin reaching out to those on our list—quietly alerting them without causing alarm."

"We'll need help," Helena adds, her gaze flickering over our assembled notes—a sea chart guiding us through perilous waters.

"We have each other," I say before I can think better of it—a statement simple but true in its depth.

They both look at me then—the inspector with his steadfast resolve; Helena with her blend of strength and grace—and something unspoken passes between us: unity born from necessity but fortified by trust—a shared determination to end this cycle once and for all.

And so we agree on our roles: De Vries coordinating with his officers discreetly; Helena using her contacts in scientific circles for more information; myself reaching out into Brugge's undercurrents where whispers flow like water through reeds.

The gas lamps flicker lower now as dawn threatens on the horizon—an approaching light that seems both hopeful and foreboding. We stand together amidst piles of parchment and maps etched with fates yet unwritten—a trio bound by purpose against an unseen foe who haunts like specters over water.

And there within those dimly lit confines, we steel ourselves for what comes next—for though uncertainty shrouds our path forward we are resolute: This murderer will be brought to light; these vengeful tides will be stemmed; justice shall reclaim its rightful place within Brugge's whispered history.

A Desperate Search

As I step inside the Brugge police station, dawn's gray fingers creep through the narrow windows. The morning air still clings to my coat. The station is hollow, with shadows huddling in the corners like silent spectators. I can smell the remnants of burnt coffee and feel the quiet tension that seems to seep from the walls. Gerard and Helena are there, hunched over a table. Papers and parchment are scattered throughout it. Their faces show concern and focus.

"Willem," Gerard greets me, his voice a low rumble in the quiet room. "We must act swiftly."

Helena's eyes, bright even in the dim light, meet mine. "Time is not our ally," she adds, pushing a lock of hair behind her ear as she turns back to the maps.

We gather around the table, an island of intent in a sea of uncertainty. Maps sprawl across the wooden surface like open palms, each line marking a potential clue. Historical records tower in unsteady piles, whispering secrets of old Brugge and its guilds.

Gerard's finger traces along one of the waterways on the map. "The pattern is clear; each murder mirrors historical injustices committed by tribunal members. If we can predict..."

His voice trails off as Helena interjects. "We need to understand who among the living might still be seen as bearing their ancestors' guilt." She spreads out a family tree so intricate it resembles a delicate tapestry. "Here," she points, "are the lines that bind present to past."

I lean closer, following her gestures as she outlines descendants linked to those long-ago tribunals – people who might now be marked by a vendetta reaching from beyond the grave.

"We cross-reference these names with current city records," I suggest, my finger hovering over one particularly entwined section of lineage. "Find out where they live, what they do."

Helena nods in agreement while Gerard's brow furrows further. His skepticism has always been his armor, but now it seems to weigh on him.

"Willem's right," he says after a moment. "We'll split up; cover more ground that way."

As dawn breaks fully, painting thin streaks of gold against the walls, we divide our tasks with solemn nods and set about threading our way through history's web in search of its most vulnerable strands.

The silence between us speaks volumes; it is heavy with shared resolve but also with the unsaid – fears for those we might be too late to save and for ourselves as we peel back layers best left undisturbed.

Maps become our guideposts; records become our breadcrumbs. Helena and I sift through them like prospectors panning for gold – every name, every date could be key to unlocking this puzzle box of lineage and legacy.

She handles each document with reverence, her touch gentle as if she fears disturbing spirits resting within their fibers. Her focus is laser-sharp, yet there's an elegance to her movements that belies the gravity of our task.

I watch as Inspector De Vries, brow furrowed in thought, taps a pencil against the edge of the map. He's like a hunter tracking an elusive prey, piecing together trails left in the underbrush. Helena stands beside him, her presence a steady flame in the dim room. She holds a list of names, her finger skimming down the column as if she could feel the pulse of history beneath the ink.

"The pattern," De Vries murmurs, almost to himself, "is not just about revenge. It's theatrical... calculated." He pauses and glances up at me, his eyes reflecting a stormy sea of thoughts. "Our killer wants to send a message, dredging up the sins of the past to stain the present."

I lean in closer, trying to follow his line of reasoning. The concept of family legacy is no stranger to me – it's been my shadow since birth. But this is different; this is someone weaponizing history for their own twisted sense of justice.

"He's targeting descendants," I say, my voice steady despite the turmoil inside. "But why these families? What's the connection that we're missing?"

Helena chimes in with a theory as elegant as it is chilling. "Perhaps he sees himself as an avenger," she suggests. "Correcting what he perceives as historical wrongs through blood."

The inspector nods slowly. "An eye for an eye... until everyone is blind." His hand comes to rest on a family crest etched into one corner of the map. "We need to think like him, anticipate his next move."

Together, we dive into the abyss of old grudges and vendettas, tracing lines that connect victims to their forebears' misdeeds. We assemble profiles of those who might fit the murderer's criteria: descendants occupying positions of influence or wealth – symbols of continued power that he might see as unjustly inherited.

"Here," Helena points out a name – De Groote – our current mayor, her ancestors with significant holdings in the textile trade centuries ago.

"And here," De Vries adds another – Claes – whose family was known for its harsh rulings during guild disputes.

I contribute my findings, marking down those who have made enemies in recent times or whose family stories are marred by darker chapters.

We compile our list with grim determination; each name is a potential bullseye for our unseen archer. With every name that crosses our lips, I can't help but feel the weight of their fates pressing down upon us.

De Vries proposes a plan that feels like setting sail in stormy waters with no compass but our instincts. "We must protect them," he says with resolve. "And speak with them. They may hold pieces of this puzzle without even knowing it."

"We cross-check everything," she says, laying out the evidence collected from each chilling scene. "Fibers, residue, anything that might link our list of descendants to the scenes. There could be a pattern we've missed."

I nod, my thoughts turbulent as a tempest-tossed sea. Guilt gnaws at me, a relentless tide eroding the shores of my resolve. The vendetta – this sequence of retribution – is rooted in the dark soil of my ancestors' deeds. How can I stand here, trying to unravel this knot when my hands are soiled by the same earth?

Gerard is already moving, gathering the samples we've kept sealed and cataloged with obsessive care. "Good idea," he murmurs, and I catch a glimmer of admiration in his eyes as he looks at Helena. Her forensic approach has already shed light on details that were once shrouded in darkness.

We set up an impromptu lab amidst the dust and echoes of an unused room in the station. It feels like stepping into a different world – one where the clarity of science cuts through the mists of fear and superstition that have long clung to my name.

Helena works with a grace that belies her focus, each movement precise as she examines fibers under a microscope or tests samples with chemicals whose names dance on her tongue like ancient incantations.

I try to follow suit, to contribute more than just brute force or local knowledge. But every fiber I place under the lens, every sample I hold up to the light is tinged with an unspoken question – am I doing this to save others or to redeem myself?

Gerard watches us both, his presence solid and reassuring. He does not speak much; his attention is fixed on piecing together this puzzle that sprawls across time like an endless tapestry.

Hours pass in silence but for the soft clink of glassware and Helena's occasional murmured observations. My hands are steady as I work, but inside I am a cacophony of doubts and fears.

"We have something," Helena eventually declares, breaking the quiet with her revelation. She beckons us over with an urgency that sets my heart racing.

I lean in beside Gerard to see what she's found – a strand of hair caught on a piece of fabric, so fine it's almost invisible against its dark background.

"It doesn't match any of our victims," she explains. "But if we can find out who it belongs to..."

"It could be our connection," Gerard finishes for her, his voice low but charged with potential energy.

Helena nods, already reaching for her notes. "We compare this with samples from our list of targets."

The possibility sends a shiver through me – are we one step closer to ending this nightmare? Or merely stirring deeper into its depths?

The weight of my family's legacy bears down on me harder than ever as we work through the night. Each name on our list is a reminder of how closely history clings to us all, and how it shapes our lives in ways we can barely grasp.

When we finally pause for breath, fatigue hangs heavy in the air like fog over the canals. Helena's face is pale but determined under the harsh light; Gerard's eyes are shadowed but unwavering.

I rub at my own eyes, feeling their burn from too many hours spent peering into microscopes and over documents. My mind races with what-ifs and maybes as I consider each descendant who might soon find themselves at the mercy of a madman seeking justice for wrongs they never committed.

"I should have seen this coming," I mutter into the quiet room.

Helena turns to me then, her gaze kind but firm. "You couldn't have known," she says softly.

"But it's my history that has brought us here," I insist, feeling that old anger rising within me like bile.

"It's our history," Gerard corrects me quietly from across the table. "Brugge's history. And we face it together."

The air in the room grows thick with the ticking of the clock, each second a drumbeat marching towards potential tragedy. Helena, Gerard, and I know the rhythm well – it's the sound of time slipping through our fingers like grains of sand. With each name on our list, a life hangs in balance, and we can't afford to let the pendulum swing towards another murder.

Helena's hands move with swift precision, arranging our findings into coherent order. Gerard stands sentinel by the window, his gaze scanning the horizon as if he could spot danger approaching from miles away. And me? I'm pacing, a caged animal tracing the same worn path, unable to still the storm within.

"We should consult with Van Eck again," I suggest abruptly, halting mid-pace. "He might have insights we've missed."

Gerard nods in agreement, and within a few hours we're seated at a corner table in a dimly lit pub. The warm, amber light flickers off the walls as Professor Jan Van Eck steps through the door, his presence commanding attention even in the casual setting.

Van Eck approaches with a grave expression, his scholarly demeanor unmistakable. As he takes a seat, his eyes reflect the weight of the stories he carries. The scent of old books and parchment seems to follow him, as though his study—filled with leather-bound tomes and towering stacks of papers—has come along for the ride. Adjusting his glasses, he leans in, ready to unravel the dark history that has brought us together.

"Inspector De Vries, Miss De Baere, Mr. Van Aarden," he greets us with a nod for each name. "I understand there's urgency."

"You could say that," Gerard replies, his voice grim. "We're trying to prevent another murder."

Van Eck leans closer, eyes intent behind thick lenses. "Tell me what you've found."

Helena takes over then, her narrative concise as she lays out our discoveries – patterns in victims' lineage linked to ancient tribunal decisions.

The professor listens, his fingers steepled beneath his chin. When Helena finishes, he lets out a slow breath that seems to carry the weight of centuries.

"The guilds wielded great power," he begins thoughtfully. "They were more than mere associations; they were akin to courts – judge, jury... executioner." He pauses as if choosing his next words carefully. "To understand your murderer's mindset... you must grasp the full extent of their influence."

I feel a chill despite the room's warmth – this man speaks of power so absolute it could dictate life and death over generations.

"Is there any record of guild members being targeted in retribution?" Gerard asks pointedly.

Van Eck nods slowly. "There are instances... whispers of vendettas taken up by those wronged or their kin."

Helena interjects with a question about specific family names – does their prominence today echo their ancestors' status?

"Some do," Van Eck confirms after consulting a tome that seems as old as Brugge. "But not all wealth or influence is easily seen."

We absorb this in silence – hidden power is the hardest to challenge.

"Professor," I interject suddenly, my voice hoarse with urgency. "Is there anything... anything at all that might tell us who is next?"

He looks at me then, and there's sorrow in those eyes – sorrow for me and for what Brugge has become.

"Willem," he says softly but firmly, "your family was not alone in suffering injustice at their hands." He shuffles through some papers before holding up one for us to see – it's another list of names but annotated with recent events: accidents that were perhaps not accidents, fortunes lost overnight...

A pattern emerges from these seemingly unrelated incidents – one that aligns with our list and sharpens its focus.

"We need more," Helena says resolutely after a moment's reflection. She's right; we need context – knowledge that can only come from those who have studied Brugge's shadows.

We need to contact more; each historian or genealogist adds pieces to our puzzle. Soon we find out that one speaks of secret meetings held under cover of darkness; another tells us about codes embedded in guild crests; yet another recounts how certain families vanished from records as if erased by an unseen hand.

I can't shake the feeling that something is off. The air around me feels heavy, charged with a tension that I can't quite put my finger on. It's as if the city itself is holding its breath, waiting for something to happen.

I've been following this case since the first murder, working closely with Inspector De Vries and Helena De Baere. We've pieced together clues like fragments of a shattered mirror, trying to make sense of a pattern that seems almost too perfect. But despite our best efforts, we've hit a dead end – or so it seems.

As I sit back at the police station the following evening, surrounded by maps and documents strewn across tables, I can't help but feel like we're missing something crucial. Something that could unlock the door to understanding this killer and put an end to their reign of terror.

Helena is deep in conversation with Gerard over by the window, their voices low but intense as they pore over evidence. They seem lost in their world, oblivious to the ticking clock and the looming shadow outside.

Suddenly, Helena looks up from her notes and gestures for me to come over. Her eyes are wide with excitement – she's made a breakthrough!

"Willem," she exclaims breathlessly, "I think I've found something!"

Her words send a jolt of adrenaline coursing through me. Could this be it? The key that will lead us to the killer and save another life?

She hands me a small bag filled with forensic samples – fibers from a piece of clothing found at one of the crime scenes, residue from a poisonous substance used in another... It's all evidence collected during our investigation but somehow overlooked until now.

"Take a look at these," she says urgently. "See if there are any connections between them."

I take the bag carefully, examining each item under the microscope as Helena watches anxiously by my side. My heart races as I search for patterns or clues that could lead us closer to our target – or even reveal who they are.

After what feels like hours of meticulous examination, I finally find what Helena has been looking for a strand of hair that matches one of our potential targets – De Groote. This isn't just any hair; it bears traces of an unusual dye used in ancient textile production techniques dating back centuries ago – techniques associated with certain guild families in Brugge.

The realization hits me like a thunderbolt – our mayor Elisabeth De Groote could be our next victim! We need to act fast if we want to prevent another murder and bring this madman to justice once and for all.

My heart pounds against my ribs as I race down the quiet streets of Brugge, the echoes of our footsteps shattering the stillness of the night. Gerard and Helena hurry alongside me, their faces etched with determination.

We have a name now – De Groote. A clue plucked from the tangled threads of evidence we've been sifting through, finally revealing the identity of our killer's next target.

There's no time to lose. Every second brings us closer to another life stolen, another chapter of history written in blood. The streets fly past in a blur as we sprint toward the mayor her estate on the outskirts of the city.

Up ahead, the sprawling manor house comes into view, its windows dark and shuttered. My lungs burn with exertion but I don't slow down. Gerard's face is fixed in a mask of concentration, while Helena's hair streams behind her like a banner leading our charge.

We approach cautiously, senses primed for any sign of danger. The grounds are cloaked in an eerie silence. My heart lurches as we spot a broken window at the rear of the house – forced entry.

I motion for Gerard and Helena to follow as I creep toward the jagged hole in the glass. Shards crunch under my boots, impossibly loud in the stillness. Somewhere inside, our killer stalks his prey.

We slip through the window, shards snagging at our clothes. I pause, listening, but hear only the rasp of our breathing. Cautiously, we make our way down a darkened corridor toward muffled sounds of movement. Gerard's hand hovers over his holster prepared to draw his weapon at the first sign of a threat.

The noises grow louder as we approach a closed door. I raise my fingers in a silent countdown – three, two, one… Gerard kicks the door open, gun raised.

"Police! Don't move!" he bellows into the room. A figure whirls around in surprise, hands clutching an antique vase. Elisabeth De Groote. Still alive.

I release a shaky breath. We've made it in time. But where is the killer? My eyes scan the room, searching shadowy corners as De Groote stammers questions.

Helena hurries over to check on the dazed man while Gerard clears the surrounding rooms. Nothing. There's no sign of our would-be murderer.

My shoulders slump as the adrenaline fades, replaced by a creeping sense of unease. Something isn't right. I turn in a slow circle, taking in details that jar against my instincts.

The broken window – too obvious. The vase in De Groote's hands – conveniently placed. The lack of any struggle or confrontation. Realization dawns on me like an icy tide.

"It's a set-up," I mutter.

Gerard's head snaps towards me, eyes narrowing. Before he can respond, a bone-chilling laugh echoes through the room. Helena gasps, grabbing Elisabeth's arm. I whirl around but see nothing except our shadows flickering across the walls.

The disembodied voice seems to come from everywhere and nowhere all at once. "Clever, Willem," it hisses mockingly. "But not clever enough."

I clench my fists, every muscle taut. Where is he? How does he know my name?

"Show yourself!" Gerard commands, gun raised towards the ceiling. Only eerie silence answers.

Helena meets my gaze, her face pale but resolute. "He wanted us to come here," she says softly. Of course – we played right into his hands.

A creak from above makes us all look up. A shadowy figure stands on the railing of the balcony overhead. Before we can react, he raises a strange device and pulls the trigger.

A projectile whizzes through the air straight towards me. I dive to the floor just as an explosion shatters the windows behind me. Ears ringing, I look up to see a gaping hole blown through the glass.

Helena rushes over, pulling me behind an upturned table. Gerard fires two shots at the balcony, but the figure is gone. The scene dissolves into chaos as we take cover from another projectile, dragging a dazed Van der Eecken with us.

"Are you hit?" Helena yells over the noise, quickly checking me for injuries. I shake my head, still in shock. Gerard is returning fire, trying to pin down our attacker.

"We need to move, now!" he orders. Nodding, I help Helena pull Elisabeth De Groote towards the door. We race from the room under a hail of debris as our assailant continues his relentless assault.

We burst out into moonlit grounds, sprinting for cover. Behind us, the manor house trembles as another explosion rips through its interior. We've escaped for now, but the killer has once again evaded our grasp.

My lungs burn and my ears still ring as we hurry De Groote to safety. But my mind is already churning, analyzing each element of the trap we've stumbled into. What game is our adversary playing? And how long until his next move?

A Tangled Web

In the cramped space of the Brugge police station, Inspector Gerard De Vries leans closer to the flickering screen, his eyes scanning the grainy images for a hint of truth amid shadows and silhouettes. Around him, officers murmur, their voices a low hum against the mechanical whir of the projector.

The night's cloak on the footage gives little away, but De Vries's keen gaze misses nothing. A figure moves across the screen, deliberate and unhurried—a ghostly imprint against the cobbled backdrop of the sleeping city. The timestamp in the corner ticks away, a silent witness to the nocturnal trespass.

"There," he points to a frame where light from a street lamp casts clarity on the intruder. "Can you enhance that section?"

A junior officer fiddles with controls, bringing the figure into sharper focus. It's a woman, her posture rigid with purpose. The tailored coat, unmistakable even in monochrome—the flair of its collar and cut—belong to one they all know too well.

Madame Blanchard.

A collective intake of breath sucks tension into the room. Her presence here, in this stolen moment caught on film, paints a stark picture—one that doesn't align with her usual facade of refinement.

Helena leans over De Vries's shoulder, squinting at Madame Blanchard's image on screen. "What would she be doing there at that hour?"

De Vries strokes his beard, mind racing with possibilities. "Madame Blanchard is no casual night stroller. Her being there... it's no coincidence."

An officer chimes in from behind them. "Perhaps she had an appointment with Rombouts?"

De Vries shakes his head slightly. "At this ungodly hour? No. She prefers her dealings in broad daylight, under chandeliers—not moonlight."

Helena taps a finger against her lips, thoughtful. "Maybe she wanted to see his latest works before anyone else?"

De Vries gives her a look that borders on admiration for her tenacity but shakes his head again. "No." His voice carries certainty like a blade. "Lucas Rombouts' paintings are darker than midnight; they'd give Madame nightmares for weeks."

Silence settles over them as they watch Madame Blanchard's figure disappear offscreen. The mystery of her presence wraps tighter around them, an enigma yet to yield its secrets.

"We need more than this," De Vries announces as he stands up straighter, stretching out the stiffness from leaning over too long. "We must question Madame Blanchard directly."

An officer hesitates before speaking up. "Sir, confronting someone of her stature without concrete evidence could backfire."

De Vries meets his gaze squarely. "We're not confronting; we're merely asking questions—out of concern for her safety, naturally."

Helena nods in agreement, catching onto his approach. "After all," she adds with a glint in her eye that matches De Vries's own shrewdness, "she might be a witness—or worse, another potential victim."

"Exactly." De Vries looks around at his team with resolve etching deep lines into his face. "Prepare for an interview with Madame Blanchard first thing tomorrow morning."

The team disperses to their respective tasks as De Vries turns back to Helena and lowers his voice just enough so only she can hear him.

"We tread carefully here; Madame has connections like spider webs—delicate but far-reaching."

Helena nods solemnly in understanding.

***

Morning light filters through the stained glass windows of Madame Blanchard's residence, casting a kaleidoscope of colors across the pristine floors. Inspector Gerard De Vries steps over the threshold, Helena De Baere at his side. The air smells faintly of oil paint and beeswax, a testament to the art that adorns every wall.

Madame Blanchard awaits them in the foyer, her attire as impeccable as her surroundings—a tailored dress that whispers of wealth and status. Yet, for all her poise, there's a tremor in her smile, a tightness around her eyes that wasn't there before.

"Inspector De Vries, Miss De Baere," she greets, voice like chimes in the still air. "To what do I owe this unexpected visit?"

De Vries offers a courteous nod. "Apologies for the intrusion, Madame. We're here on official business regarding recent events in our city."

Madame Blanchard leads them to the drawing room, where velvet drapes and plush furnishings speak of luxury few can afford. She seats herself gracefully on an ornate chaise lounge, arranging her dress with meticulous care.

"Please," she gestures to the chairs opposite her, "be seated."

They comply, and De Vries leans forward, elbows resting on his knees. He watches as Madame's hands begin their dance upon a silk scarf, twining and untwining with subconscious anxiety.

"Madame Blanchard," he begins, his tone deliberate and calm, "we have reason to believe you were near Lucas Rombouts' gallery on the night his exhibit was vandalized."

Her laughter rings out—a practiced melody meant to dismiss. "Surely you jest, Inspector. Why would I vandalize Mr. Rombouts' works? His art is quite... unique. It brings a certain flavor to Brugge's scene."

De Vries doesn't flinch at the deflection. "No one is accusing you of vandalism outright," he assures her. "But your presence at such an hour raises questions."

Madame's fingers pause their ballet on the fabric of her scarf—a flicker of doubt crossing her features before she masks it with a practiced smile.

"I often take late walks to clear my head," she explains. "The night has a beauty all its own."

Helena interjects softly but firmly. "It's an unusual time for a walk, especially alone."

The Madame's gaze sharpens on Helena but softens again as if remembering herself. "A woman in my position learns to appreciate solitude."

De Vries notes the careful choreography of her responses—the way she parries their queries with elegance befitting her station.

"We understand your appreciation for solitude," he says with gentle insistence. "However, we must consider all possibilities."

Madame Blanchard stands abruptly; her movements betraying a flash of irritation as she moves to pour herself a glass of water from a crystal decanter.

"I assure you, Inspector," she says over her shoulder, "my late-night strolls are nothing more than they appear."

Helena leans in slightly, watching Madame's reflection in a gilded mirror. "And yet they coincided with an act of malice against an artist whose works depict truths some would rather keep hidden."

The glass makes a soft clink as Madame sets it down too quickly on the tray—water sloshing over its brim.

"You imply much with little evidence," Madame Blanchard counters with forced composure as she retakes her seat.

De Vries remains silent for a moment—letting the tension hang between them like heavy drapes before speaking again.

"Madame Blanchard," he says softly but with an undercurrent of steel, "the night is indeed beautiful and mysterious—but it also veils deeds meant for darkness."

Her hands clutch at the scarf now—a lifeline against waves of scrutiny—her knuckles whitening with each twist.

"You paint me as some nocturnal creature skulking in alleys," she retorts sharply. "My life is devoted to art and beauty—not petty destruction."

De Vries leans back slightly; eyes never leaving Madame Blanchard's face—a face now etched with lines of stress no amount of finery can hide.

"Your devotion is well known," he acknowledges respectfully. "Yet devotion can lead us down unexpected paths."

Helena rises smoothly from her chair; her movements echo De Vries's earlier lean—poised yet assertive.

"Might there be anyone who can confirm your whereabouts that night?" she asks gently.

Madame Blanchard's eyes dart toward Helena then back to De Vries—an animal caught in the light yet too proud to scurry away.

"No," she admits after a beat too long—her voice finally betraying the strain. "I value my privacy."

De Vries observes Helena as she scrutinizes Madame Blanchard. Her eyes, sharp and probing, sweep the room, pausing at each piece of art with a scientist's precision. He's come to rely on her keen observational skills throughout the investigation. Her gaze lingers on a painting—a splash of color that stands out from the rest of Madame Blanchard's collection. It's a storm of emotion on canvas, dark and foreboding.

"That's a remarkable piece," Helena remarks casually, tilting her head. "It seems out of place among the rest."

Madame Blanchard follows her gaze, a flicker of discomfort crossing her features. "Oh, that? A trifle I acquired recently. A rather impulsive purchase."

De Vries steps closer to the painting, feeling the pieces of the puzzle click into place in his mind. The brushwork is unmistakable—raw, visceral, almost violent in its execution. It bears a striking resemblance to Lucas Rombouts' signature style—the very artist whose gallery had been vandalized.

"Indeed," he muses aloud, "it's quite reminiscent of Lucas Rombouts' work."

Madame Blanchard's fingers twitch against her scarf. "Is it now? I wouldn't know. I buy what pleases my eye."

Helena moves nearer to the painting, her fingers hovering just inches from the canvas as if she could touch the truth hidden within its layers of paint.

"But this piece," she continues with feigned nonchalance, "it has a particular... intensity that's quite characteristic of his recent series."

De Vries watches Madame Blanchard closely as Helena speaks. There's a tightening around her eyes—a mask slipping to reveal the first signs of panic.

"Lucas is an artist who evokes strong emotions," Madame Blanchard replies hastily. "Perhaps it's merely a coincidental resemblance."

Helena glances at De Vries, giving him a subtle nod—confirmation of her suspicions.

De Vries turns back to Madame Blanchard with deliberate slowness. "Madame, would you mind terribly if we took a closer look at this piece? It may hold relevance to our investigation."

Madame Blanchard stands abruptly, her composure crumbling like dry earth. "You have no right to—"

"Please understand," De Vries interjects with gentle firmness, "we seek only to clarify matters."

The room grows tense as they wait for her response. Madame Blanchard seems to wrestle with an internal struggle before finally gesturing toward the painting with resignation.

"Very well," she concedes with bitterness creeping into her voice. "Do what you must."

Helena steps forward and examines the painting meticulously. Her eyes trace over every detail—each brushstroke and hue scrutinized under her discerning gaze.

"It's not just similar," she concludes after a moment, turning to face them both. "It's one of his—of Lucas's paintings from his 'Whispers in Water' series—one that was reported defaced."

Madame Blanchard sinks back onto the chaise lounge as if her legs can no longer bear her weight. Her hands clutch at her scarf—a lifeline frayed by too many tugs and pulls.

"I... I don't understand how it came into my possession," she stammers, but the words lack conviction—a rehearsed script gone awry.

De Vries takes a measured breath before speaking. His voice is soft but carries an undercurrent that brooks no evasion.

"Madame Blanchard," he says firmly, "it's time for honesty."

She looks up at him then—at Helena—and there's something raw and unguarded in her eyes now—something akin to fear or perhaps desperation.

"I did it," she whispers finally—a confession pulled from deep within.

De Vries steps closer as she continues, words spilling forth like water breaching a dam.

"I was jealous," Madame Blanchard admits, tears brimming in her eyes but not yet falling. "Lucas's work began to overshadow mine—to overshadow everything I built here."

Helena listens intently as Madame Blanchard unravels before them—the polished exterior giving way to reveal the turmoil beneath.

"He was becoming the talk of Brugge," Madame continues with a bitter laugh that holds no humor—only pain and regret. "His name was on everyone's lips at every salon and gathering."

De Vries nods slowly; he understands all too well how envy can poison reason—how it can lead one down paths they never thought they'd tread.

"I couldn't stand it—the thought of him rising while I... while I became nothing more than an afterthought." Her voice cracks—a dam breaking under pressure.

"So you vandalized his gallery?" Helena asks gently but firmly—an inquiry rather than an accusation.

As Madame Blanchard's confession continues, Inspector De Vries takes note of every detail she reveals. Her jealousy towards Lucas Rombouts and her subsequent actions to discredit him is clear, but there's more to this story.

"Madame Blanchard," he says calmly, "you mentioned a shadowy figure connected to the guild. Can you tell me more about this person?"

She hesitates before responding, her eyes darting nervously around the room. "It's... it's someone who wants to maintain control over Brugge's artistic scene," she finally admits. "They believe that by discrediting artists like Lucas, they can preserve their power."

De Vries nods thoughtfully. The guild has been known for centuries, but he's never heard whispers of such extreme measures being taken to maintain influence. He knows he needs to delve deeper into this aspect of the case.

"Can you describe this person?" he asks again, his voice steady and professional.

Madame Blanchard looks down at her hands—the same hands that held a paintbrush so skillfully just moments ago—and shakes her head. "I don't know much," she confesses. "Only that they have connections within the guild and beyond."

De Vries leans forward slightly—he can sense the fear in her voice, but he also sees an opportunity to uncover more information about the mysterious figure and their motives. He knows that time is of the essence; he must tread carefully so as not to alert the figure or anyone else involved in this conspiracy.

"Madame Blanchard," he says gently yet firmly, "I need you to remember everything you know about this person—every detail, no matter how small or insignificant it may seem." He pauses for a moment before continuing, "And if you can recall anything else—any conversation or encounter with them—please share it with me."

She nods slowly, tears glistening in her eyes as she realizes the gravity of her situation. De Vries gives her a reassuring smile before turning his attention back towards Helena De Baere and Lucas Rombouts. The room seems to grow colder as they continue their interrogation of Madame Blanchard—the air is thick with tension and uncertainty.

Inspector Gerard De Vries studies Madame Blanchard as she wrings her hands, a mannerism so at odds with her usual composed self. The once-immaculate silk scarf she twists in her fingers has creased beyond recognition. He can see the toll of her confession etching lines of worry on her forehead, her lips a thin line of reluctance.

"Madame Blanchard," he urges softly, hoping to coax out the information lodged in the crevices of her fear. "Any detail could be crucial. Think back. What did you hear about the guild's plans?"

She draws a shuddering breath, eyes flitting to the corners of the room as if expecting shadows to spring to life. "It was during an exhibition," she starts, voice barely above a whisper. "A private showing for Brugge's elite... There were whispers—"

"Whispers?" De Vries prompts, leaning in.

"Yes," she nods, seeming to gather the shards of her shattered poise. "Conversations drenched in wine and shadowed by art. They spoke of reclaiming Brugge's cultural throne, of purging the unworthy."

De Vries feels a chill that has nothing to do with the draft seeping through the antique windows. "Purging? Are we speaking metaphorically or—"

"I don't know!" she cuts in, a hint of the old steel returning to her voice. "But it was clear they would go to great lengths to maintain their vision for Brugge."

"And this contact of yours," he probes further, "the one who wanted Lucas's reputation tarnished—did they give any indication they were part of these plans?"

Madame Blanchard hesitates, then nods almost imperceptibly. "I believe so. They moved with confidence as if backed by a powerful force."

De Vries straightens up, feeling the weight of responsibility settle on his shoulders like an old, familiar coat. He needs to protect this woman, despite her misdeeds; she's become an unwitting player in a game that predates them all.

He turns to Helena, who's been quietly observing their exchange. "Miss De Baere, please make arrangements for Madame Blanchard's protection immediately."

Helena nods and steps away to confer with officers waiting outside the drawing-room door.

Returning his attention to Madame Blanchard, De Vries reassures her with calm authority. "You're safe now. We'll have officers stationed discreetly nearby at all times."

Madame Blanchard's shoulders drop slightly—a release of tension she's been holding since they arrived. "Thank you," she murmurs.

"But remember," De Vries continues with gentle sternness, "you must stay within reach and inform us immediately if you recall anything else or if anyone contacts you regarding these matters."

"I understand," she says, lifting her chin in a semblance of her former resolve.

***

The following day, In the study, walls lined with canvases whisper secrets of a bygone era. De Vries stands, a sentinel amidst the masterpieces, his sharp gaze dissecting each piece as if it might spring to life and confess its creator's sins. Madame Blanchard sits across from him, a portrait of distress framed by her lavish trappings. Helena paces like a caged intellect, her mind racing through the implications of their discoveries.

De Vries turns over Madame Blanchard's words in his mind, letting them settle like sediment in still water. The guild—once guardians of Brugge's cultural sanctity—now casts a shadow far more menacing than any ordinary criminal syndicate.

"Madame Blanchard," he says, voice resonating with the gravity of their situation, "you've told us much about the guild's influence in the art world. But what of the city itself? The people?"

She clasps her hands tightly, knuckles whitening as if grasping the edge of a precipice. "Inspector," she begins, her voice a tremulous note amidst the silent audience of oil and canvas, "the guild does not limit itself to artists and galleries. Its tendrils wind through Brugge like roots through the soil."

Helena stops pacing and turns to face them both, her eyes alight with an understanding that sends a shiver down De Vries's spine. "The drownings," she murmurs. "Could they be part of this 'purging' you mentioned?"

De Vries considers this, the pieces of an ominous puzzle clicking into place with an almost audible finality. The murders had struck at the heart of Brugge, seeding fear and suspicion among its people.

Madame Blanchard nods slowly, eyes haunted by the realization that her vendetta against Rombouts may have dovetailed with a much darker scheme. "It's possible," she concedes. "The guild is obsessed with preserving what they deem to be the city's purity."

"And yet," De Vries muses aloud, turning to glance at an opulent landscape painting that seems to mock them with its serene beauty, "they are willing to stain their hands with blood."

The irony is not lost on Helena as she interjects, "Their vision of purity is tainted by their actions."

De Vries nods in agreement. The contradiction gnaws at him—a dissonance that clashes with his every belief in justice and order.

He approaches Madame Blanchard once more, leaning in so that only she can hear him over Helena's quiet mutterings as she deciphers notes from her father's apothecary journals.

"Madame," he says firmly yet not unkindly, "the guild may have influenced your actions against Lucas Rombouts, but I need to know if they directed them."

She recoils slightly from the intensity of his gaze but holds his stare. "No," she asserts after a fraught pause. "My actions were my own—born from personal spite and professional jealousy."

De Vries nods again—her admission aligning with his sense of her character: proud and ambitious to a fault but not a puppet dancing on the guild's strings.

Turning away from Madame Blanchard, De Vries steps closer to Helena. He keeps his voice low as he shares his thoughts.

"Helena," he says contemplatively, "we must consider every angle—the political climate of Brugge, its financial institutions... everything could be woven into this tapestry of corruption."

Helena meets his gaze squarely—a reflection of his determination mirrored in her eyes. "We will unravel this tapestry thread by thread if we must," she promises.

Their attention is pulled back to Madame Blanchard as she rises abruptly from her seat—a caged bird desperate for flight yet aware there is nowhere safe to land.

"Inspector De Vries," she pleads, desperation seeping into her tone despite her efforts at composure. "I've told you all I know."

He nods once more—a silent pact forged between them that no further secrets will remain buried within these walls.

"Stay vigilant," he advises before turning to leave. "We will be in touch should we require anything further."

Madame Blanchard sinks back into her chair—a wilted flower amid a garden of grandeur—as De Vries and Helena make their way out of the study.

In the hallway outside, De Vries pauses beside Helena; both are acutely aware that they stand on precarious ground.

"The guild's reach extends further than we imagined," he says gravely as they walk through corridors lined with centuries-old grandeur. "They have infiltrated not just the art scene but Brugge itself—its very lifeblood."

Helena nods somberly—the weight of their task etched upon her features like fine lines on parchment.

"We're facing an adversary deeply embedded within our city's fabric," De Vries continues as they step out into the daylight—a stark contrast to the dim opulence they leave behind.

"The canal murders..." Helena trails off; then adds resolutely: "They could be just one part of a larger scheme—one rooted in history and hunger for power."

De Vries agrees silently; thoughts swirling like dark waters beneath Brugge's tranquil canals.

A Crushing Setback

The cobbled streets beneath my boots carry centuries of secrets. Tonight, we're about to coax one more into the dim glow of the gas lamps. Inspector De Vries, Helena, and I stand huddled in an alleyway, the cold seeping through our coats. The inspector's eyes are sharp, cutting through the darkness as he secures a tiny device onto Helena's cloak.

"This will keep you within our sights," he murmurs. His voice is steady, but there's an edge to it—a blade hidden beneath velvet.

Helena nods, her face a mask of determination, but I catch the quick dart of her eyes toward me. There's fear there, no matter how brave she's trying to be. She's about to walk into the lion's den, and she knows it.

We split up then, as planned. Inspector De Vries melts into the shadows across the canal, a figure in a dark coat dissolving into the night. I take my position on a higher vantage point—a secluded balcony overlooking Helena's path. From here, I can see everything without being seen, a ghost haunting my own city.

Below me, Helena steps out from the alley and onto the street. She walks with purpose but not haste—a perfect imitation of confidence that's meant to be alluring prey for our unseen hunter.

I've never felt so torn. Part of me is on that balcony, silent and watchful; another part strides beside Helena on the street below. My fingers twitch at my side, ready to leap into action should anything go wrong.

I peer through the gloom and spot Inspector De Vries on the opposite side. Even from this distance, I recognize his posture—the rigid set of his shoulders as he observes Helena through a pair of compact binoculars.

The plan is simple: follow Helena discreetly until our quarry shows themselves. Then swoop in and end this nightmare that's been choking Brugge for too long.

The night is quiet—too quiet—with only the occasional clop of horse hooves or distant murmur of conversation to break the silence. A mist creeps over the canals like spilled milk, softening edges and swallowing sounds.

I scan every shadow, every doorway. My eyes are drawn to movement—a cat slinking along a wall; a late traveler hurrying home; nothing out of place.

Helena rounds a corner and my breath catches. For a moment she disappears from view and I'm left staring at empty space where she should be. Panic flares up like a struck match before she reappears further down the street, still unhurried, still alone.

The tracking device—no bigger than a coin sewn discreetly into her cloak—sends back signals to a contraption in De Vries's possession. A marvel of modern ingenuity that feels like witchcraft itself to me.

My fingers brush over my jacket where I've hidden my own piece of ingenuity—a small whistle designed to mimic the call of a nightjar. It's our signal if things turn sour; one sharp note to cut through silence and bring De Vries crashing through from his hiding place.

Minutes drag on like hours as Helena continues her performance, playing her role with an actress's grace but none of their insincerity. Each step she takes is measured and deliberate—each one drawing her further into danger for all we know.

I watch her pass beneath lanterns that paint her in light and shadow by turns until she looks like she's walking between worlds—one foot in safety, one in peril.

A shape detaches itself from an alcove some distance behind her—a man stepping out onto the street. My heart leaps into my throat as I grip the railing before me with white-knuckled intensity.

He follows at a discreet distance—too discreet for someone simply heading home or off to meet friends at this late hour.

My eyes flicker across rooftops toward De Vries's position—I can't see him now but I know he's there—and back down to Helena who remains blissfully unaware of her follower.

She's approaching an intersection where four streets meet—a crossroads that offers too many choices for an escape route if need be. The man behind her is closing in; deliberate now as if he's made up his mind about something.

I lift the whistle to my lips ready to blow it if he makes another step towards her—

But then he pauses; looks around suspiciously as if sensing something amiss in this game of cat-and-mouse we've laid out for him; something that tells him this prey might not be as vulnerable as she appears.

He steps back into shadow and vanishes as quickly as he appeared leaving nothing but disturbed air where he once stood.

Helena continues forward oblivious still playing her part even though our would-be attacker has withdrawn—for now at least.

My heart slowly climbs down from its perch in my throat allowing me to breathe again though not deeply—not yet.

I watch from my perch as Helena's lone figure traverses the cobbled streets, a beacon of bait in the sinister game we're playing. She's been walking for what seems like an eternity when a chill that has nothing to do with the night air runs down my spine. From the shadows, they come—cloaked figures, silent and swift, converging on her like dark waves crashing against a solitary rock.

My heart hammers against my ribs, a trapped bird desperate to escape. This isn't part of the plan. Inspector De Vries and I never anticipated this; we expected a lone predator, not a pack. The inspector is out there, somewhere in the dark, but these figures have materialized so suddenly that even he seems caught unawares.

There's no time to think. My hand clenches around the whistle, ready to sound the alarm, but I hesitate. Will it only hasten her peril?

Helena stops in her tracks as the figures form a circle around her. Even from this distance, I see her posture straighten—a doe bracing for hounds. There's no fear in her stance; she's calm, almost eerily so.

She speaks then, her voice carrying across the silence of the night. "Good evening," she says with a clarity that belies our precarious situation. "Perhaps you could help me? I seem to have lost my way."

The figures don't respond. They inch closer, an oppressive ring of malice. Yet Helena doesn't flinch; she stands resolute as if rooted to the very stones beneath her feet.

"What is it you want?" Her question hangs in the air unanswered, as if words are foreign to these specters encircling her.

I need to act—now—but what can I do against such numbers? My mind races as fast as my pulse, scrambling for a plan that doesn't end with Helena enveloped by this midnight shroud.

Her head turns slightly, and though I can't see her eyes from here, I know she's searching for De Vries or me—some sign that we're still here with her.

I take a quiet breath and ready myself to descend into the fray when something remarkable happens. Helena begins to walk slowly in place, turning on the spot as though inspecting an invisible gallery of curiosities around her.

"It's such a beautiful night," she muses aloud. "The stars above Brugge always seem to shine with an extra glimmer."

The cloaked figures pause their advance. They're puzzled—perhaps even unnerved—by her lack of panic.

"Wouldn't you agree?" Helena prompts again after a moment of uneasy silence from her would-be assailants.

Her tactic is clear now—she's trying to humanize herself before them, become more than just prey. But they're statues carved from night itself; they give nothing away.

Still, there's something in their stillness now—a hesitation that wasn't there before. It's working; she's buying us time.

I mustn't waste it.

With careful movements that make no sound, I start making my way down from my vantage point, keeping close to the walls where shadows are thickest.

Below me, Helena continues her strange waltz within the circle of cloaked figures who seem unsure how to react to this unexpected performance.

"Do you not find peace in such moments?" she asks them again with gentle insistence. "A pause from whatever drives you?"

A shiver courses through me—not from cold but anticipation and fear mingled together into a bitter cocktail that threatens to choke me. What drives them indeed?

One of the figures steps forward slightly—a leader or simply more curious than his companions—and it feels like we've been granted a small victory within this tense standoff.

But then something changes—a shift in their demeanor that tells me our time is running out.

Helena senses it too; I see it in the subtle tightening of her shoulders—the way she draws herself up even taller as if making herself ready for whatever comes next.

It's now or never.

I reach ground level just as Inspector De Vries emerges from his own hiding place across the canal like a phantom called forth by urgency alone.

Inspector De Vries is already on the move, a ghostly figure darting from one pool of darkness to another. We're both drawn to Helena, moths to a flame that we fear might be snuffed out at any moment.

Helena's voice cuts through the tension once more, clear and unwavering. "It's said that every star is a story," she tells them, her words painting pictures in the void. "Perhaps you have stories too?"

One of the figures steps closer. I can't make out his face beneath the hood, but there's a menace to his gait that sets my heart pounding harder.

I'm close now, so close I can almost reach out and snatch Helena away from them.

But then they act.

With sudden ferocity, they surge forward. The leader's hand flashes out, seizing Helena by the arm. She lets out a gasp—not of fear, but surprise—as if she can't quite believe they've shattered her calm facade so easily.

"Helena!" My voice is a hoarse whisper lost in the rush of my own blood.

De Vries and I surge forward in unison, driven by the same impulse to protect, to save. But our path is suddenly blocked by more figures emerging from the mist like specters conjured by an evil will.

They're between us and Helena now, an impenetrable wall of malice. We've been outmaneuvered—lured into a trap not just for Helena but for us all.

"Go!" De Vries barks at me across the distance that separates us. His eyes are aflame with urgency as he grapples with one assailant who dared to come too close.

I don't hesitate. Ducking low, I charge at the barrier before me with all the force of a tempest unleashed. They're ready for me though; they meet my onslaught with a cold precision that belies their numbers.

I feel hands like iron clamps grip my arms, pulling me back even as I strain forward with every ounce of strength left in me. A blow catches me off guard and pain explodes in my side—but it's nothing compared to the agony of watching Helena being dragged away into an alley as narrow as a slit throat.

De Vries fights like a man possessed, his every move honed by years on streets far crueler than these. But even he can't break through alone; we're outnumbered and outflanked.

I twist and turn, fighting against the hands that bind me, but it's like struggling against chains forged from night itself—they give no quarter.

"Helena!" I call again, louder this time, but there's no answer save for the mocking echo off ancient bricks.

They're moving fast now—the figures dragging Helena away as if she weighs nothing at all. Her feet stumble over cobblestones slick with mist; her head turns back towards us just once before she disappears around a corner.

That look—it sears itself into my memory like a brand: her eyes wide not with fear but pleading for us to follow, to find her.

We will—I swear it on every star above us—we will find her.

But first we must break free.

With renewed fury I lash out at my captors, catching one off-guard enough to loosen his grip on me for just an instant. It's all I need—I wrench free and dive forward towards where Helena vanished.

De Vries is beside me again somehow; together we're an unstoppable force cutting through resistance as if it were nothing but air. We reach the alley entrance just in time to see the last flicker of Helena's cloak vanish into darkness beyond.

We give chase without thought for our own safety—for there's no room for caution when desperation takes hold.

The alley twists and turns like a serpent coiling upon itself; shadows leap at us from doorways that might hide friend or foe—we can't tell which anymore.

We push ourselves harder than we've ever done before—muscles screaming protest and lungs burning for air that seems too thick to draw in properly here amongst these narrow confines where light fears to tread.

But it doesn't matter—nothing does except finding Helena before these devils do whatever it is they have planned for her.

Our footsteps echo hollowly on stone—too loud in this silence that feels like it's waiting for something terrible to be born from within its depths.

Ahead there's another turn—a sharp right—and as we take it we come face-to-face with emptiness; an empty street that might have never known Helena's presence at all had we not seen her taken down this very path not moments ago.

They're gone—all of them—as if swallowed by Brugge itself into secrets held tight since medieval times when darkness was a thing alive and breathing just beyond men's firesides.

I lean against a wall trying to catch breaths that come too fast and ragged while De Vries paces back and forth like a caged animal searching for any sign any clue that might tell us where they've taken her.

I stand amidst the chaos of an ambush that has already faded into the night, feeling like a phantom in my own city. The inspector's men swarm the site, their lanterns casting an uneasy glow on cobbled stones that refuse to give up their secrets. De Vries is a storm of motion and orders, his silhouette sharp against the flickering light.

"We comb every inch!" he commands, his voice slicing through the murk. "Sewers, alleys, every damned nook! She's here—she has to be."

I move through the aftermath, my gaze searching for something overlooked, a clue forsaken in haste. But there is nothing—only the silence that mocks us with its emptiness.

De Vries catches my eye and motions me over. His face is a mask of resolve chiseled from years of chasing shadows just like these. "They won't get far," he assures me, though I see the edge of doubt gnawing at him.

I nod, grasping at the certainty in his words like a lifeline. We move together to where his men huddle around the device meant to lead us to Helena.

One of them, a young officer with eyes too wide for his face, holds it out to De Vries. "It's still transmitting," he reports, his voice betraying his disbelief.

"Then we go now," De Vries states flatly, as if it were as simple as stepping into daylight. But this is Brugge at night—a labyrinth cloaked in shadow and deceit.

We set off at a pace that borders on reckless. The inspector leads with the device in hand, its faint beeping a heartbeat in the dark. I follow close behind, my own heart thundering with a cocktail of fear and fury.

The streets are a blur as we pass; each twist and turn draws us deeper into Brugge's embrace. We are hunters—predators driven by desperation—but it's Helena who's caught in the snare.

De Vries checks the device constantly, swearing under his breath each time it leads us down another empty street or barren alleyway. He's a man possessed by the need to make things right—to undo this one dark thread in an otherwise meticulous tapestry of justice.

Our chase leads us beyond familiar paths into parts of Brugge that feel untouched by time. Buildings loom like silent judges; canals whisper secrets just beneath their calm surfaces.

Then suddenly, as we round a corner where ivy clings to old stone like memories too stubborn to fade, the device falters.

De Vries stops so abruptly I nearly crash into him. He taps the contraption with a growing urgency until finally it falls silent—no more beeps to guide us through the night.

He curses—a rare crack in his composed facade—and shakes the device as if willing it back to life by sheer force of will.

But there's nothing—just silence where once there was hope.

The inspector looks up at me, and I see it—the same helplessness that's been gnawing at my insides since Helena was taken. It's an unfamiliar look on him—one that doesn't belong on a man who's made a career out of certainty.

"They knew," he says softly—more to himself than to me—"They knew we'd track her."

We stand there for a moment suspended in time—two men lost without our lifeline in a city that feels like it's closing in around us.

But De Vries isn't one to linger in doubt for long. He snaps into action once more, eyes scanning our surroundings as if seeing them for the first time.

"We keep moving," he decides with renewed determination. "They can't have gotten far—not on foot."

So we press on without our beacon, each step an act of faith in darkness that offers none in return.

The streets here are narrower—more intimate—as if sharing their confidences only grudgingly with those who dare wander them at this ungodly hour.

We split up then—De Vries heading down one path while I take another—our paths diverging and converging like threads weaving through Brugge's fabric.

Each shadow I pass could conceal friend or foe—I no longer trust my own instincts which seem dulled by panic and dread.

Every sound sets me on edge—a distant laugh that could be mocking or merry; the scuttle of rats that might be something else entirely; even my own footsteps seem too loud betraying my presence to anyone who might be listening.

I find myself calling her name into empty spaces knowing full well she won't answer but unable to stop myself all the same. "Helena!" It echoes off walls that have stood silent for centuries absorbing countless cries just like mine but offering no comfort or solace in return.

I meet back up with De Vries at an intersection where four streets meet like old friends sharing secrets over drinks long past due. His face is drawn tight with frustration—a map of roads not taken; clues missed; time lost irretrievably into night's gaping maw.

"We'll find her," I say though I'm not sure which one of us I'm trying to convince more. It feels important though—to speak it aloud—to make it real somehow amidst all this uncertainty and fear.

Helena's Resolve

Helena woke with a start, her head throbbing. As her eyes adjusted to the dim lighting, she realized she was in an unfamiliar place. She tried to move but found her arms and legs tightly bound to a chair. Panic rose in her chest as she took in her surroundings - she was in a large, empty warehouse, with dusty wooden crates stacked along the walls.

A single light bulb swung from the ceiling, casting ominous shadows across the concrete floor. How did she get here? Her mind raced to remember. The last thing she recalled was being ambushed. Rough hands grabbed her, a cloth pressed to her face, and then darkness.

Helena tested her restraints, but they held fast. She spotted a rusted nail protruding from the arm of the chair and carefully maneuvered her wrist to rub against it. The metal was rough but sharp. As she sawed slowly back and forth, the rope fibers started to fray and snap.

Finally, her left hand came free. She quickly untied her other limbs and stood up on shaky legs, peering into the gloom. There was no sign of her captors. She had to get out of here before they returned.

Keeping to the shadows, Helena crept to a nearby stack of crates and crouched down, listening intently. Somewhere, a door creaked on its hinges, and muffled voices echoed through the warehouse. Steeling her nerves, she tiptoed in the opposite direction, towards the back of the building.

There, behind a tower of old machinery parts, she spotted a small window near the ceiling. If she could reach it, it might offer a way out. Glancing around, Helena dragged a crate beneath the window and clambered up. With trembling fingers, she unlatched the window and slid it open.

The cool night air washed over her face as she hoisted herself up and through the narrow opening. She emerged into a dark alley, the silhouette of a church spire visible down the street. This was the outskirts of Brugge. Keeping to the shadows, Helena hurried away from the warehouse, wary of any sounds of pursuit.

Each time she emerged from an alley, Helena scanned her surroundings, alert for any threat. But the city remained still and silent as the grave.

***

A sudden knock at the door jolts me from my thoughts. I glance around the small, dimly lit cottage, my heart pounding in my chest. Visitors are rare, and unexpected ones even more so.

I approach the door cautiously, my hand resting on the worn wooden handle. The knock comes again, more insistent this time. I take a deep breath and pull the door open.

Helena stands before me, her clothes disheveled and a bruise darkening her cheek. Relief washes over me, quickly followed by shock at her appearance.

"Helena!" I exclaim, reaching out to steady her. She winces as my hand brushes her arm, and I quickly pull back. "Are you alright?"

She nods, her eyes meeting mine with a determination that belies her battered state. "I'm fine, Willem. I managed to escape."

I usher her inside, closing the door behind us. The cottage feels smaller with her presence, the air thick with unspoken questions and fears. She sinks into the worn chair by the fireplace, her hands trembling slightly.

"Tell me everything," I say, crouching down beside her.

Helena takes a deep breath, her gaze fixed on the flickering flames. "They took me to a warehouse... I don't know where."

Her voice wavers, but she continues, recounting her capture and daring escape. I listen in silence, my mind racing with questions and concerns. When she finishes, I lean back, absorbing the gravity of her words.

"You're lucky to be alive," I murmur, my voice barely above a whisper.

She nods, a wry smile tugging at her lips. "I had some help from a rusty nail and my apothecary skills."

Despite the circumstances, I can't help but smile at her resilience.

Guilt gnaws at me as I watch Helena, the bruises on her skin a stark testament to the danger she's faced – all because of me. She's here, in this rundown fisherman's hut, her elegance out of place among the nets and hooks, because she chose to help clear my tarnished name. I owe her my life, yet I've repaid her with peril.

"I'm sorry," I say, the words heavy with the weight of my regret. "You shouldn't be caught up in this mess. It's my battle to fight, not yours."

Helena looks up at me, her eyes steady and resolute. "Willem," she begins, her voice firm despite the fatigue etching her features, "this is bigger than just you or me. It's about justice, about shining a light on the truth that has been shrouded in darkness for far too long."

I shake my head, feeling the pull of despair. "Maybe it's time for me to leave Brugge. Start anew somewhere else where my past doesn't haunt me, where it doesn't put others in danger."

"Do you think really think that leaving everything behind will change anything?" she challenges softly. "The shadows will only stretch further if you run from them. We have a chance to make things right – not just for your family but for all those who have suffered under the weight of these secrets."

I sigh, my gaze drifting to the window where Brugge lies beyond, silent and watchful like a sentinel of my fate. The city has always been my home, yet now it feels like a prison.

"Every step I take seems to draw more innocent people into harm's way," I confess, the admission burning in my throat.

Helena rises from her chair and moves closer to me. "Willem," she says, placing a hand on my shoulder with surprising strength. "I chose this path freely. The moment I saw the fear and injustice clouding our city, I knew I couldn't stand idly by."

Her touch steadies me, and I find myself drawn into her resolve.

"We are on the brink of exposing something vile that has festered in Brugge for centuries," Helena continues. "If we abandon our quest now, we let fear win. We allow history to repeat itself – and what kind of life would that be?"

I look into Helena's eyes and see not just compassion but a fire that refuses to be quenched by the darkness we're facing.

"You've been alone in this fight for too long," she says gently but with an iron edge that tells me she won't be swayed. "But you're not alone anymore. We stand together – against ignorance, against fear."

Her words stir something within me – a flicker of hope amidst the storm of doubt.

"I can't promise we'll come out unscathed," Helena admits with an earnestness that pierces straight through to my soul. "But imagine a Brugge free from whispers and shadows; imagine being able to walk through these streets without your head bowed under the weight of false accusations."

The image takes root in my mind – a life unmarred by stigma; it's a life worth fighting for.

"And what if we fail?" The question escapes me before I can hold it back.

"Then we fail knowing we did everything in our power to confront what many wouldn't even dare acknowledge." Her voice doesn't waver; it's infused with strength born from facing adversity head-on.

I nod slowly, absorbing her conviction. Her belief in our cause – in me – anchors me back to purpose when I'm adrift in a sea of guilt.

I am immersed in the stillness of the moment, my eyes fixated on the dancing embers of the fire. As Helena's voice resonates in the air, her face is bathed in the warm glow, casting ever-changing shadows. Her every word slices through the fog of uncertainty in my mind, each one bearing the weight of undeniable truth. For so long, I've carried the burden of my family's dark history and the persistent rumors of witchcraft. The thought of breaking free from it all seemed like a distant, unattainable fantasy. But here stands Helena De Baere, bearing the physical marks of her own struggles, embodying the very essence of bravery.

Her determination ignited something within me, a spark that I thought had been extinguished by years of solitude and suspicion. It's a strange sensation, unfamiliar but invigorating. For so long, I've been adrift in a sea of fear and resignation. But Helena's resolve serves as a beacon, guiding me back to the shores of purpose.

I take a deep breath, letting her conviction fill my lungs like fresh air after being submerged for too long. "Alright," I say finally, my voice steadier than I expected. "You convinced me we should continue."

Helena's eyes light up with fierce joy. "I knew you wouldn't give up," she says.

We move to the old wooden table in the center of my cottage – a place where I've cleaned countless fish but never plotted the course of justice. It's strewn with maps of Brugge and scattered notes; evidence of our quest to untangle the web of deceit spun through our city's streets.

I lay out the maps before us, tracing the canals with my finger. "The murders all happened here," I point out, "along these waterways."

Helena leans over the table, her hair falling over her shoulder as she studies the map closely. "There must be a pattern we're missing," she muses.

I nod in agreement. "We need to revisit the scenes. There could be something we overlooked – a clue left behind."

"We also need more information on the guilds," Helena adds, tapping a finger on a list of names we've compiled – descendants of those ancient brotherhoods that once ruled Brugge from the shadows.

I glance at her list and then back at the map. "Perhaps there are properties or businesses that have been passed down through these families."

Helena pulls a ledger towards us – a record of local trades and addresses that we've been using to track our suspects' movements. She flips through it rapidly, her fingers pausing on certain pages as if feeling for secrets hidden between the lines.

"And Lucas Rombouts," I remind her. "His paintings... they might not just be art; they could be messages or warnings."

Her eyes meet mine, and there's an unspoken understanding between us – that art often speaks where words cannot.

We work in tandem now, piecing together fragments into a coherent picture. We discuss every detail we know about each victim: their lives, their families, and their connections to Brugge's history.

The night deepens around us as we delve into theories and scenarios, our conversation punctuated by moments of silence as we ponder deeper implications. The cottage is quiet except for our voices and the crackling fire – an island of light in a sea shrouded by darkness.

A Dark Revelation

Inspector Gerard De Vries leaned back in his creaky wooden chair, letting out a deep sigh as he surveyed the mess of papers and books spread out on the desk before him. After hours spent poring over dusty guild records in the basement archives of the Brugge police station, his eyes ached from squinting at the faded, cramped handwriting. But finally, buried among reams of tedious transactions and meeting minutes, he had found it—a crucial connection that breathed new life into the stalled investigation.

The discovery had come just as frustration threatened to overwhelm him. For days, De Vries had painstakingly combed through the archives, hoping to uncover some link between Brugge's medieval guilds and the recent canal murders. But each promising lead had fizzled out, leaving him grasping at shadows. Until now.

Stretching his stiff limbs, De Vries picked up the yellowed parchment that had cracked open the case. It was an official guild tribunal record from the late 1600s, detailing the charges brought against a Brugge family called the Deroo—allegations of embezzlement and fraud that led to public disgrace and financial ruin. As De Vries cross-referenced other records, a chilling picture emerged.

The Deroo family's downfall bore all the hallmarks of the guilds' notorious ruthlessness in dealing with those who defied their authority. Whispers and rumor-mongering destroyed the family's standing. Their assets were seized, and their reputations shattered beyond repair. The Deroo name all but vanished from Brugge's records after the trial, the broken family forced to flee the city under cover of darkness.

Until now, De Vries mused, turning the parchment over in his hands. According to the police census, a Deroo family still lived in Brugge—direct descendants of the disgraced ancestors, quietly persisting through the centuries. De Vries grabbed another book, rapidly flipping through the pages until he found the entry. There it was: Denis Deroo, his wife, Marguerite, and their teenage son, Luc. An ordinary family, on the surface. But perhaps the lingering echoes of the past had caught up with them.

De Vries felt the thrill of a break in the case, but uncertainty tempered his excitement. Much was still unclear, the gaps in the story yawning before him like Brugge's shadowy canals. Had the Deroo family's presence provoked the canal murders—an act of long-delayed retribution by someone connected to the medieval guild? Or were the DuBois themselves involved, orchestrating violence out of a desire for revenge against the descendants of their persecutors?

Either possibility pointed to the murders' roots in the distant past, confirming De Vries' suspicions. But speculation would not suffice. He needed evidence, facts, something concrete to move the investigation forward. The Deroo connection was promising yet fragile, just the first loose thread in a tangle of secrets centuries old.

Glancing at his watch, De Vries grimaced. It was already past midnight, and exhaustion clouded his thoughts. The archives' musty stillness suddenly felt oppressive, heightening his longing for fresh air and activity. He would revisit the problem in the clear light of morning when revived energy would help him sift through the questions.

***

Helena leaned over the desk in her makeshift laboratory, peering intently through a microscope. Arrayed before her on the worn wooden surface were various glass vials, pipettes, and reagents - the tools of her scientific trade. A single oil lamp provided dim illumination in the cramped room. This was her private sanctuary, where she pursued her amateur forensic inquiries away from the bustle of the apothecary.

Tonight, her focus was the DNA sample retrieved from the latest canal murder. Inspector De Vries had managed to secure a few traces of biological material caught on a jagged rock near the water's edge. Though crude by modern standards, Helena's equipment and knowledge allowed her to extract and amplify the precious DNA fragments.

For hours she had been poring over the sampled sequences, scrutinizing each nucleotide base pair, looking for any clues that might identify the killer. Suddenly she paused, adjusted the magnification, and leaned even closer to the eyepiece. There it was - a distinctive marker on the Y chromosome that she recognized from her past genetic studies. It was a sequence found only in males of the Deroo bloodline, an old Brugge family intertwined with the city's medieval history.

Helena's pulse quickened with excitement and apprehension. This forensic breakthrough suggested a Deroo descendant could be behind the murders, perhaps enacting some long-held intergenerational vengeance.

The link to the city's past was too salient to ignore. But she needed more evidence before raising an accusation that could ruin lives.

Meticulously, Helena replicated the DNA amplification and analysis to confirm her results. She cross-checked her reagents for contamination. Satisfied with the accuracy of her findings, she tidied up her equipment and slipped the vials holding the precious DNA samples into her apron pocket. It was late, but this news couldn't wait till morning.

Hurrying through the darkened streets, Helena made her way to Inspector De Vries's temporary office near the city square. She found him, as expected, still hunched over his desk, documents strewn around him. He looked up wearily as she entered.

"Inspector, I've made a breakthrough with the DNA sample," Helena announced.

De Vries sat up straighter, alertness returning to his eyes. "Go on."

"I found a Y chromosome marker that traces back specifically to the Deroo family line. It strongly suggests the killer is a male descendant."

"Are you certain?" De Vries asked intently.

"I've triple checked the results and I'm confident they're accurate. Here, see for yourself."

Helena opened her apron and retrieved the vials, handing them to the Inspector. He held them up to the light, gazing at the precious contents within.

"If this is true, we finally have a solid lead," De Vries murmured. He swiveled to face Helena.

"Excellent work, Helena. Your skills have proven invaluable."

She smiled, warmed by the rare praise from the typically reserved Inspector. This affirmation of the importance of science in solving crime strengthened her resolve.

***

I gaze out at the still waters of the canal as the first hints of dawn light up the morning mist. Despite the tranquil scene, my thoughts are heavy with the revelations from yesterday. Inspector De Vries believes he's found a solid lead tying the Deroo family to the recent murders, but the shadows of history stretch long, and I know well the suffering inflicted upon that family so many generations ago.

As we gather today to discuss the investigation, I see the inspector's eyes alight with the thrill of the chase. He has the scent of his quarry. The clues point to vengeance from the past, and I know I must speak, to shed light on the injustices that may have spurred this bloody retribution.

"Inspector, if we are to untangle the truth, you must understand the tragedy of the Deroo family," I begin. The words feel rusty in my mouth, tales meant to be forgotten, but necessary to exhume now. I recount the story burned into my memory since childhood.

Centuries ago, the Deroo family rose to prominence as master stonemasons, their work shaping much of Brugge's iconic architecture. But with success came scrutiny from the stonemasons' guild, who grew wary of outsiders threatening their power. When the Deroo family turned down an invitation to join the guild, dark forces conspired against them.

First came rumors, and whispers that the Deroo had gained their skills through witchcraft and unholy means. Then, sightings of strange rituals, acts of vandalism, and the death of a guild member while working on a Deroo site. The accusations flew, each one a nail in the family's coffin, forged by the guild's machinations. The trial was a sham, the verdict predetermined. The Deroo patriarch was burned at the stake, and his wife and sons hanged at the gallows.

We sit in solemn silence as I finish recounting the tragic fall of the Deroo. Helena's eyes glisten with tears, while the inspector strokes his beard. "A likely genesis for a revenge plot centuries in the making," De Vries mutters. Finding justice has always been my hope, but breaking this cycle of violence is now my prayer.

Shifting the mood, Helena clears her throat. "We should investigate any living relatives. Besides Denis Deroo, there was also a Julien Moreau you found, Inspector, he could hold some answers."

De Vries nods, retrieving a folder from his briefcase. "Julien Moreau, born and raised here in Brugge. He's in his mid-thirties, single, and works a job at the archives. The quiet type, a bit of a loner." I listen intently as De Vries reviews the profile, hungry for any scrap that takes us closer to the truth.

"I did some poking around," the inspector continues. "Turns out Moreau's mother was a Deroo descendant. Took her husband's name when they married. The family history's all there."

Helena furrows her brow. "Do you think he knows about his lineage, about what happened to his ancestors?" It's a critical question - this knowledge would be a potent motivator.

***

Under the cloak of night, Inspector De Vries and his team approach Julien Moreau's residence, a brooding structure on the outskirts of Brugge. The home looms, silent and watchful, as if it anticipates the intrusion. The inspector signals to his team, and they fan out, securing the perimeter.

De Vries's heart hammers against his ribcage. Every fiber of his being screams that this is the place where answers lie hidden, ready to unravel this mystery of murder woven through the city's history. He takes a breath, steadying himself, before giving a firm nod to proceed.

The door gives way under the firm push of a battering ram, and they flood into the residence. Dust particles dance in the beam of their lanterns as they sweep through room after room. Each step echoes with a sense of urgency.

In the study, amidst a clutter of papers and open books, De Vries finds what he's been searching for: an array of old guild artifacts—seals, ceremonial daggers, and faded documents with wax crests. His fingers graze over each item, feeling for the pulse of history that throbs within them.

"Look at this," one of his officers calls out.

De Vries turns to find a stack of cryptic notes scrawled with names and dates that stretch back centuries. They speak of debts unpaid and justice unclaimed—a ledger of grievances against the guild's descendants. His eyes narrow as he absorbs each word, feeling the weight of hatred in every line.

The team gathers around, sharing uneasy glances as they pore over Moreau's collection. There's no doubt in De Vries's mind; they've stumbled upon a well-nurtured vendetta.

As dawn threatens to break, another piece of information catches De Vries's eye—a scribbled reference to the Deroo crypt. The handwriting trembles with fervor. It doesn't take long for him to decide their next move.

"Pack everything up," he orders briskly. "We're not done tonight."

They move like shadows across Brugge, towards the ancient cemetery where generations of Deroo rest in peace—or so it was believed until now.

The crypt stands solemnly apart from its neighbors; ivy clings to its stone face like desperate hands. De Vries feels a shiver crawl up his spine despite himself as they approach with caution.

He can't shake off the sense that they are not alone in their quest—that someone else stalks these graves with intentions far darker than their own.

They split up to cover more ground, Helena pausing at the entrance to gather her thoughts before venturing into the crypt's gaping maw.

Inside, De Vries's lantern reveals signs of recent visits: fresh footprints in the dust, candles burnt down to stubs, and walls etched with frantic lines that chart out family trees long forgotten by most.

"This is an obsession," Helena whispers from behind him.

De Vries nods silently. Whoever has been coming here is not merely paying respects; they're searching for something or perhaps communing with ghosts only they can see.

But Julien is not here now—only his shadow lingers in the form of these disturbing discoveries. Their suspect has been one step ahead all along.

De Vries motions for his team to collect evidence before stepping out into the first light of morning. He looks towards the horizon where night retreats and realizes this chase has only just begun.

***

In the quiet morning, before the day had fully begun, Helena was already busy in the apothecary, meticulously preparing for the tasks ahead. Her workspace, cluttered with various herbs and tools, was a testament to her dedication. Her father, observing from a distance, couldn't help but notice how engrossed she was in her work. The look on her face, one of determination and focus, spoke volumes about her commitment to her cause.

"You're deep in this now, aren't you?" he asked, his voice laced with concern. It was a gentle question, one that sought to understand rather than accuse. He could see the weight of her responsibilities reflected in the way she carried herself, a burden he wished he could lighten.

Helena paused in her grinding of herbs, acknowledging his observation with a simple nod. "There's more at stake than I realized," she responded, her tone serious. It was a rare moment of vulnerability, revealing the depth of her concerns about the work she had undertaken.

Her father moved closer, a step that seemed to bridge not just the physical space between them but also the gap of understanding and worry. He placed a reassuring hand on her shoulder, a gesture meant to comfort and remind her of his unwavering support. "Just remember, this town has long memories; not all are fond ones," he warned his advice stemming from a place of love and a lifetime of experience.

Helena offered a small smile in return, a silent acknowledgment of his concerns. She appreciated his advice, understanding the wisdom behind his words. Despite the risks, she was determined to continue, driven by a sense of duty that went beyond personal safety.

Their exchange was brief, but it was a meaningful connection amid their complex reality. As Helena resumed her work, her father watched her for a moment longer, filled with a mixture of pride and apprehension.

Then, quietly, he left her to her tasks, carrying with him the hope that his daughter would navigate the challenges ahead with strength and wisdom.

***

Later that day at the police station, Helena sits at a borrowed desk cluttered with papers and notes. The air is thick with tension; even the walls seem to hold their breath as she pieces together a profile of Julien Moreau.

De Vries leans against the doorframe, watching her move pins on a large map peppered with notes and colored strings stretching across it like veins.

"He's been shaped by history," Helena muses aloud. "Imagine living your life defined by an ancestral grudge."

De Vries crosses his arms. "Do you think he believes in his cause?"

Helena pauses to consider. "I think he believes he's righting wrongs—avenging his family."

A constable interrupts them with fresh reports from the townspeople. De Vries skims through them, his frown deepening.

"Any mentions of Moreau?" Helena asks without looking up from her work.

"A few sightings," De Vries responds. "Mostly rumors and shadows."

Helena places another pin on the map where Moreau was reportedly seen last night.

"The pattern is erratic," she observes. "But there's purpose behind it; he's following a narrative only he fully understands."

De Vries nods slowly as Helena continues to weave a psychological tapestry from fragments of evidence and whispers of history.

"It's personal for him," she adds. "Each act is meticulously planned—symbolic retribution."

Helena rises to pin another string to the map when her father enters unexpectedly. His face wears worry like an unwelcome mask.

"I've heard talk," he begins cautiously. "People are afraid that bringing up old vendettas will reignite feuds long buried."

Helena turns to face him squarely. "If we don't unearth these secrets now, they'll fester." She glances at De Vries who nods in agreement.

"The truth can be painful," De Vries adds softly. "But it's necessary."

The apothecary nods solemnly before leaving as quietly as he came in.

Helena returns to her profiling, piecing together Moreau's potential mindset. She ponders over letters found in his residence—lines filled with anger and sorrow.

"He feels justified," she concludes aloud. "To him, this isn't murder; it's reparation."

De Vries watches Helena work with an admiration he does not voice; instead, he steps back into action mode.

"We need to predict his next move," De Vries says decisively. "If we understand his motivations clearly..."

"We can anticipate his target," Helena finishes for him.

They lock eyes for a moment—two minds in sync amid chaos—and then return to their shared task: stopping Julien Moreau before history repeats itself through his hands.

***

My family's tale is a dark one, whispered in hushed tones by those who remember. We were once proud, our name synonymous with integrity and hard work. But fear and suspicion twisted fate's arm, branding us as pariahs, practitioners of dark arts we never dabbled in. I was but a boy when they were taken from me – my mother, father, siblings – all because they said we were different.

And now, another family's name emerges from the shadows of the past – the Deroo. Accused and executed for their defiance against the guilds' iron grip, their blood seeping into the very stones of this city. Their descendant's actions, if indeed Julien Moreau is their kin, strike a familiar chord within me.

I walk along the canal's edge, watching as it mirrors the tumultuous sky above. The water whispers secrets of its own, secrets I've spent countless hours trying to coax from its depths as I cast my nets. But tonight, it's not fish I'm after; it's understanding.

How easy it would be to succumb to the bitterness that has undoubtedly consumed Moreau. How simple to let rage fuel my actions as it does his? But something within me fights against that darkness; a flicker of hope that refuses to be snuffed out. Maybe it's because I've seen what vengeance can do – how it can twist a man until he becomes unrecognizable even to himself.

Helena's words come back to me then, her voice firm yet tinged with compassion as she recounted her findings about the DNA linking Moreau to the Deroo line. Her dedication to truth is unwavering – she doesn't just want justice; she needs it like air.

"We'll find him," she had assured me earlier in Inspector De Vries's office, her eyes meeting mine with fierce determination. "And we'll end this cycle of retribution."

I recall nodding in response, though doubt clawed at my insides. Can such cycles truly be broken? Can wounds carved so deep ever truly heal?

As I ponder these questions, I sense someone approaching from behind – steady footsteps echoing on stone. I turn to see Inspector De Vries's tall figure emerging from the darkness.

"Willem," he calls out softly, mindful not to startle me.

I wait for him to reach my side before responding. "Inspector."

He gazes out over the canal beside me for a moment before speaking again.

"I've been going over everything we know," he begins. "Moreau's history... his possible motivations... It's a tangled web we're unraveling."

His voice holds an edge of frustration but beneath it lies an undercurrent of resolve that commands respect.

"I understand your connection to all this," he continues, his eyes locking onto mine. "The past isn't just history for you; it's personal."

The understanding in his tone surprises me – De Vries is more than just an inspector hunting down leads; he sees the people behind the crimes.

"I want you to know," he says firmly, "that while we share a desire to see justice done for these victims and your family... our methods must differ from Moreau's."

I nod slowly; words are unnecessary when his conviction speaks volumes.

"We'll find him," De Vries states with an assurance that borders on an oath. "And we'll do it by honoring what is just and right."

I feel something shift within me at his declaration – perhaps it's trust blooming where suspicion once took root.

"Brugge has endured much," De Vries continues after a pause. "It's time for old wounds to be mended and for peace to be restored."

I watch him then as he sets his jaw in determination, readying himself for whatever lies ahead in this twisted tale that has bound us all together – victim and investigator alike.

We stand there for several moments more before De Vries breaks the silence once again.

"I'll see you at first light," he says simply before turning on his heel and walking away into the night.

His departure leaves me alone with my thoughts once more. The night is quiet but inside me is turmoil – fear and hope warring within my chest like two relentless tides clashing against each other in stormy weather.

As Brugge braces itself for what might be unveiled next in this saga of historical revenge, so do I brace myself for whatever role I'm yet to play in bringing closure not only to these murders but also to the chapter of suffering written so long ago in my family's blood.

But tonight, there is no resolution – only reflections on still water and a heart heavy with conflicts old and new.

Willem's Despair

The night hung heavy over Brugge, its cobbled streets deserted and silent. I sat alone in my cottage, the walls seeming to close in around me as I wrestled with the events of the day. Helena's capture had shaken me to my core, and now, I couldn't shake the feeling that I was next.

I paced the small room, my mind a whirlwind of thoughts and fears. The locket, the canal murders, the secret society we'd uncovered - it all felt so overwhelming. And yet, at the center of it all was my family's dark past, a past that had haunted me for years and now threatened to consume me.

I couldn't stay indoors any longer. I needed air, and space to think. So, I grabbed my coat and stepped out into the night. The cool air was a welcome relief as I walked through the deserted streets, my footsteps echoing off the ancient buildings.

As I made my way through, I passed landmarks that reminded me of my childhood. The bakery where my mother used to buy fresh bread, the park where my father taught me to fish, and the church where I was baptized. Each one was a reminder of happier times before the shadow of my family's past had engulfed me.

I continued walking, my thoughts consumed by the past. I recalled the day my family was taken from me, accused of witchcraft, and executed without mercy. I remembered the look of terror on my father's face as he was led away, and the tears that streamed down my mother's cheeks as she held me close.

And then there was the day I was exiled from Brugge, my reputation tarnished by the sins of my family. I had been forced to leave the only home I'd ever known, my heart heavy with grief and anger.

As I walked, I couldn't help but wonder if I was doomed to suffer the same fate as my parents. Would I too be accused of witchcraft and executed, my name forever tarnished? Or would I be able to clear my family's name and finally find peace?

I stopped at the cemetery. It's been years since I last stood here, yet the path to my family's grave is etched into my memory like the lines on my weather-beaten hands.

The gravesite is modest, an unassuming stone marking the final resting place of those who once gave me life and love. I kneel before it, the dew-soaked grass chilling my knees through my trousers. My fingers trace the cold, weathered letters of their names.

"Mother, Father," I whisper into the silence, "I stand before you a man still haunted by your shadows, still fighting to clear our name." My voice falters as my emotion thickens. "I need your guidance now more than ever. The town still whispers of witchcraft, and I feel their stares burn into me as they did into you."

I let out a breath I didn't realize I'd been holding, my gaze lingering on the etchings as if expecting them to speak back to me. "Forgive me for not coming sooner, for not tending to these stones that carry your legacy. I've been lost, adrift in a sea of suspicion and fear."

The air shifts around me as the cemetery begins to stir with the morning breeze. "Help me find justice," I continue, my voice barely above a murmur. "Help me find peace."

A sense of connection fills me – not just to my parents but to all those who came before me. Their suffering feels palpable in this sacred space, their struggles interwoven with mine across time.

I rise slowly, my body stiff from the cold and from years of labor on the canals. As I turn to leave, casting one last glance at the grave, a sliver of warmth touches my heart – perhaps their silent blessing or just the comfort of being heard.

The journey back takes me through Brugge's awakening streets. The city is beautiful at this hour; even its shadows seem softer with sleep. It's in these quiet moments that I remember why I fight so hard for her – this city is more than just cobbled streets and dark waters; it's home.

"Willem?" The voice startles me out of my reverie. It belongs to Clara, an old friend from childhood whose path diverged from mine long ago. Her face shows genuine concern as she steps closer.

"Clara," I reply with a nod, surprised by her presence.

"You're up early," she remarks softly.

"Just paying respects," I say, gesturing vaguely in the direction of the cemetery.

She looks at me closely, her eyes searching mine for something unsaid. "How are you holding up?" There's an edge to her voice that suggests she already knows part of the answer.

"I'm managing." The words feel hollow even as they leave my lips.

We begin walking side by side in comfortable silence until she breaks it again. "The whole town's talking about... everything." She hesitates before continuing. "But some of us remember who you were before... before all this."

A bitter laugh escapes me before I can stop it. "And what do they say?"

"Some fear you," Clara admits quietly. "Others think you're being blamed for things beyond your control."

"And what do you think?"

She stops walking and turns to face me fully. Her expression is earnest when she speaks. "I think you're trying to right a wrong that was never yours to bear."

Her words wash over me like a balm for wounds too long left untended.

"I just wish there was something I could do to help," Clara adds after a moment.

"You believe in my innocence," I say slowly. "That's more than most are willing to offer."

Clara reaches out tentatively and places her hand on my arm. Her touch is light but filled with empathy and an unspoken promise of support.

"I should go," she says after a pause, dropping her hand back to her side. "But please know that not everyone has turned their back on you."

I nod in acknowledgment as we part ways.

***

I sit on a worn bench, its wood weathered by time and countless storms. The first light of dawn casts a soft glow over the water, turning it into a canvas of oranges and pinks. It's in these quiet moments that I can almost forget the turmoil that surrounds me.

As I gaze at the calm surface, I see my reflection looking back at me. There's an irony in finding peace in a place that has brought so much pain to my life. The canals, once a source of livelihood for my family, now hold memories of loss and accusations that echo through the generations.

The water is like glass this morning, undisturbed by boats or swans. It's a stark contrast to the chaos that lies beneath – bodies once floated here, lives cut short, their stories ending in these murky depths. And yet, here I am, seeking solace where others met their end.

I pull my coat tighter around me as a chill runs through the air. The mist hangs over the water like a shroud, hiding the city from view. It feels as if Brugge herself is mourning, her tears collecting on the cobblestones and slipping silently into the canal.

I think about my family – my mother with her kind eyes and gentle smile, my father with his strong hands and quiet strength. They loved these waters just as much as I do. It was here that we found joy in simple things: the thrill of a good catch, the beauty of a sunset reflected on the surface.

But now those memories are tainted by what came after – the fear that spread through our home like a plague, the neighbors who turned their backs on us when we needed them most. And finally, that fateful night when they were taken from me.

The accusation of witchcraft was like a death sentence in Brugge. No trial was needed; no evidence was required. Just whispers and suspicion were enough to seal their fate – and mine along with it.

As I lost my family to superstition and ignorance, I also lost my place in this community. The isolation was suffocating; it wrapped around me like chains I couldn't break. Even now, as I try to clear our name and bring justice to those who have suffered as we did, I feel its weight upon me.

A swan glides past me now, breaking my reflection into ripples that spread across the canal. It's a reminder that life goes on despite our tragedies – that beauty can still be found even in places marred by sadness.

I let out a long breath, watching as it forms a cloud in the cold air before dissipating into nothingness. That's what I am afraid of becoming – nothing more than a breath in the cold air, forgotten by time and history.

But Helena... she gives me hope. Her determination to uncover the truth is unwavering; her belief in justice is unshakeable. She sees beyond my family's stained legacy to the man I am trying to be – one who fights not just for himself but for all those wronged by fear and falsehoods.

Inspector De Vries too has shown me an unexpected kindness. He could have easily written me off as guilty; instead, he looks beyond appearances, seeking truth amidst lies and deception.

Together we stand against currents of suspicion and doubt; together we seek light in Brugge's darkest corners.

A soft splash catches my attention – a fish breaking through the surface before diving back into its watery world. It's moments like these that remind me why I continue this fight – not just for myself but for every innocent soul who has felt the sting of injustice.

As I walk away from the water's edge, leaving behind its deceptive calmness for another day's challenges, I carry with me both the pain of my past and the promise of tomorrow – both reflected in these timeless waters that whisper secrets only few can hear.

***

I stood in the middle of my small cottage, the fading light of dusk casting long shadows across the sparse furnishings. This place held the memories of a lifetime – every notch in the wooden table, and every scuff on the stone floor was a reminder of the moments, both joyous and sorrowful, that had played out within these walls.

Now I was leaving it all behind.

I sighed deeply as I looked around, taking in the space that had been my sanctuary from the cruelties of the outside world. Here, I could shut out the accusing stares and whispered gossip that followed me everywhere in town. Here, I could remember my family without the cloud of suspicion that shrouded their memory.

My gaze fell upon the carved oak trunk in the corner. It contained what few possessions I had left to my name – the last remaining artifacts of a family torn apart and a life irrevocably damaged.

I knelt before it and unlatched the rusty clasps, lifting the heavy lid slowly as if unveiling something sacred. Inside were the remnants of our past – my mother's embroidered shawl, now faded and frayed; my father's worn leather boots that I had not had the heart to discard; stacks of letters bound in twine, their penmanship no longer legible but their sentiments still heartbreakingly clear.

Each object was a snapshot from a different time. As I sifted through them, memories washed over me, vivid and bittersweet. I could almost hear my mother humming as she stitched delicate flowers onto this shawl. I could see my father stamping the mud off these boots after a long day on the canal. And the letters...I remembered the anticipation I felt as a boy each time a new one arrived, thrilled at any word from my cousins in Antwerp.

My fingers closed around a wooden box nestled at the bottom of the trunk. It was the one that held our most treasured possessions – passed down through generations and gifted on occasions of great meaning.

The latch creaked as I opened it slowly, almost reverently. Inside were pieces of my history that I had not laid eyes on in years. My great-grandfather's compass was tarnished but still steadfast after guiding so many journeys. The prayer book my grandmother had pressed into my hands the day I left Brugge, its pages thin as butterfly wings but the prayers within still holding power. And there, tucked into the silk lining – my mother's locket, the one my father had given her as a wedding gift.

My breath caught as I rubbed a thumb over the delicate engraving. She had worn it every day until…until the end. I had kept it all this time, this small piece of her that I could not stand to part with.

Looking at these objects now, I was overcome with indecision. They were a burden, weighing me down, chaining me to a past I needed to leave behind. But they were also my history, my lineage, the last remnants of the people who had loved me into being. Was I ready to sever those ties completely?

For a long moment, I sat motionless, the locket still cupped gently in my palm. Around me the cottage was growing darker, the sun slipping below the horizon. Soon there would be nothing left but shadows.

With great care, I placed the locket back in its velvet case and returned the box to the trunk. I would not discard my family's legacy, even if leaving it behind would lighten my load. Some burdens are meant to be borne.

The last of my packing was done mechanically, my mind already starting to detach from this place. I moved through each room, taking in the empty spaces that had once held pieces of my life.

On the mantel sat a whittled figure, the first one my father had ever carved for me. It was an otter, slick and playful. "Like you," he had said with a smile, tousling my hair. I left it where it was. That memory, at least, I would carry with me untarnished.

At last, there was nothing left but to close the door one final time. I stood on the threshold, peering into the home that had sheltered me through life's tempests. Here, I had found solace. Here, I had nursed my wounds. And now, here I would leave behind all I had ever known.

"Thank you," I whispered into the silence. It felt woefully inadequate but somehow necessary. This place had been my refuge. Now it would become someone else's. I could only hope they would find the same peace within these walls that I did.

With a heavy heart and limbs leaden with regret, I stepped over the threshold. The click of the lock sliding into place reverberated with finality. I did not look back as I walked away, leaving the last remnants of my life in Brugge behind me. The future awaited, tenuous, and unknown.

***

The chill of the early morning air bites at my skin as I stand in the shadow of the Brugge bus station, a place of departures and arrivals, of hellos and goodbyes. I clutch the ticket in my hand, its edges crumpled from the tightness of my grip. This thin piece of paper is my escape, a path away from the suspicions that cling to me like a second skin.

Around me, people bustle with purpose, their destinations certain, their intentions clear. I envy that clarity. For me, this ticket represents a crossroads – to flee from a town that has been both my heart and my prison or to stay and face the ghosts that haunt me.

I close my eyes, feeling the weight of my family's history on my shoulders. The murmurs of witchcraft, the scornful looks from those who once played at my side as children – all these years later, they still see me not for who I am but for the stigma that darkens my name.

I could board the bus and leave it all behind: the whispers, the fear, the memories etched into every corner of Brugge. Yet even as the thought crosses my mind, an image of Helena surfaces – her determination fierce, her belief in justice unwavering. She stands by me when others step back, and sees in me not a man marked by misfortune but one worthy of standing beside her.

My thoughts are interrupted by the rumble of an engine. The bus to Antwerp pulls into its berth with a hiss of brakes and a belch of exhaust. The driver steps out, his face obscured by a cap pulled low over his brow. Passengers begin to line up, their tickets ready, their luggage in tow.

I should join them. I should take this chance to start anew where no one knows the name Van Aarden or whispers it like a curse. Yet even as I step forward, another image halts me: Father Emile's somber face as he recounted his role in our town's dark past and how it intertwined with my own family's tale.

My hand trembles as I bring the ticket closer to my eyes, reading over the departure time that now looms over me like a judge's verdict. This decision is more than just about leaving; it's about surrendering – admitting defeat against forces greater than myself.

But then there's Inspector De Vries with his meticulous search for truth amidst a tangle of lies and secrets. He looks beyond the surface, refusing to accept easy answers when deeper injustices lie hidden.

And what about Lucas Rombouts? His art was vandalized for mirroring too closely the darkness seeping through our city's veins. If I leave now, would I be abandoning him too? Leaving him to fend off shadows that we should be dispelling together?

The line shortens as more passengers board the bus. The driver glances at his watch with an impatient frown – time waits for no one.

I think of my parents then; their love was unconditional, their strength unyielding even in the face of ultimate despair. They wouldn't have fled; they would have stood firm, rooted like the ancient oaks that line our canals.

The realization hits me like a gale-force wind off the North Sea – I cannot leave Brugge behind because it is etched into who I am. It is in its waters that I find reflections not only of pain but also of resilience.

My fingers move on their own accord now; they work at tearing the ticket slowly at first and then with conviction until it lies in pieces at my feet like fallen leaves. A silent declaration was made amidst diesel fumes and muted farewells.

I step back from the queue and feel an unexpected weight lift off me with each torn shred that scatters on the ground – this is not to surrender; this is defiance.

Helena needs me. The Inspector needs me. Lucas needs me. Above all else, I need to confront this storm head-on if I am ever to emerge on the other side where sunlight might once again warm my face without casting shadows behind me.

With resolve fueling each step, I walk away from the bus station leaving behind what could have been for what must be done. My pace quickens as if to match the heartbeat pounding in my chest – an echo of newfound determination reverberating through me.

As I return to my cottage through streets that begin to fill with life under morning's light touch, each familiar sight reinforces my decision to stay: Madame Blanchard opening her shopfront shutters; young Pieter racing down cobbled lanes delivering milk; old Gertrude sweeping her doorstep while casting suspicious glances towards passersby – all threads in Brugge's tapestry that I'm woven into whether by fate or by choice.

Once inside my cottage again – its solitude both comforting and chilling – there's no triumphant sense of victory; there's only quiet acceptance and steeling myself for what lies ahead.

I light a small fire against morning's chill and sit staring into its flickering dance contemplating battles yet fought and sacrifices yet made. And as flames cast long shadows against stone walls around me; they remind me starkly - this fight is far from over.

But neither am I...

The Final Confrontation

It's a cold morning, and I can feel the chill seeping into my bones as I walk towards the boathouse that's hidden away from the usual paths, where the water is still and covered in mist. It's early, with dawn just starting to show, hinting at the light of a new day and maybe even the possibility of new hope. When I get there, I find Inspector De Vries and Helena already waiting. They look determined, ready to face whatever comes next, but it's obvious that the past few nights haven't been easy on them. They're showing clear signs of not getting enough rest.

De Vries greets me with a nod, his eyes scanning the area for any signs of unwanted attention. "We have to be quick. We can't afford to draw attention."

Helena's hands are steady as she carefully spreads out a map of Brugge on an old table. The map shows the city's canals, which crisscross through it, resembling the network of veins in a body. "According to our findings, we expect the next attack to occur along this stretch," she says, pointing to a narrow section of the canal bordered by overhanging trees.

"The guilds used patterns in their retributions," De Vries adds, his finger tracing an invisible line between historical sites of power and tragedy. "It's not just random violence; it's calculated."

My chest tightens at the thought of being bait. It's a role I'm familiar with – bait for scorn, for whispers behind my back, for accusations without proof. But today, it's for justice, not just for me but for all those silenced by fear and vengeance.

"I'll be on the boat," I say, more to convince myself than them. "If our murderer follows the pattern, he'll strike there."

Helena reaches out, her touch light on my arm. "We'll be close by," she assures me.

I look into her eyes, seeing the same resolve that's carried us this far. It's what makes me trust her – that and her brilliant mind that sees beyond what most dare to notice.

De Vries hands me a small device. "Keep this on you. If anything happens—"

"I know," I interrupt him before he can finish. "Press it and wait for you lot to come running."

He doesn't smile at that; there's no room for humor in what we're about to do.

As the morning progresses from dawn to full daylight, we initiate our carefully laid out plan. De Vries and his team of undercover officers quickly vanish into the crowd, merging seamlessly with the bustle of the city, as unnoticeable as shadows when evening falls. Meanwhile, Helena occupies herself with her collection of equipment, handling various vials and tools with a familiarity that's beyond my comprehension, yet I have complete trust in her expertise.

And then there's me – alone again on my boat, drifting down the canals that have been both my livelihood and my curse.

I push off from the dock quietly; no engine today – just an oar and the ripple of water against wood. My heart beats in time with the stroke of the oar; every splash is a second ticking away in our trap.

The canal feels different today; it knows something is about to happen. Or maybe that's just me projecting my fears onto these ancient waters that have seen too much already.

I keep my eyes peeled for anything unusual as I row under bridges and past homes where Brugge begins its day unaware of what lurks beneath its calm surface.

Time passes – an hour or two – but it feels like an eternity with each turn I take down these winding paths carved by history and tragedy.

My hands work the oar with a rhythm born of years on these waters. Every stroke is smooth, every turn calculated to appear casual to any prying eyes. I've become a master at wearing masks, and today my facade is that of indifference.

I glance at the windows lining the canal, watching life unfold within as I pass by. They're like paintings in motion, each frame a story untold. But it's not the warm glow of hearth fires or the clatter of breakfast dishes that hold my attention—it's the shadowed doorways and narrow alleys where danger could be lurking.

The sun climbs higher, and with it, my apprehension grows. The plan was simple: draw out the murderer by presenting an irresistible opportunity—me, seemingly alone and vulnerable on the water. But simple plans have a way of becoming complicated quickly.

I round a bend, and there it is—a cloaked figure emerges from the shadows between two ancient buildings. It's like watching a specter take form from the mist—a presence both there and not there, cloaked in secrecy and silence.

The figure moves with purpose, confident yet cautious. He hugs the wall, aware of his surroundings—aware of me. His head is down, but I can tell he is watching me with an intensity that sends a shiver down my spine.

A flicker of movement catches my eye from above—a subtle shift behind an upper window's curtain. Helena. She must have spotted the figure too.

In an instant, her quick observation becomes our lifeline. Her keen eyes have picked up on something crucial—the figure doesn't match Julien Moreau's build or gait. This isn't our main suspect; it's someone else entirely.

My grip tightens on the oar as I fight to keep my breathing steady. My pulse thrums in my ears like a drumbeat, each thump echoing against the canal walls.

Helena's voice crackles through the communication device hidden beneath my jacket. "Not Moreau," she says tersely.

I don't respond; I can't without giving myself away. Instead, I focus on keeping my movements natural as if I haven't noticed anything amiss.

Inspector De Vries's voice follows Helena's, calm and controlled. "Stay the course, Willem."

So we continue this deadly dance—me on the water, them watching from their hidden perches—and all the while, this cloaked stranger draws nearer.

They're close now—too close for comfort—yet they make no move to strike or call out. They simply walk parallel to me along the canal bank as if taking a stroll in broad daylight.

Who is this person? A new player in this twisted game? A minion sent by Moreau to do his dirty work? Or perhaps just a local out for a walk? No—that last thought is dismissed as quickly as it forms. There's intent in this figure's steps; I can feel it like electricity in the air.

I row steadily past another bridge and glance sideways discreetly. The figure stops and seems to consider his next move.

My heart pounds against my ribs as I draw closer to the figure, his face still obscured beneath the hood. I have to end this dance, to confront the demon that's been haunting Brugge.

With a final stroke, I bring the boat parallel to the walkway where the figure stands motionless. Before I can talk myself out of it, I leap from the boat onto the stone steps.

"Show yourself!" I demand, my voice echoing off the canal walls.

The figure jerks back, startled, but quickly regains its footing. We stand face to face, the chill morning air thick with tension.

I step forward, hands clenched. "Who are you? Why are you following me?"

No response, just the unnerving stillness of that hood pointed at me like the barrel of a gun.

My nerves are frayed my patience is at its end. I lunge forward and grab the figure's cloak. "Answer me!"

We grapple for a moment, the fabric twisted in my fists. And then suddenly, the hood slips back, and I stumble back in shock.

It's Clara staring back at me, her eyes ablaze with fury and anguish. My childhood friend, now unrecognizable in her rage.

"Clara?" I gasp. "What is this? What are you doing?"

Her lips curl into a bitter smile. "Finishing what you don't dare to start, Willem."

I shake my head, trying to make sense of her words. Clara had always been sweet and gentle - nothing like the venom in her voice now.

She steps closer, her face inches from mine. "Yes, Willem. It was me. I killed them - the guild descendants. I avenged our families, while you did nothing!"

My mind reels, flashing through memories of Clara and me as children, oblivious to the tragedy awaiting us. She had lost her parents in a tragic accident. Just as I did, what are the odds?

I grab her shoulders. "Clara, listen to me. This isn't justice - it's madness. More blood spilled cannot erase the past."

Angry tears stream down her cheeks. "You don't understand. For years I've lived with the screams of our dying families ringing in my ears. No more. The guilty will pay for their crimes."

"Innocents died, Clara!" I plead with her to see the reason.

She shoves me back violently. "Innocent? Their hands are stained with the blood of our families! Yours and mine!"

Her voice breaks, raw emotion pouring out. "We suffered while they sat in their gilded halls and stepped over our misery. I will have vengeance for the fallen."

"Vengeance only breeds more vengeance," I urge her. "Killing them makes you no better than their ancestors who wronged us."

Clara shakes her head bitterly. "I knew you wouldn't understand. You never dared to do what was needed." She turns away. "But I did. And I will finish this, with or without you."

She moves to leave, but I grab her arm. "I can't let you kill again, Clara."

Her eyes flash with defiance. "Then you'll have to stop me."

She shoves me back once more and I lose my footing, tumbling into the icy canal waters. I break the surface, sputtering, in time to see her fleeing form disappear into the morning mist.

I'm suddenly submerged in water, its coldness and unyielding nature hitting me with the harsh reality of my situation. I find myself gasping for air, my physical response outpacing my mental realization of what has just happened – a betrayal. As I struggle, Clara's form recedes into the morning mist, disappearing like a specter. Her recent revelation lingers in my mind, a haunting presence that disturbs me even more than the icy embrace of the canal water.

I claw my way to the edge, my fingers gripping the slimy stones. With every heave of my chest, I pull myself out of the water, but it feels like I'm trying to escape more than just the canal's grip—I'm trying to escape a truth I don't want to face.

My teeth chatter as I sit on the bank, drenched and shivering, not just from cold but from shock. How could Clara, who played with me in these very streets as children, be capable of such darkness? The signs—were there signs I ignored?

Before I can chase that thought, a flurry of activity erupts around me. Inspector De Vries and Helena appear out of nowhere, their faces tense with urgency. Behind them, officers move swiftly to secure the area.

"Willem!" Helena's voice cuts through my daze. She kneels beside me, her hands gentle as she checks for injuries.

I meet her eyes briefly before looking away, unable to hold her gaze with the weight of what I've just learned. "It's Clara," I manage to say through quivering lips. "She's the one behind it all."

Helena's expression shifts from concern to disbelief. "Clara? But how—"

"There's no time," Inspector De Vries interrupts, his hand on his earpiece as he listens to updates from his team. "She can't have gone far."

He barks orders at his officers and they scatter like hounds on a hunt. Then he turns back to me with a grimace. "Stay with him," he instructs Helena before following after his team.

Helena wraps her coat around me as we hear distant shouts—signs of a pursuit in progress. "Willem," she says softly, "we'll get through this."

Her words should offer comfort but instead, they echo hollowly in my ears. Get through this? How do you get through discovering your childhood friend has been killing in the name of vengeance? How do you reconcile memories of laughter with acts of cold-blooded murder?

"Willem," Helena prompts again, her tone insistent.

I shake my head as if it might shake loose the images flooding my mind—Clara's smile as we ran through these streets, innocent and free from the shadows that would later define us.

My thoughts are interrupted by shouts growing louder, and closer. Inspector De Vries reappears at the end of the alleyway with Clara in tow—two officers gripping her arms tightly. Her face is defiant still but there's fear there too—fear that maybe she realizes what she's become.

A brief standoff unfolds before my eyes as Clara struggles against her captor's grip. She locks eyes with me across the distance and for a moment we're not killers and witnesses; we're just two lost souls trying to navigate a world that's been cruel beyond measure.

De Vries steps forward authoritatively. "Enough!" His command reverberates off the walls and Clara ceases struggling.

They bring her closer and something inside me wants to reach out—to find that little girl who once shared secrets with me under the willow trees by these very waters—but that world is gone now.

Clara stops before us, panting from exertion or perhaps fear now that she's caught. "Willem," she whispers, her voice cracking with emotion. "You don't understand."

Understanding? Is that what she wants from me? To understand why she chose murder over mercy? My silence must speak volumes because she looks away first, defeated.

Inspector De Vries doesn't wait for an emotional reunion; he's all business as he nods to his officers and they begin to lead Clara away.

My gaze follows her retreating form until she disappears around a corner—a part of my childhood vanishing with her.

I turn back to Helena; she's watching me closely now, trying to read my expression. "Willem," she starts again but stops herself when she sees something shift behind my eyes—a torrent of emotions I can't quite articulate yet.

"I should have seen it," I murmur more to myself than to her. "All those times we talked about justice… I never imagined…"

Helena reaches out tentatively but then draws back unsure how to console someone whose world has just been upended.

Inspector De Vries approaches again; his face softened somewhat by what he's just witnessed—a personal tragedy amidst a professional victory.

"You did well today," he says quietly—not as an inspector but as someone who understands loss and pain all too well.

His words are meant to be reassuring but they land awkwardly between us—what is good about any of this?

"We'll take care of everything from here," De Vries continues, gesturing towards where Clara was taken. "You should get warm."

I watch numbly as Clara is led away, the officers' steps echoing off the damp cobblestones. She doesn't resist now; the fight has gone out of her. Her admission hangs heavy in the air, a dark revelation I'm still struggling to comprehend.

My mind flashes through memories of our childhood—lazy summer days playing in the meadows, nights huddled together for warmth and comfort. We were just children then, unaware of the tragedy that awaited us. When did that innocence turn to vengeance inside her? How did I not see the signs?

I'm jolted back to the present by Inspector De Vries's voice cutting through the fog in my mind. "We need to secure the scene," he says, already scanning the area with a trained eye.

Helena places a gentle hand on my shoulder, guiding me to sit on a stone bench lining the canal. I feel numb like I'm sleepwalking through a nightmare I can't wake from.

Around us, officers fan out, gathering evidence, taking photos, and documenting every detail of this site that's now a crime scene. Yellow tape goes up, closing off sections methodically. It all seems strangely mundane for what just transpired.

Helena kneels beside me, her face creased with concern. "Willem," she says softly. "I know this is a lot to process right now, but we're here for you, okay?"

I just nod mutely. Her words float past me, unable to penetrate the shock settled over me.

Inspector De Vries approaches, flipping his notebook closed. "The scene is secure," he reports. "We'll need your full statement, but that can wait until tomorrow."

I glance up at him, seeing past the professional exterior to the empathy in his eyes. He understands the pain of betrayal perhaps better than anyone.

"For now, go home. Get some rest," De Vries continues. "We'll take it from here."

Home. The thought of returning to my cold, empty apartment is unbearable. But I don't argue. I simply stand on unsteady legs, Helena's hand supporting me.

We make our way down the canal path silently. All around us, officers catalog and collect their evidence. The horror of what happened here feels strangely removed, like it's part of someone else's life.

Up ahead, the canal bends and blue lights dance across the water—an array of police vehicles gathered at the scene. As we approach, I see Clara seated in the back of a squad car.

Our eyes meet through the window. Hers are bloodshot, haunted. Mine must look much the same. She raises her hand slightly, as if to reach out to me, then lets it drop heavily onto her lap.

I force myself to look away. Even now, seeing her pain cuts into me like a knife. She made her choices, I remind myself. But it offers little comfort.

Helena's grip on my arm tightens, grounding me. We bypass the car silently.

The area around the canal is now illuminated by an unsettling light as officers go about their business, taking photographs and recording details of the scene. This routine procedure feels oddly trivial considering the magnitude of what has happened, how it has forever altered the lives of everyone involved—Clara, myself, and even the city of Brugge.

Inspector De Vries approaches us again. "We'll take it from here," he repeats gently. "Get some rest, both of you."

He looks between Helena and me with a knowing sadness. We three make an unlikely trio, brought together by tragedy. But bonded now by a commitment to truth and justice, however painful.

Helena nods, then turns to me. "Come on," she urges softly. "Let's get you home."

I let her guide me down the canal path without argument, away from the flashing lights and grim proceedings. Brugge feels different now—a collective innocence lost.

At the end of the path, I chance one last look over my shoulder. Clara is gone, the squad car pulling away down a side street. Officers walk the scene methodically. And in the middle of it all stands Inspector De Vries, his face unreadable as he surveys the ripples of this revelation spreading through Brugge.

When we reach the main road, Helena hails a carriage to take me home. Neither of us speaks as it rumbles down the cobblestone streets. What is there to say?

Helena walks me to my door when we arrive. Her eyes search my face, but I have no words of comfort or closure to offer her.

"Get some rest," she says again, giving my hand a final squeeze before leaving me.

Alone again, I sink onto my bed heavily. Through the window, I can just make out the distant police lights still pulsing beyond the rooftops.

Rest—that seems unlikely tonight. My mind is far from quiet, still churning through fragmented memories of my childhood with Clara. Her laughter echoes down the years, haunting me now.

I should have seen the signs. I should have stopped her before it came to this. The guilt sits like a stone in my chest, crushing the air from my lungs.

But dwelling on what I should have done won't undo what's been done. Clara made her choices—horrific as they were. Now we must find a way to move forward, though the city itself feels fractured by this legacy of violence and secrecy.

Somehow, tomorrow, we'll have to pick up the pieces. Brugge's spirit has been tested before, its resilience runs bone-deep in these ancient streets. But for tonight, I will grieve. I will rage. I will try to make sense of how innocence gave way to such depravity.

And I will wonder, as I stare at Clara's faded initials carved into the willow tree of our childhood, whether redemption can ever find root in such poisoned ground.

The lights continue to flicker beyond my window as the night wears on, echoing the unsettled state of my soul.

The Truth Unveiled

Inside the police station, the interrogation room has the atmosphere of a tightly locked vault where secrets are kept hidden away, and I find myself merely a shadow against its walls, observing the unfolding scene. Clara is there, confronting Inspector De Vries, her hands shaking and her eyes scanning the room, desperately searching for something solid to hold onto amidst her confusion and fear. De Vries, on the other hand, exudes patience, his voice maintaining a consistent and soothing cadence that appears to ease the tension in the room.

"Clara," he starts, his gaze never leaving her face, "I know this is difficult, but your insight is crucial. We need to understand the full scope of the guild's actions."

She nods and takes a deep breath. I see her steeling herself against the weight of her words. "It's not just what you think," she begins. "The guild... they didn't just control trade or uphold traditions. They shaped history with bloodied hands."

De Vries leans forward slightly. "Tell me about their influence over justice."

Clara swallows hard, her voice barely above a whisper. "The trials... they were spectacles. The accused had no chance. Evidence was planted, witnesses coerced—"

"Like with Willem's ancestors?" De Vries interjects.

Her eyes meet mine for a fleeting moment before dropping to her lap. "Yes," she admits. "The Van Aardens were convenient scapegoats. Feared for their independence, their refusal to bow to the guild's demands."

My heart pounds in my chest like a drumbeat of old rage, echoing through time. I clench my fists until my nails dig into my palms.

"How did they justify it?" De Vries presses on.

Clara's face crumples for a second before she composes herself again. "Witchcraft was an easy accusation then—impossible to disprove. It created fear, kept people in line."

De Vries writes something down in his notebook, his expression unreadable.

"And the drownings now?" he asks.

Clara hesitates, biting her lip until it whitens under the pressure.

"The guild... their descendants believe they're purging shame," she reveals with difficulty. "They think they're cleansing their lineage by targeting those related to the old tribunal members—the ones who passed judgment centuries ago."

De Vries leans back in his chair; I can tell he's digesting every word.

"Was there any resistance within the guild? Anyone who saw the injustice?"

She nods slowly. "There were always whispers of dissenters who disappeared or met unfortunate ends."

"And your family?" De Vries questions softly.

Tears brim in Clara's eyes as she confesses, "My great-grandfather tried to help those accused... he paid with his life."

I remember whispers of such stories from my mother when I was young—a legacy of secret kindness and hidden bravery amid widespread cruelty.

De Vries rises and offers Clara a glass of water; she takes it with shaking hands.

"We need evidence, Clara," he says gently but firmly. "Documents, artifacts—anything that can prove what you're telling us."

"I have something," she says after a long pause. "Letters from my great-grandfather detailing his opposition to the guild's practices." Her voice strengthens with resolve. "I'll bring them to you."

De Vries gives her a nod of gratitude and assurance that seems to ease some tension from her shoulders.

As they wrap up their conversation and Clara stands to leave, escorted by an officer, I feel an odd sense of camaraderie with her—a bond forged by our ancestors' suffering under the same tyrannical shadow.

Once we're alone, De Vries turns to me.

"Willem," he says solemnly, "this could be the breakthrough we've been waiting for."

I can only nod as hope battles skepticism within me.

"We're going to set things right," he promises with a conviction that makes me want to believe him more than anything else in this twisted world.

The inspector leaves shortly after to prepare for Clara's return with the letters; I remain in the interrogation room a while longer—alone but for ghosts of past injustices whispering along the walls.

Finally ready to face whatever comes next, I step out into the corridor where Helena waits for me; her presence is like a lighthouse on this dark and stormy night of our investigation.

We exchange looks that say more than words ever could—about fear and hope and determination—and together we walk out into Brugge's evening chill, ready to confront history's demons and claim justice for both our families and all those wronged by concealed truths now coming into sharp relief under Inspector Gerard De Vries' relentless pursuit.

***

Sitting across from Inspector De Vries, I feel the weight of generations on my shoulders. Spread between us on the table are Clara's letters and the historical records that may finally shed light on my family's past. Helena places a supportive hand on my arm before sorting through the documents, focused as always.

I brace myself as the inspector summarizes Clara's confession - how the Stonemasons' guild targeted my ancestors to eliminate competition, manipulating superstitions to accuse them of witchcraft. Evidence taken out of context, suspicious accidents staged, witnesses intimidated - all machinations of the powerful guild that led to the execution of my ancestors.

Inspector De Vries' voice anchors me back to the present. He recounts Clara's admission that the guild strongarmed the tribunal into convicting my parents. The so-called evidence was fabricated, and the trial was a mere performance to justify the predetermined verdict.

I feel a flare of anger at the injustice and the callousness with which they destroyed my family. Helena's hand squeezes mine in silent solidarity. I meet her earnest gaze and sense she understands my turmoil.

Taking a deep breath, I study the documents. Faded letters between tribunal members discussing the mounting pressure from the guild, worried whispers of dissent brutally silenced. Records of payments to witnesses coached to echo the guild's version of events. My heart pounds as the truth is gradually exposed.

Helena traces her finger over a notation describing threats to a tribunal member's family should he refuse to convict my parents. Her eyes flash with anger, lips pressed in a hard line. "This proves they coerced the judges. Your family never stood a chance."

Inspector De Vries nods solemnly. "A gross perversion of justice. But one that has haunted this city for too long." He meets my gaze. "On behalf of the authorities, I sincerely apologize for what your family endured."

I swallow hard, overcome with emotion. After a lifetime of stigma, here sits a representative of the law acknowledging the injustice. The weight on my shoulders lifts, if only slightly.

"Thank you, Inspector. Your efforts to uncover the truth mean more than you know." I take a shaky breath. "Now that you have confirmed what happened, my family can finally rest in peace."

A charged silence settles over us as we reflect on the revelations. Helena squeezes my hand once more, grounding me. I give her a small, grateful smile. Her unwavering support through this ordeal has been my lifeline.

Glancing at the stained glass windows, I notice the light fading outside. "Let us resume the investigation tomorrow with clear heads and renewed determination." He stands, shaking my hand firmly. "Get some rest, Willem. And thank you for your trust - it will not be in vain."

I bid the inspector goodnight before walking Helena home, our steps echoing on the cobbled streets. She slips her hand into the crook of my arm, a comforting warmth in the evening chill. Neither of us speak, content with the silent companionship.

At her door, Helena turns to me, eyes bright with emotion. "I'm so pleased for you, Willem. The cloud over your family has finally lifted."

I take her hands in mine. "I could not have endured this without you, Helena. You gave me the courage to pursue the truth."

She smiles softly. "Your strength and resilience are what saw you through this. But I'm honored to stand by your side."

We linger in the moment, this remarkable woman and I, brought together by tragedy but united now in justice and understanding. I sense a new beginning ahead, one unburdened by the past.

I take a deep breath as I enter the crowded auditorium, the buzz of hushed conversations washing over me. Today, Inspector De Vries will publicly disclose the findings of our investigation, exposing the guild's crimes and clearing my family's name. A mix of anticipation and unease roils within me.

Helena gives my hand a supportive squeeze before we take our seats in the front row.

***

A hush falls over the room as Inspector De Vries steps up to the podium. His eyes meet mine briefly before he begins.

"Citizens of Brugge, thank you for being here today. Recent tragic events have shaken our city and forced us to re-examine our history..."

As the inspector summarizes the canal murders, I relive the darkness that descended on Brugge. The fear in people's eyes, the suspicion cast my way. I rub my clammy palms on my trousers, steadying my nerves.

"...Our investigation uncovered a disturbing truth. Historical records show the medieval guilds abused their power, manipulating superstitions to target innocent families."

Murmurs ripple through the crowd at this revelation. I keep my gaze fixed straight ahead, shoulders taut.

"Among their victims were the Van Aardens, wrongfully accused of witchcraft due to the stonemasons' guild's campaign against them. Their entire family was unjustly executed."

I close my eyes briefly against the painful memories. Helena's hand finds mine again, grounding me.

"Today, I formally apologize to their last descendant, Willem Van Aarden, for this unconscionable miscarriage of justice."

I feel hundreds of eyes turn to me. Drawing myself up, I meet their gazes unflinchingly. The truth is out now. There is no more need to hide.

Inspector De Vries goes on to highlight Adeline's brave opposition to the guild. Shocked whispers ripple through the room at the revelations. I glance at Eva and see tears glistening in her eyes as her ancestor's secret sacrifices are acknowledged.

As the inspector concludes, a charged silence hangs over the auditorium. I observe the crowd, struck by the range of emotions on their faces - dismay, incredulity, shame. This is a collective reckoning generation in the making.

Reporters barrage the inspector with questions. Flashbulbs pop as photographers capture the historic moment. I remain seated, listening to the voices clamoring to understand, to make sense of revelations that have upended everything they thought they knew about their city.

Amidst the chaos, I feel a sense of catharsis. The truth is out now for all to see. My family's name has been cleared at last. Whatever comes next, I have reclaimed my rightful place in Brugge's history.

Helena stays loyally by my side as we make our way out, declining requests for interviews. I meet the eyes of various townspeople, seeing in them sympathy, remorse, and even admiration for my perseverance.

Outside, I pause to take in the crisp air, gazing at the Gothic facades that have been the backdrop of so much suffering and redemption. I feel Helena studying my profile.

"How are you feeling?" she asks gently.

I consider the question. The lifting of a burden long carried, yet also the uncertainty of a new path ahead. But underneath it all, a sense of hope.

I turn to Helena with a small, weary smile. "It is a new day in Brugge."

**

I take a deep breath as I gaze out the window of the police station, watching the sunset over the canals of Brugge. So much has happened in these last few weeks that it almost feels like a dream. Or more accurately, a nightmare. The canal murders, Helena's kidnapping, Clara, the revelations about the guild...it has all been so much to process.

Yet now, in this moment of stillness, I try to make sense of it all. Helena and Inspector De Vries stand on either side of me, lost in their thoughts as we reflect on the complexities of justice and the need to confront historical wrongs.

Helena is the first to speak, her voice soft but resolute. "True justice requires acknowledging the mistakes of the past, no matter how painful." I know she speaks not just of my family's tragedy, but also of the many innocent lives ruined by the machinations of the guild over the centuries. The depth of their corruption is still coming to light.

Inspector De Vries nods slowly, sadness etched on his face. "Justice must be blind to status and reputation. The law must apply equally to all." I sense this case has shaken his faith in the institutions he has long revered.

When I finally added my voice, I am surprised by the steadiness of my words. "The truth can hurt, but lies and secrecy only breed more injustice. We must confront our history before we can move forward."

Helena reaches over and gives my hand a gentle, reassuring squeeze. Despite all she has endured, her strength and compassion remain unbroken.

We stand in contemplative silence for a few more moments before a knock at the door stirs us from our thoughts. It is Eva, a mix of nervousness and excitement shining in her eyes.

In her hands is the locket that started her on the journey to uncovering her family's hidden past. She managed to preserve Adeline's legacy and, in doing so, helped expose the guild's misdeeds.

Eva suggests we take a walk by the canals before sunset. The three of us readily agree, suddenly eager for fresh evening air to clear our minds.

As we stroll along the water's edge, I can't help but think of all the secrets these canals still hold. We have dredged up many truths from their murky depths, yet so much of our history remains submerged in shadow.

When we pause by the stone bridge, Eva turns to me, locket cradled gently in her palms. "After all these years, justice for your family. I hope they can now rest peacefully." Her words are simple but heartfelt.

I nod, a lump forming in my throat. Thanks to her discovery, my family's name will finally be cleared. "The past can never be changed, but at least now we can tell the true story. Their memories will live on, unstained by lies."

Eva clasps the locket tenderly. "We must remember, not just the injustices but also those who fought against them. Like my grandmother. It's the only way forward."

I know she speaks wisdom. Too long have we tried to bury the past; now we must learn from it. Together, we will write a new story for this city.

As the last glimmer of sunset fades over the canals, I feel a cautious hope rising within me. With truth as our guide, perhaps Brugge can leave the shadows of its history behind and step into a more just future. It will not be quick or easy, but for the first time, it feels possible.

A new Dawn for Brugge

As the Belfry bells echo across Brugge, their sound matches the rhythm of my own heartbeat. A crowd has formed in the city's main square, their whispered conversations flowing through the gathered mass, reminiscent of ripples spreading across a body of water. I'm standing there too, my feet set firmly on the cobblestones that have been smoothed over by the passage of time, anxiously awaiting Elisabeth De Groote's appearance on the platform. This day holds the promise of redemption; the once-stained reputation of my family has the chance to be restored to its rightful honor.

Elisabeth's voice rings out, clear and authoritative, yet there's a gentleness to her words today. "Citizens of Brugge," she begins, her eyes sweeping over the assembled crowd before settling on me. "We stand here in the light of truth, a truth that has been shrouded in darkness for far too long."

The square is silent now; every breath held seems to honor the gravity of this moment. "The Van Aarden family," Elisabeth continues, "wrongly persecuted and condemned for crimes they did not commit, are hereby exonerated." A pause lingers in the air. "We acknowledge the grave injustice they suffered and extend our deepest apologies to Willem Van Aarden."

I draw a breath as if surfacing from deep underwater. Apologies echo through the square, reaching me like a distant tide. Elisabeth descends from the platform and approaches me with open palms. "Willem," she says softly, "on behalf of Brugge, I am sorry."

Her apology hovers between us like mist over morning canals. I nod, a gesture that carries more weight than words could muster.

One by one, townsfolk approach – bakers I've known since childhood who would turn their gaze when I walked past; fishermen who shared silent nods across the water but never a conversation; women who whispered behind hands as I passed by their windows. Each apology lands differently.

"Willem," old Pieter from the bookshop grasps my hand firmly. His eyes don't waver as he speaks. "For what it's worth, I hope you can find it in your heart to forgive our blindness."

I search his face for traces of sincerity and find an open book. "Thank you, Pieter," I reply.

A young mother comes forward with her daughter clinging to her skirts. The girl offers me a small bunch of wildflowers with a shy smile. "For your family," she whispers.

Their scent is simple and pure – forgiveness in its most innocent form. I crouch down to her level and accept them with a nod. "Thank you," I say softly.

As more people come forth with handshakes and murmured regrets, my heart beats a rhythm that is both liberating and sorrowful. Relief washes over me like gentle waves against a steadfast shore; yet beneath it all is an undercurrent of grief for what can never be returned – time lost and love extinguished.

Helena stands at the edge of the square watching – her presence is a beacon as it has been throughout this ordeal – and Inspector De Vries leans against an ancient oak with arms folded across his chest, observing but not intruding.

The morning sun climbs higher as the last of the townsfolk return to their daily lives, leaving me standing there with my hands full of apologies like so many fishing nets returned empty.

Helena walks over to me then; her steps are measured but sure. She doesn't speak immediately but stands beside me in silent solidarity until words find their way out.

"We've unearthed something rotten here in Brugge," she says quietly. "But perhaps now healing can begin."

De Vries joins us after a moment; his eyes hold a weariness from bearing witness to too many truths that were never meant to see daylight.

"Willem," he says in his gruff way that somehow manages to carry warmth today, "I believe this city owes you more than apologies."

His words hang between us – an offering without form yet filled with possibility.

"And what would that be?" I ask.

De Vries shrugs slightly. "A start would be remembering your family not as victims or villains but as pillars of this community." He extends his hand towards me.

I take it; his grip is firm and sure like an anchor in stormy seas.

Helena's hand finds my other arm gently squeezing it in reassurance or perhaps encouragement to accept this new beginning.

We stand there together – inspector, scientist, fisherman – bound by threads of justice and truth interwoven through our fates like Brugge's own canals through its heart.

A chapter closes today; one where my family's name is finally freed from its shackles allowing them to rest at last in peace if not in presence. And here I am still standing among these ancient stones with old and new friends by my side ready.

I breathe deeply taking in the crisp air filled with promises and newfound camaraderie allowing myself just this moment before looking ahead because while exoneration is sweet it's just one step on the long road towards redemption.

***

Lucas Rombouts took a moment to step back and take in the entirety of his gallery space, which was softly illuminated by carefully arranged spotlights that highlighted each piece of artwork. Following weeks filled with intense creativity, countless late nights spent in his studio, and meticulous planning and arrangement, his latest exhibition was ready for viewing. Feeling a profound sense of pride, Lucas recognized that this show marked a pivotal moment in his journey as an artist, especially considering the upheaval and significant events he had experienced in Brugge.

The theme of "Reconciliation and Understanding" was a marked departure from Lucas's usually macabre subject matter. But the recent unfolding of the canal murders and their ties to the city's dark past had profoundly impacted Lucas, forcing him to grapple with difficult questions of justice, truth, and letting go.

Lucas glanced at the painting nearest him, an impressionist scene of sunlight dancing on the canal's surface. Its warmth and vibrancy evoked a sense of hope. Nearby hung charcoal sketches of Brugge's architecture, honoring the city's beauty rather than its shadows.

At the exhibition's center sat Lucas's most ambitious piece - a triptych titled "Brugge Reborn." Its panels depicted the city embroiled in the chaos of the witch hunts, then a solemn funeral procession under brooding skies, and finally, risen with renewed spirit beneath rays of light. Lucas hoped its narrative of suffering, grief, and redemption would resonate.

The opening hour approached, and Lucas took a deep breath, pushing down nerves. His last show had ended in vandalism and scorn. But this felt different - a chance at understanding.

As patrons began trickling in, Lucas was relieved to see many familiar faces - fellow artists, friends, and even some former critics. Madame Blanchard arrived, offering Lucas a graceful nod.

The crowd grew, engaging with Lucas's artwork in thoughtful discussion. There were smiles, clasped hands, and even tears. Lucas caught snippets of conversations about healing, humanity, and honest expressions of regret.

Inspector De Vries and Helena appeared, paying their respects to Lucas. "Your work honors this city's spirit," remarked De Vries. Helena squeezed Lucas's hand warmly.

Lucas noticed Willem Van Aarden viewing "Brugge Reborn," standing with humble dignity. Lucas approached him. "I hope this does justice to your family's truth." Willem studied the panels, and then met Lucas's eyes. "You've conveyed what words cannot," he replied simply.

As Lucas surveyed the room, the atmosphere hummed with an energy he'd never experienced before. People connecting, walls coming down, unity through understanding. Art's power to transform. This was worth everything.

***

Helena De Baere stepped back and admired the progress of the museum exhibit. As curator, she had worked tirelessly with local historians to bring this important history to light. The large central panel displayed images of key figures who had opposed the oppressive guilds in medieval Brugge. Most prominently featured was Eva's grandmother, Adeline, along with details of her secret fight for justice.

Smaller panels branching off told the stories of other dissenters punished by the guilds. Their faded portraits seemed to gaze knowingly at Helena, as if grateful she was restoring their legacies. She hoped this exhibit would vindicate them and inspire visitors to defend the truth, however challenging.

A young historian named Peter approached Helena, holding an old box. "We found more of Adeline's personal effects," he said eagerly. "Letters, notes, even her grandmother's locket."

Helena's eyes widened as she opened the box. "Incredible," she murmured, carefully lifting out the tarnished silver locket. It still contained the hidden manuscript that had cracked open this dark history.

She turned the fragile pages, envisioning Adeline wearing this locket as she covertly aided the persecuted. This new trove would enrich the exhibit, bringing life to a woman who epitomized courage.

The curator in Helena swelled with excitement about these artifacts. But the scientist in her knew she must verify their provenance before displaying them. Gently setting the locket back in its box, she thanked Lukas for the find and promised to properly authenticate the items.

As Peter left, Helena's gaze returned to the panels. Her joy dimmed slightly, remembering those who wouldn't see this exhibit realized. She wished Eva's grandmother and Adeline were still alive to witness these heroic acts memorialized. And Willem...this redemption had come too late for him.

***

Inspector Gerard De Vries walked along the cobblestone streets of Brugge, his steps making solitary sounds in the quiet of the early morning. Dawn was breaking, bathing the city's ancient buildings and the intricate network of canals in a soft, golden light. While the city presented a picture of tranquil beauty, De Vries's mind was troubled, consumed by the case he was currently handling. The recent spate of violent murders by the canals had plunged the city into fear, each incident more perplexing and horrifying than the one before, leaving De Vries with a deep sense of unease as he pondered over the mysteries yet unsolved.

The case had taken a toll on him, both physically and mentally. He had spent countless nights poring over files and evidence, his eyes strained and his mind clouded with doubt. But he had persevered, driven by a sense of duty and a determination to bring the perpetrator to justice.

Now, as he walked through the town, he couldn't help but feel a sense of accomplishment. He had solved the case, uncovered the truth, and brought the killer to justice. But at what cost?

Brugge was a town steeped in history, its streets lined with well-preserved Gothic architecture and its canals whispering of secrets long forgotten. It was a place that had seen its share of tragedy and triumph, and the recent murders had left a deep wound in its collective psyche.

As De Vries passed by the homes and shops of the town's residents, he couldn't help but notice the tension in the air. People went about their business, but their faces were drawn and their eyes were haunted. The town was still reeling from the horror of the murders, and it would take time for the wounds to heal.

De Vries knew that his job was far from over. He had to help the town recover, to restore its sense of safety and security. He had to ensure that the killer's legacy didn't cast a shadow over Brugge's future.

As he walked, he couldn't help but think of Willem Van Aarden, the tormented man who had been at the center of the investigation. Willem had lost his family to a witchcraft accusation, and the pain of the accusations had never truly left him. De Vries had seen the toll that the investigation had taken on Willem, and he couldn't help but feel a sense of responsibility for his well-being.

De Vries knew that he had to do more than just solve the case. He had to help Willem, and the rest of the city, find a way to move forward. He had to help them heal.

As he continued his walk, he came across the cemetery where Willem's family was buried. The graves were old and weathered, the names on the headstones barely legible. De Vries stood in front of the Van Aarden family plot, his mind filled with memories of the investigation and the pain it had caused Willem.

He thought of the day when he had exonerated the Van Aardens, clearing their name of the witchcraft accusations that had led to their deaths. It had been a bittersweet moment, a victory tinged with sadness. He had known that the truth would not bring back Willem's family, but he had hoped that it would bring him some measure of peace.

But as he stood there, looking at the graves, he couldn't help but wonder if the truth had been enough. He wondered if Willem would ever be able to move on, to find a way to live with the pain of his past.

As De Vries left the cemetery, he made a promise to himself. He would do everything in his power to help Willem, and the rest of Brugge, heal. He would work tirelessly to ensure that the town's future was brighter than its past.

He knew that the road ahead would be long and difficult, but he was determined to see it through. He would not rest until the wounds of the past were healed, and Brugge was once again the thriving, vibrant city it had always been.

As he walked back to the police station, his steps were heavy with the weight of his responsibility. But he carried that weight with pride, knowing that he was doing what was right for the town and its people.

***

Eva Van Der Meer, a seamstress from Brugge, had uncovered her ancestor Adeline's mysterious past, which involved a covert society opposed to the oppressive guilds of medieval Brugge. Eva, determined to honor her ancestor's legacy, set up a small exhibit in the town's historical archive.

The exhibit was modest but impactful, with a central display of the locket that had belonged to Adeline and excerpts from the historical manuscript she had left behind. The locket, an intricate piece of jewelry with a hidden compartment, contained the manuscript that revealed the truth about Adeline's life and the corruption that plagued Brugge.

Eva had carefully arranged the exhibit to be both informative and respectful, creating a space that told the story of her ancestor's bravery and the fight for justice that she had been a part of. The exhibit was a testament to the strength and resilience of those who had stood up against the oppressive guilds, and it served as a reminder of the importance of truth and justice.

As the exhibit opened, it drew the interest of local school groups and visitors alike. Students from nearby schools were brought in to learn about the history of Brugge and the role that Adeline and her covert society had played in shaping the town's future. They were captivated by the story of the locket and the manuscript, and many of them left the exhibit with a newfound appreciation for the power of truth and the importance of standing up for what is right.

Visitors to the exhibit were also intrigued by the story of Adeline and her fight for justice. Many of them were locals who had heard about the exhibit through word of mouth, and they were eager to learn more about the town's history and the role that Adeline had played in it. Others were tourists who had stumbled upon the exhibit while exploring the historical archive, and they were equally captivated by the story of the locket and the manuscript.

The exhibit was a success, and Eva was proud of the way that it honored her family's legacy. She felt a sense of satisfaction knowing that Adeline's story was being told and that her bravery and determination were being recognized. The exhibit served as a reminder of the importance of truth and justice, and it inspired those who visited it to stand up for what they believed in and to fight for a better future.

As the days went by, the exhibit continued to draw interest from both locals and visitors. Eva was touched by the way that people were connecting with the story of Adeline and the covert society, and she was grateful for the opportunity to share her grandmother's legacy with the world.

In the evenings, after the exhibit had closed, Eva would sit in the quiet of the historical archive and reflect on the impact that the exhibit was having. She would look at the locket and the manuscript, and she would think about the bravery of Adeline and the others who had fought for justice in Brugge.

As she sat there, Eva couldn't help but feel a sense of pride and accomplishment. She had created a space that told the story of Adeline and the covert society, and she had inspired others to stand up for what they believed in and to fight for a better future.

The exhibit had become more than just a tribute to her family, it had become a symbol of hope and a reminder of the power of truth and justice.

***

I never imagined I would find myself back in Brugge, let alone standing in front of a group of eager children at the community center, ready to share my family's history. After years of shame and exile, it feels surreal to finally have the chance to restore my family's name.

As I gaze out at the young, expectant faces, I take a deep breath and begin. "Let me tell you about the Van Aardens, who were once honored stonemasons in this very town..."

I recount my ancestors' skills as master craftsmen, and architects of Brugge's iconic buildings. The children listen, wide-eyed, as I describe the beauty my forefathers helped create.

Then I speak of the envy and greed that festered within the stonemasons' guild. How they coveted my family's talents and contracts. How they conspired to eliminate the competition.

"One day, the guild accused my great-grandparents of witchcraft. They were tried and executed, all based on lies and deception."

A somber mood settles over the room. I explain how the Van Aardens were stripped of their livelihoods and good name, and forced to the margins of society.

As I share our tale, I feel a burden lifting, replaced by a sense of purpose. My family's truth can finally be known.

Afterward, a shy girl approaches me. "Your family was really brave," she says softly. I'm touched by her words. If only my parents could have heard such sincere sympathy.

Other children ask questions about my parents, my exile, and if the prejudice remains. I answer openly. Their curiosity gives me hope. Perhaps the future generation can learn from the past.

***

Weeks later, I stand beside Lucas Rombouts in the town square, looking up at the monument we've created together. The marble pillar bears the engraved names of those persecuted by the guilds.

Lucas and I make an unlikely pair. An eccentric artist and a disgraced stonemason. But our shared desire for justice united us.

His artistic talents captured what I could not express alone - the lost potential of those condemned, the ripples of their absence in the community.

We crowd around the memorial with other citizens on dedication day. I spot Inspector De Vries and Helena in the audience. This moment would not have come without them.

As the veil is lifted, a hush falls over the crowd. The pillar stands tall and dignified. Lucas has crafted an exquisite memorial, as only he could envision.

I scan the engravings, pausing at each name with a silent tribute. Tears prick my eyes as I find my parents' names. Finally, their suffering is acknowledged.

Mayor De Groote speaks of righting past wrongs. I hardly hear her words, lost in the enormity of this moment.

When Lucas and I are invited to say a few words, I defer to him. He voices what we both feel - grief over lost lives, hope that truth can heal, and determination to defend justice.

Later, townspeople approach us with gratitude. Some even ask my forgiveness, which I graciously give. The past is the past.

At day's end, Lucas and I stand alone at the memorial. We do not need to speak. A glance conveys our shared pride in this accomplishment.

Perhaps the greatest gift is seeing young people gathered here, reading the engravings. A teacher explains the history to her class. The children's faces reflect a dawning awareness.

I know my parents can finally rest peacefully, their names and memories preserved here. Our family history will not be forgotten.

This memorial ensures that though the guilds' injustice can never be fully undone, it will always be remembered. If we forget the past, we are doomed to repeat it.

Thanks to Lucas, there is now a tangible tribute to those we lost, and a warning to guard against prejudice. It will serve as a lesson for generations to come.

As we turn to leave, I rest a hand on the cool marble. "Thank you, my friend," I say to Lucas. He simply nods, his face reflecting the depth of emotion we both feel.

No more words are needed. Together, we have turned a painful history into something meaningful. Out of darkness, there is now light.

***

The sun sinks low over Brugge, casting the historic buildings and winding canals in a warm, golden glow. As I make my way along the cobblestone streets, the setting sun reminds me of the closing of one chapter and the dawn of a new era for this charming city.

All around me, the sights and sounds of daily life fill the air. The clip-clop of horses pulling carriages, the chatter of neighbors catching up, the laughter of children weaving through the crowds. Merchants pack up their stalls after a busy day's work, while friends gather at cafés to share a drink and lively conversation as the day winds down.

Despite the idyllic scene, I know that darkness lingers beneath the surface of this picturesque town, shadows from generations past. But today, bathed in the soft hues of sunset, Brugge feels full of hope.

I spot Lucas, my new friend, the passionate young artist, sketching canal-side, capturing the beauty around him. We exchange smiles - kindred spirits bound by our desire to revive Brugge's light.

As I walk on, I pass Eva's parent's bakery, the delicious scents of fresh pastries wafting into the street. Eva has honored her family's courageous legacy. Despite her modesty, her contributions, like mine, have helped Brugge chart a new course.

Nearing the bustling main square, I see children laughing as they chase pigeons between stands full of flowers, produce, and handmade crafts - innocent joys, far removed from the troubles of the past.

I notice Inspector De Vries patrolling nearby. Our eyes meet and he gives me a nod of understanding. An unlikely ally, he represents the new era of justice dawning in Brugge.

Despite lingering wounds, today the shadow over Brugge feels lighter. What once divided us has given way to a spirit of unity. This town, bearing witness to humanity's best and worst, now turns the page to a new chapter. One defined by truth, reconciliation, and community.

As I look out across the canal, the water mirrors the reddish-gold tones of the darkening sky. A pair of swans glide by, untroubled by the ripples beneath.

I think of my parents and whisper, "We did it." I wish they could be here to see Brugge reborn and our family name restored. But I know they're watching over me and this town.

The sun disappears below the horizon. Dusk deepens, ushering in the night. Windows and streetlamps cast a warm glow over the canal-side promenades now bustling with people heading to the theater, opera, and art galleries - simple pleasures once denied to many.

I spot Helena's distinctive silhouette in the crowd and catch up to her. Side by side, we walk in comfortable silence, our shared past connecting us like the intricate web of canals flowing through Brugge.

Up ahead, a street musician plays a hopeful melody on his violin. The sweet notes resonate through the streets, mingling with the chatter and laughter of people strolling by.

Helena and I pause on a bridge overlooking the canal. Boats lit up with lanterns glow like fireflies, floating by as people dine and share drinks on the water. Above us, stars peek through gathering clouds.

"It's beautiful isn't it?" Helena says softly.

I nod, taking in the scene. "It's a new chapter for Brugge."

She squeezes my hand, understanding the deeper meaning of my words. This town, now at peace with its past, can look to the future. And so can I.

"Helena," I began, my voice husky with emotion, "I..."

She placed a finger on my lips, a gentle smile playing on her lips. "No need for words, Willem. I know."

Her words sent a thrill of joy coursing through me. I reached out and took her hands in mine, feeling the warmth of her skin against mine.

"I love you, Helena," I confessed, my heart pounding in my chest.

Her eyes sparkled with unshed tears. "I love you too, Willem."

We stood there for a moment, lost in each other's gaze, the world around us fading into insignificance. Then, as if drawn by an invisible force, we leaned in and our lips met in a tender kiss.

It was a kiss that sealed our bond, a promise of a future together, a vow to heal each other's wounds and to face whatever life threw our way as a united front.

As we pulled away, Helena whispered, "We'll make a life together, Willem. A life filled with love, laughter, and understanding."

I nodded, my heart overflowing with emotion. "Yes, Helena. Together, we will."

Rebirth

Brugge breathes a gentle rhythm, like the ebb and flow of tides I know so well. These streets, once corridors of suspicion and whispers, now echo with the laughter of my children as they chase each other around the cobbles. Helena watches them from the doorway, her smile a beacon of warmth in the cool evening light.

"Luc, Anouk, be careful near the canals!" she calls out, her voice laced with the mirth of a mother's love tempered by caution. They heed her words, their games never straying too far from safety or her watchful gaze.

The past feels like a different lifetime. The murky waters of suspicion have cleared, revealing a life I never dared to dream of—a family, a home, and a town that finally knows my name not as a curse but as one of their own.

Helena steps beside me, her hand finding mine. "They're growing up so fast," she says. I squeeze her hand in agreement, feeling the weight and wonder of every moment we've shared.

"Remember when we first met?" I ask. Her eyes meet mine—those windows to a soul as brave as it is kind—sparking memories of our first encounter by the canals.

"How could I forget? You were the most brooding fisherman I'd ever seen." Her laughter dances in the air. "And now look at you—Willem Van Aarden, husband, father, and respected member of our community."

The journey from there to here wasn't easy. The shadows that clung to me after my family's wrongful persecution were stubborn. With Helena's unwavering support and Inspector De Vries's relentless pursuit of justice, we unearthed truths that reshaped not only my life but the very fabric of Brugge.

Helena nudges me gently. "You're lost in thought again."

"Just thinking about how far we've come," I admit.

We turn our attention back to Luc and Anouk. Their innocence is something I cherish—a gift from this town that once threatened to take everything from me.

Helena's eyes shimmer with unspoken understanding. "We did it together," she says softly.

I nod. It was Helena who stood by me when fear and superstition sought to sever my ties to Brugge forever. She saw beyond the stigma; she saw me.

"We should start heading back," Helena suggests. "Dinner won't cook itself."

We gather our children with promises of their favorite meal—stewed eel, a recipe passed down from my mother—and begin our walk home. The narrow streets are familiar friends now, lined with shops closing for the day and windows lighting up for the evening.

Our house is modest but filled with love and laughter—a haven we built together from the remnants of my fractured past. As we approach, I see Helena's apothecary sign swinging gently above the door—a symbol of her contribution to our community and our livelihood.

Inside, Luc helps set the table while Anouk assists Helena with stirring pots on the stove. The aroma is comforting—a blend of herbs and spices that only Helena knows how to wield into something magical.

"Did you have fun today?" Helena asks them as they chatter about their adventures by the canals.

"The best!" Anouk exclaims with a wide grin that mirrors her mother's.

Luc nods enthusiastically. "We played knights defending Brugge from dragons!"

I ruffle his hair affectionately. "Well done, knight," I say with pride.

As dinner progresses amidst stories and shared laughter, I feel an overwhelming sense of contentment. This family is my greatest accomplishment—not one forged through hardship alone but through resilience and love.

After tucking Luc and Anouk into bed with tales of brave ancestors and legendary heroes of Brugge—stories where good always prevails—Helena and I retreat to our room upstairs.

"Do you ever miss it?" Helena asks suddenly as we gaze out at the moonlit canals from our window.

"Miss what?"

"The solitude," she clarifies. "The silence on your boat at dawn."

I ponder her question—a life spent alone on those waters had its moments of peace—but shake my head decisively.

"No," I answer truthfully. "Not when it meant being apart from you or our children."

Helena smiles softly before leaning into me. We stand there in comfortable silence, knowing that while the past will always be part of us, it doesn't define us—not anymore.

"We've made quite a life for ourselves," she murmurs.

"We have," I agree. The gratitude in my voice isn't lost on either of us; it's been earned through trials that tested every fiber of our being.

A gentle breeze wafts through our open window, carrying with it the faintest scent of saltwater mingled with blooming nightflowers—an amalgam only Brugge could provide. It reminds me that life continues at its steady pace just as it always has—the bad with the good—and somehow finds balance in between.

In those quiet moments before sleep claims us, we revel in the stillness that now signifies peace rather than loneliness—a peace we fought hard for and won together.

As sleep beckons with its soft embrace, one last thought lingers in my mind: this happiness was worth every struggle faced in those shadowed times when light seemed scarce—because ultimately, it led us here—to each other and to a future once shrouded but now shining bright under Brugge's starry sky.

Also By

Project Celestia

Following the enigmatic depths of "The Canal Whisperer," Stefaan Declerck unveils a new realm of intrigue in "Project Celestia." Dr. Emma Sterling's life takes a dramatic turn with the discovery of a hidden alien artifact, unraveling the mystery behind her father's disappearance and revealing a universe brimming with secrets.

Joined by Captain Adrian Kane and Zara, an alien torn between worlds, Emma finds herself at the epicenter of a prophecy that could alter humanity's subservience under alien oversight. "Project Celestia" is a thrilling narrative of courage, clandestine power, and the quest for autonomy against the backdrop of an alien-dominated Earth.

This compelling tale merges the boundless curiosity of a scientist with the audacity of a leader poised to ignite a revolution against cosmic overlords. Venture with Emma from the halls of academia to the frontlines of an interstellar conflict, where the destiny of our planet is intertwined with the mysteries of the universe.

Prepare for a journey through "Project Celestia," where advanced alien technology, hidden alliances, and the quest for freedom converge in a battle for the soul of humanity.

About the Author

From a young age, Stefaan Declerck was a kid who always had his nose buried in a book. Whether it was under the covers with a flashlight past bedtime or curled up in a corner when he should have been doing chores, stories were his escape and joy. As he grew up, this love for stories didn't wane; it simply evolved. He swapped books for the screen, devouring movies and series with the same hunger he once reserved for novels.

Life took a creative turn when Stefaan picked up a camera. Suddenly, he wasn't just consuming stories; he was capturing them, frame by frame, as a photographer and videographer. This new profession cracked open a door to a world he hadn't explored yet—writing scenarios and scripts. It was like finding a secret passage in a familiar room, leading him to a fascination with crafting stories, not just capturing or watching them.

But it's not all about the stories. At home, Stefaan is a dedicated dad to three lively boys and a loving partner. Juggling family life with creative pursuits could be a plot twist he never saw coming, yet it's one he wouldn't trade for the world. It was amid this beautiful chaos that he realized writing was more than just a hobby; it was what he was meant to do. Drawing from his vast experience with visual storytelling, Stefaan finally took the leap from scripts to novels, weaving together tales that reflect the vividness and depth of the worlds he's always loved to explore.

Now, as he embarks on this journey of novel writing, Stefaan brings all these threads together—his childhood love for stories, his eye for capturing moments, and his heart, full of the love and laughter of his family.

Printed in Great Britain
by Amazon